Also by Zoraida Córdova

On the Verge Series
Luck on the Line

Diversion Books
A Division of Diversion Publishing Corp.
443 Park Avenue South, Suite 1008
New York, New York 10016
www.DiversionBooks.com

For more information, email info@diversionbooks.com

First Diversion Books edition May 2015.
Print ISBN: 978-1-62681-665-7
eBook ISBN: 978-1-62681-580-3

LOVE
on the
LEDGE

ON THE VERGE: Book Two

ZORAIDA CÓRDOVA

DIVERSIONBOOKS

For Goody Horbs, Goody Higgins, and Goody Rosado—
My daily inspirations, troublemakers, and soul sisters.
To more adventures, lobster bibs, and alotta whiskey.

CHAPTER 1

The first time I'll wear white to a wedding, I won't be the bride.

I turn in the full-length mirror, admiring the way the soft white satin hugs my Hamptons-summer-kissed skin. When I tried the dress on back in April, it was snug on my hips. Then, I was in Boston working night shifts at a hospital that included a steady supply of pastries, cold pizza, and coffee. When I wasn't working the graveyard shift, I was clinging to the arm of my perfect boyfriend with one hand and downing cocktails with the other. I'll say one thing about this break-up—it's the only one that's ever caused me to lose weight instead of pile it on.

That and wedding planning.

Wedding planning is a stressful business, especially when the groom is your uncle, and your entire family gets to see your life plans spectacularly come apart at the seams.

At least I can say my bridesmaid dress fits.

Maybe it's the dress, but I start to think about myself walking down the aisle as the bride. How next year it could have been me. How I would have chosen the same color palate. That's a spiral I don't want to go down again. So instead I focus on the little things like the wrinkles along the hem, the fingerprints on the mirror, the specks of dust that flutter around the room. I run my fingers through it. I wonder how dust, sneezy, dirty dust, can look so beautiful when a beam of light hits it. I guess anything can be beautiful at a certain angle, like perfect boys that turn out to not be so perfect.

"Sky!" Leti bangs on the door. "Are you dressed yet?"

The doorknob turns, a reminder that I can kiss privacy (and silence) goodbye. For a whole two months, I had the house to myself. Sure, it belongs to my uncles, but because they're both such workaholics, it felt like I was by myself. One by one, the family's started to arrive for the big day. Before today I'd get a daily call from my mother reminding me that I'm man-less and jobless and homeless. Only two by choice. Well, actually all by choice. It's one thing to get nagged over the phone. It's another to get nagged in person.

My cousin Leti runs in wearing the same dress as me, only it's too narrow around her knees so she does a weird wobble, like a mermaid trying to walk on land. Her brown eyes go wide when she sees me. She presses a hand on her giant breast and sighs.

"*Giiirl*, you look like the bride. I'm feeling like a beached whale. I mean, it's a lot better than my initial expectations after seeing his spring collection of neon circus chic, but really? Why is he doing this to me?"

"Because our uncle is gay and has no idea what it's like to wear a dress?"

She laughs in that thunderous way of hers—a belly rumble boom. A tiny gold star on her left canine glints in the angel dust light coming through the window. She got the star in Sweden during her semester there last year. Apparently it's a *thing* there. Teeth bling is *not* a thing in our family, and she got a load of grief from Las Viejas—the old ladies—our moms and aunts and grandmas, the Ecuadorian chorus to the tragi-comedy of our lives.

I should have gone with her to Sweden when I had the chance, but I chose Boston over traveling. Now's not the time for regrets, but regrets always have a way of finding their way into the present.

"I don't know about Tony," she says, "but Uncle Pepe used to wear dresses all the time."

"Whatever," I say. "Are we sure we can't convince them on something in an empire waist?"

A third white dress, more like second-skin than fabric, saunters into my room. My best friend, River, leans against the doorframe. Her wild honey curls tumble down her back. I can smell the ocean on her clothes. Her skin is even tanner than mine, only mine is genetic and hers is one step closer to skin cancer. The smatter of golden-brown freckles on her high cheekbones makes her blue eyes just that much sharper.

"Remind me again why we're wearing white?" River asks. She tiptoes in, the material stretching so tightly I'm afraid the seams are going to rip.

"Because," Leti says. Leti speaks with her hands. She swings them all over the place. Ever since we were little she's been like that, a loud firecracker on the loose. "Pepe and Tony are going to wear all the color. Did you see the suits? Navy with turquoise and white accents. It's pretty much adorbs."

"You know," River says in her smoker's voice, "it's a testament to my love for Pepe and Tony that I'm here right now. I was at the beach, and I almost couldn't tear myself away from those surfers."

She licks her lips in a way that makes Leti bat her eyes and say, "Oh, how I've missed you, River. I can't wait for everyone to get here."

I groan. "The *whole* family, plus Uncle Tony's family we've never met, plus all their snooty fashion friends? I wonder which of the neighbors is going to call the cops first."

"It's like *My Big Fat Greek Wedding*," River says. "Only the groom is Italian, the other is Ecuadorian, and they're both gay."

"My Big Fat Italian-Ecuadorian Gay Wedding," Leti giggles. "It's going to be so romantic. I wish we had dates."

I did have a date. I try not to let my face crumple up and cry. I'm done crying. I'm done feeling sorry for myself. Or, mostly. I'm done letting *other* people see me cry and feel sorry for me. But these aren't other people. Leti's my first cousin. River's my biffle. They're the closest things I have to sisters, and I can't lie to them.

"I'm sorry, Sky," Leti says. "I didn't mean—"

I nod. I hate that I'm this way. I hate that I can't shake the sadness. It wears me like an ugly dress I can't unzip myself out of.

"I should be over it," I say. "But it's Bradley, you know? He was everything to me for such a long time."

We try to sit, but the dresses are so tight that sitting cuts off our air supply. So we stand in front of the wide, full-length mirror. More white particles flake down on us. Leti sneezes and gets into a fight with the dust. The dust wins.

"What is that?" she asks. "It sounds like a stampede."

"The roofers have been tramping around for two days. There was a small hole when they cut down the tree for the wedding, and then they found rot. Just what we need."

"Hey," Leti says, "if all of River's numbers are dead ends, we can ask some of them to be our dates. At least they'll be good with their tools."

"You're impossible," I say.

"Aww, come on, Sky," she says. "I just don't want you to be sad."

"Listen," River tells me, "if you want to feel sad then you should feel sad. Bradley was a piece of shit who deserves to have his dick cut off, ground up, and then fed to him. He cheated on you with an old lady!"

Leti shakes her head. I don't know who she's more terrified of, River or me with my break-up face. "I stopped watching Stella's cooking show as soon as you told me she slept with Bradley."

River leans against the wall, digging her pinky in her ear. A tiny trail of sand falls to the floor. "This whole time I thought you were worried about the daughter. What's her name? Rainbow?"

I laugh. "*Lucky*. And no, she's cool. We're sort of friends now."

"Ugh," she says. "Always the objective one, you."

"I don't want you to be sad anymore, Sky," Leti says. "You've done so much for the wedding. This is your baby. You need to enjoy it."

"Nothing like planning a dream wedding for someone else after you've been dumped."

"Hey!" River says. "Shut the fuck up. Don't you talk about yourself like that. You dumped him."

"Isn't that the shit part? Even after everything. After he groveled and promised it was only one mistake, that he wanted another shot, that I should give him a chance to be better. After

I told him I never wanted to see him again, *I* still feel like the one who got dumped?"

"Fuck it," River says. "No more moping. I hate that I can't fix your broken heart. Or that I can't murder Bradley with my bare hands this minute. Or that he's probably out on some yacht having a grand old time while you're sad. But I can stop you from wallowing in your own misery."

"How are you going to do that?" I ask.

"Haven't figured it out," she says. "Isn't it enough that I can kill him with my mind?"

It's funny how cursing and death threats against a man who wronged me can lift my spirits a little.

"However," River says, "you've been here for two months since you left Boston, and you haven't even had rebound sex. I've been here for a week and I've already gathered a *bunch* of healthy prospects."

"For you or me?"

"For all." There's that twinkle in her eyes. River's always been the wild card, and she loves every minute of it.

"The summer's almost over. And I have the wedding. And I have to figure out what I'm supposed to do after that. I'm considering spending the fall and winter holed up here, though. Fresh Direct delivers, and that coffee place is only a ten minute walk for my chai addiction."

River shakes her head. "No."

"What do you mean, no?"

"I can't have this talk from you," she says. "That's quitter talk. Thomases don't quit."

I bark a laugh. "I'm not a Thomas. I'm a Lopez. Lopezes quit all the time."

"Stop it, Sky," River says. "I'm going to find you a man so fine you'll want to dip him in chocolate and lick his toes."

"Can I get that too?" Leti asks.

"First of all," I say, "I don't like chocolate. Second of all, I *hate* feet. Third, the kind of guy I need right now isn't a rebound. I don't need any guy. I need perspective. I just want to be alone. My head is a mess. Anything that needs my attention had better involve flower arrangements and catering."

"Honey," River says, "I love you, but you need a rebound. A rebound covered in so much suntan oil that you'll be able to fry him up like bacon."

"I really don't know if I'm hungry or horny," Leti says. "Hmm. Maybe both."

"I get what you're saying," I say, zipping down the white bridesmaid dress so I can breathe. I pull it down, and the girls suck their teeth when I don't have to wiggle it past the hips. "But the kind of guy I want right now is a dream. And you know what? I'm okay with dreaming. I thought I had that with Bradley for three whole years, and it was the biggest hurt of my life. I can't do it again. Not without becoming bitter, like River."

"Hey!"

Leti shrugs at her.

River sighs. "Well, you're not wrong."

"It might seem stupid and naïve. I just want a good guy. A truly, really, *good* guy."

River and Leti exchange glances as if I'm the most hopeless thing in the world. Maybe I am.

"I hate to break it to you, *nena*," Leti says, "but nice guys don't just fall from the sky."

"That's why I don't pray for miracles."

I reach for my sundress to change into, but a loud noise makes me jump back. Sunlight filters through the ceiling, which is strange because there isn't a skylight. River grabs Leti and falls back just as the ceiling gives way. There's a scream, the snap and crunch of wood, the shattering of glass, and a sack falls through the hole in the roof. Dust and sheetrock fill the room with tiny clouds. I cough when I accidentally inhale it. That can't be healthy.

"Are you guys okay?" River asks.

The sack moans a response.

I jump back.

It's not a sack.

It's a guy.

A very beautiful, shirtless, unconscious guy.

CHAPTER 2

I run to the guy on the pile of sheetrock and shingles.

Behind me, the girls run to go get help. The other construction workers are already clambering inside, shouting after their colleague.

I press my fingers on his pulse.

"Let me get him," a guy says, standing over me.

"Don't move him," I say.

"It's all right, sweetie," he says.

"Which one of us is a nurse?" I stand. Even without my heels, I'm taller than he is. His sweaty face wrinkles and he takes a step back.

A pained groan comes from the pile at our feet.

"Don't try to sit up," I say. "You probably have a concussion."

Maybe even a worse head injury, because he's just lying there staring at me. Against his skin, golden from days and days of working shirtless on top of roofs or lying out in the sun, his blue eyes are startling bursts of light.

He blinks repeatedly. There's blood where a nail has skewered his shoulder, but he doesn't seem to notice. He just keeps staring.

At the door, River and Leti are in a fit of giggles.

My mom, aunt, and uncles run into the room. An older man with a beer belly follows at a leisurely pace. His shirt has the white letters "Robertson Roofing & Co." printed across it.

"Sky!" my mom shouts. Her brown eyes are manic and wide. In Spanish she yells, "*Ponte decente!*"

"What?"

When I look down, I realize I'm naked. Or mostly naked. I've got on a demi-bra and a thong. I can feel my skin turn hot and red. *Shit. Shit. Shit.*

I point a finger at my Uncle Pepe. "It's his fault. What else are we supposed to wear when the dress is practically see through?"

"Don't blame the artist, honey," Pepe says.

Save face, I think. Even though my hands are trembling and I'm trying to avoid my friends snickering at my predicament, I grab my pajama shirt hanging from the doorknob (my sundress is covered in sheetrock) and put it on. It falls down to my knees. I try not to think that this shirt used to be Bradley's. That I promised myself I'd throw it out.

"Did anyone call an ambulance?" I ask evenly.

The old man clears his throat, more angry than afraid for his employee. "Aw, not to worry, dear. He hits his head alda time. Never fell tru a roof before. This one's a first."

"Am I the only one who thinks he needs medical attention?"

All the onlookers take turns staring at each other. That's the problem with people. No one wants to take action unless it's approved by someone else. I see it all the time at the hospital. People would bring their injured friends in too late, and when we would ask why, they just "weren't sure." I've been surrounded by unsure people for too long.

The injured guy in question now groans some more. "I'm okay," he says.

"Sit back," I tell him.

But he ignores me. "No, really. My dad's right. I hit my head a lot."

Under his breath the father says something like, "Knocked the sense out of him long ago."

I can't believe that's his father. If I got a paper cut my mom would insist we go to the ER. Sure, she's a borderline hypochondriac, and maybe her smothering might *possibly* be linked to my failed relationships, but at least I know she cares.

When he stands, he's the tallest person in the room. Not as tall as Bradley. Bradley was slimmer too. This guy, with his blond hair that reminds me of polished gold, is built like someone who's spent his whole life working hard. His broad chest, covered in sheetrock, sweat, and a little bit of blood from the scrapes on his way down, wasn't built at the gym, but by carrying loads of—well, whatever roofers carry, I guess.

"Really, I'm okay." he says. His voice is brighter than I thought. You know when you look at a guy and you expect this gruff, brooding voice to come out of his mouth? This guy is the opposite. His voice is *light* if that's possible. Not high-pitched or anything. Just bright. Light. Carefree. "Thanks for your concern, everyone."

He looks at his dad, who has already turned around and is in a huddle with Uncle Tony, probably about turning the small job into a bigger one. Pepe screams when he sees my bridal gown in the heap. He pulls it out of the rubble.

The Fallen Roofer winces. "Sorry about that."

Pepe looks him up and down. He wants to say, "It's okay." But he just shakes his head and carries the gown out of the room.

"Okay, party's over, people," I say.

When River, Leti, and Las Viejas don't move, I snap. "Get out of my room!"

They all hold their hands up at my vitriol and turn away.

"Not *you*," I tell the Fallen Roofer.

He turns around, massaging his neck. He quirks an eyebrow and points to his chest in a "who me?" kind of way.

"If you're not going to get that hard head of yours checked out, then at least let me help with the bleeding."

He's backing away slowly, twisting and turning his torso. I know he's trying to stretch out the kinks, but all it does is make the muscles in his abdomen ripple. Why are muscles so delicious to look at? Underneath the skin it's just soft tissue and cells and…what was I talking about again?

In this light, with those big blue eyes, golden skin, and lush blond hair, he's almost angelic. The kind of angel that falls out of heaven for being too beautiful. Or falls through a roof. Same diff. All I know is looking at his six-pack, I'm thinking I'm going to need an extra ice pack. One to put on his neck, and one to smack myself with. Am I *blushing*?

"Sure thing, Doc." His periwinkle eyes are the kind of eyes that are always smiling.

I go to the bathroom and pull the first aid kit out from under the sink. "I'm not a doctor. Nurse. Sit."

"Are you sure?" He points to the white couch. "I'm dirty."

"Just sit down, okay?" I say in the voice I use on my patients who don't want me to change their lines and don't want to stay still.

"Yes, Nurse." He says nurse in a way that makes my belly tingle.

Then I realize something. "Hold this."

I run into the bathroom and pull on the pajama pants discarded on the floor. When I come back out he looks a tad disappointed.

"Harvard girl," he says, looking at my oversized pajamas.

This time the blush comes with a dull pain and a familiar headache. I shake my head. How can I say these are not my pajamas without seeming like a crazy ex-girlfriend who still sleeps in her ex-boyfriend's old college rags?

"I went to Stony Brook, actually," I say.

"Local girl." He watches every step I take from the bathroom and back to him.

My room is huge. Bigger than the studio I had in Boston. But the way he looks at me makes it feel teeny tiny. It's like he takes up all of it with his bare chest and golden hair.

Without another word I clean the back of his shoulder where a nail got a good dig. I take a pair of tweezers and pluck out tiny bits of plaster and wood. When I rip open an antiseptic wipe he jumps up.

"I'm good. Great, actually. I'll be fine. I have to go back out and help the guys load up the truck."

"Don't be a baby."

He groans, making him look all of twelve. "I'm a twenty-five year old baby, thank you very much."

But he sits, and before he can jump away again I press the wipe on the cut. I can't help but laugh.

"I'm glad my pain is funny to you," he says.

"I'm not laughing *at you*. I'm laughing at the fact that you're this big guy who fell through a roof, but this you have a problem with."

"It's a certain kind of pain that I don't like. I can take punches. It's just those little pains, like pouring chemicals on an open wound or lemon in a paper cut or stubbing your toe when you're fumbling around in the dark on the way to the bathroom. Those little pains are the worst."

I make a face I'm glad he can't see. I take a square bandage and tape it on the back of his shoulder. "Then I'm glad you've never had necrotizing fasciitis."

"Me too," he says, rolling his eyes like he totally understands me. "Sounds terrible."

"Well," I say, walking back around him, "do you have bandages at home? Put another on after you shower. If it gets infected your whole shoulder is going to come off."

"You're the meanest nurse in Nurse Town," he tells me.

I bite the smile from my lips and turn away from him. "You're dismissed."

He stands and walks backward toward the door. "That's it? I don't get a lollipop or a kiss or something?"

Kiss. The word makes my stomach flutter in a way River saying "laid" never could. I busy myself with putting the first aid kit back together. He stands at the door waiting for me to say something. Flirt. He's flirting. Why can't I, even if I kind of want to?

"You can have someone clean up the mess you made," I say.

He scratches the back of his head and winces at the pain he discovers there. "Sure thing. I just need your name so I can fill out a cleaning order."

I give him The Eye. "Nurse."

"Nurse," he says. "Is that a family name?"

I don't laugh. I mean, I'm laughing, but I don't let the laugh leave my lips. My inner self is kicking my outer self. He's gorgeous. He's dirty and will probably be blooming with black and blues tomorrow, but he's absolutely gorgeous. It radiates from inside of him.

"I'm Tripp," he says. "In case you were wondering."

"That's not a real name. I refuse to call you that."

He looks affronted and stands a little taller. "Hayden Robertson the Third. Tripp? Like triple?"

Now I can't help but let the laugh out. "I thought it might be Tripp like in triple shot of espresso. You have enough energy."

He smirks. It's a lovely smirk. "It's kind of my superpower."

"Mine's wedding planning."

He takes a step closer, away from the door. My senses are on alarm. He should stop being charming. Stop doing what he's doing because it makes the hairs on my arms stand on end. Makes my stomach do jumping jacks. Makes me want to take these stupid Harvard pajamas off, and not just because it's about time, but because he is the most beautiful creature I've seen in a long time, or maybe ever.

But then his dad stands at the doorway, and he stops mid-step. "Tripp, let's go. Hill and Sanders are going to clean up. Get your sorry ass packing up the truck."

The old man nods at me and storms out of the house.

"See you tomorrow, Nurse," Tripp says, lingering.

I swallow the nervous laughter bubbling up in me and wave, hoping he doesn't see how much he's rattled me.

CHAPTER 3

Because my room has permanently become a construction site, I get to upgrade to the balcony room upstairs. Pepe was going to use it on the eve of the wedding so the groom wouldn't see the groom before the ceremony, but now he's relocated to the pool house.

The upside to my new digs is that I have a direct view of the lawn and pool. The downside is that's where my cousins inevitably take over, and their loud mouths will ruin my peace and quiet.

When Uncle Tony bought this house in his twenties, this part of the neighborhood wasn't as ritzy as it is now. The Hamptons are, of course, the summer getaway for celebrities and for New York's richest. The house might be a wing short of a mansion, but when he bought it, it was abandoned, and over time he renovated it himself to his liking. Thirty years later, he met the man of his dreams—my Uncle Pepe, the only openly gay member of our immigrant, Catholic, Ecuadorian family.

Tony worked in stocks and retired early. Pepe is a fashion designer who has every starlet wearing his gowns on red carpets. They're the American dream, and they treat me like the daughter they never had.

Pepe even named me. I owe him a huge one. If it wasn't for him, I'd be Guadalupe Lopez, and I got enough shit in middle school ranging from "Are you J.Lo's cousin?" to "She thinks she's too good for us because she's light skinned," to my favorite, "Her ass ain't even all that."

The downside of being named Sky is that in college the people asked, "Wow, where is that from?"

"It's English, you idiot," I wanted to say. But it was their polite way of asking my race without seeming rude. Tan skin and light eyes really seem to confuse people.

My eyes, the bipolar green-hazel, and my last name are the only things I inherited from my father before he left us high and dry. In solitary moments like this, standing at my balcony sipping a cold cup of milk and coffee, I briefly wonder where he is.

The morning after the famous roof accident the workers are right back at it. I crane my neck to see the guys working on the roof. Three of them, and none of them are Hayden Robertson III. There's no way in hell I'd ever call him Tripp, even to myself.

Bradley was Bradley Edward Thorton IV. Before I let myself go down that spiral, I run back inside where the air conditioning is a sweet respite from the heat.

"Sky!" Leti yells from downstairs. "Breakfast!"

Before everyone started arriving for the wedding, I could sit by the pool without having to listen to the chitter chatter of Las Viejas discussing my break up in Spanish. It's a good thing I don't speak it, and only just understand it. They're worse than a high school cafeteria gossip squad, because after they discuss my failure to maintain a man, they cross themselves and pray for my soul.

"I'm coming!" I shout down the stairs.

I kiss my dreams of a few laps in the pool goodbye. Missing breakfast would require an explanation. They'd think I was skipping meals. They'd think I was in my room crying (again). I throw on a pair of plaid shorts and a surf-green polo. I tie my hair back in a ponytail and skip my contacts for glasses. I'll make it to a body of water eventually.

Down in the dining room, Las Viejas, Uncle Pepe and Tony, Leti, and cousin Maria are already eating.

"Good morning," I say as cheerily as I can.

Maria is a teacher at a Catholic high school in the Bronx. She dresses like she's a middle-aged real estate agent, and acts like she's one of Las Viejas instead of twenty-five and single.

Only when she waves at me, she makes sure I see the rock

on her finger. Make that twenty-five and engaged.

"So," Maria says, "I hear you're taking time off?"

My mom makes a face. She touches the gold necklace she always wears—a gold stamp of the Virgin Mary.

"Yeah," I say with a smile on my face. I take the orange juice and pour myself a glass. "There wasn't really room for me to grow in the unit. I'm thinking of going into social work."

"Wouldn't you have to go back to school?" Maria asks.

There are people in your life who are secretly rooting for you to fail. They disguise themselves with smiling faces and fake wishes of success. Maria is this person in my life. Ever since she was little she was right beside me competing for grades, Uncle Pepe's attention, Abuela Gloria's favor.

"Only for a year or two," I say. "I was going to get my master's no matter what. At least I would be doing something I actually want this time."

Uncle Pepe holds out his glass. "Whatever you need, love. I'll be there for you if you want ten master's."

I smile sheepishly, and Maria's lips pinch like she ate a lemon.

"Isn't it scary?" Maria asks. "Starting over?"

"I'm not starting over," I say, adding extra cream cheese to my bagel.

She shrugs and takes sliced cheese and ham onto her plate. She butters her bread with the thinnest layer. "New school, new career. You'd hardly have time to have a life."

My left eye twitches. It's the Maria twitch. Every time she finds a good dig, my eye does an irritated cha-cha. "I like to think of it as a continuation of the path I was on."

Leti yawns loudly. "You could also come with me to Amsterdam. They have medical schools there. Way better than here, FYI."

I give Leti a look that I hope will calm her. The two of them have hated each other since Maria told on Leti about Leti's belly button piercing in high school. There was nothing we could do to get back at Maria. She's saint-like, in addition to being a judgmental, nosy biatch.

"Leti!" my mom groans. "Don't put ideas in her head."

Yes, God forbid I get ideas of traveling the world.

Aunt Salomé nods. "Just because you abandoned your mother doesn't mean Sky has to do the same."

"Ma," Leti says, giving her mom a smothering hug. "I didn't abandon you."

"What's in Amsterdam?" Maria asks.

"Hookers and ganja," Leti says, winking her long lashes at Maria.

Aunt Salomé slaps Leti's arm playfully. Pepe giggles to himself. My mom purses her lips and cuts her breakfast sandwich in half. Sometimes it's hard to believe they're siblings.

Maria grumbles deeply. "Sky doesn't need that in her life on top of everything."

My ears burn. My mom says that your ears burn when someone is talking about you behind your back. It's some superstitious crap—Maria's not doing it behind my back.

"What's that supposed to mean?" I drop my fork and it clatters against my plate. I feel someone place a hand on top of mine, but I pull my hand away.

"I mean your life is kind of a mess," she says. "I'm sorry, but someone has to say it. You had a good job, a relationship. Now you're living at home again. Running around a city like Amsterdam isn't exactly going to do you any favors."

I stand so quickly that my chair falls backward onto the floor and echoes in the quiet of the dining room.

"Sky," they call after me. "Come back."

All except Maria.

I walk out back where the ruckus of hammers and wood provides a barrier between my family and me. I go past the crystal blue pool and the lawn that's going to be the stage for the wedding in a few weeks, until I reach the line of trees that leads to a small patch of woods.

In the shade of a tree, I sit on the grass and lean my head back against the trunk. I wonder whether, if I sit here long enough, a deer will come out from the woods. I'll be like the Snow White of West Hampton Beach. When we were in high school, Leti and I would sit really still and wait for deer to sneak into the backyard to eat the leaves on Uncle's Tony's fancy bushes.

The rustle behind me makes me jump up. I'm expecting to see an animal, but instead there's him.

Hayden Robertson the Third.

Tripp.

Don't call him that, Sky, I tell myself. *That's not a real name.*

He's wearing a t-shirt that covers that glorious torso, and that charming smile. There's a toolbelt around his waist. He's like a blue-collar Batman.

"Nurse," he says, "I'm so glad you're here. I have this pain I want you to take a look at."

I glance at the house. They're all still at breakfast. No one's going to come for me.

His eyes are so blue. Bluer than the summer sky. Bluer than the pool. So blue I want to jump into them and swim as many laps as it would take to get lost.

"Yeah?" I ask, laughing. Usually when guys say this to me it sounds smarmy. When Hayden says it, I know he's just being cute. "Where?"

I love the way he looks at me. It's like he takes in every part of my body. My face, my neck, my breasts, my thighs. He lingers everywhere.

He takes the pencil tucked behind his ear and taps it once, twice, over his heart.

I laugh. "That's terrible. How did that happen?"

He shrugs. "You wouldn't tell me your name."

And just like that all the ugliness I was feeling vaporizes with a turn of his smile.

"It's pretty easy to guess," I say. "All you have to do is look up."

His brow furrows. He parts his lips to say something. I could just tell him. It's not that big of a deal. But there's something about him that makes me want to be playful. Something I haven't felt in such a long time. It's wonderful and ridiculous.

"Tripp!" Mr. Robertson walks towards the tree line and

stops when he sees me. "Sorry to bother you."

I shake my head. "No bother. I was just taking a walk."

Hayden taps his toolbelt. I forgot he's working and didn't just appear to brighten my day because I keep thinking about him.

"I have the measurements, Dad."

"Then get to it. Stop bothering the young lady."

"He's not bothering me," I say.

The old man furrows his brow and turns around as if I didn't say anything. "Get back to work. You've got a lot of free labor to do."

Hayden follows after his dad, but not before he winks at me and digs the end of his pencil into his chest one more time.

I roll my eyes and pretend he doesn't make my insides flutter like petals in a sweet breeze. He doesn't take his gaze off me as we walk parallel to each other across the lawn. So to hide from the blazing sun, the sear of his blue eyes, and the gossiping tongues of my family, I do the one thing I've wanted to do since I woke up—I dive headfirst into the pool, clothes and all.

CHAPTER 4

I hold a white lily up to my mother's nose. "I like this one."

"Too funeral," my mom says, batting it away. We're picking out flowers for the wedding, and my mom insisted on coming along.

"Didn't you hear?" I tell her. "That's what my generation calls getting married. Sorry Pepe."

"You don't have to tell me, *nena*." He faux pushes me away. "I'm the last person I thought would ever get hitched."

"Because all your ex-boyfriends could populate Texas?"

He sucks his teeth, and my mom doesn't look amused.

"Don't encourage her," my mom says.

Pepe isn't a typical uncle. Most of my uncles are middle-aged with mustaches and bellies that show how many beers they've had over the years. Pepe is fit from his days as a celebrity trainer. He's middle-aged but doesn't act like it. He's more like a brother than anything else. Hence, I'm his maid of honor.

"And don't talk like that, Sky," my mom says, followed by an exasperated sigh. "It'll happen for you. I got married late—twenty-three."

It's hard to think that at my age my mother already had a husband and a child on the way. That life is so far away from my plans, yet here it is being shoved in my face while I plan someone else's happily-ever-after.

Pepe's hip starts to flash. His phone is programmed to do that when it rings, which is seizure-inducing. "It's Paris," he says excitedly, then puts his hand over the phone and adds, "The *country*."

He's not usually so boastful, but the family deserves it after the way they treated him growing up.

My mom shakes her head, and I can see her clutch her purse tightly, the way she does when she wants to make the sign of the cross over her body and say a prayer. But she doesn't. Instead, she takes all of that pent-up family guilt and turns it over to me. I'm such a winner.

"We've been trying to pick wedding flowers for hours. It's not your wedding, and they both said they like the sunflowers," I say.

"Sunflowers don't say wedding by the beach. It says wedding on a farm."

"Ma, no it doesn't. And also, the ceremony is at their house, not on the beach. Just trust me, okay?"

"Why are you in such a hurry?"

I have a flashback of my mother standing in my way at the door to our old apartment, back when she had two jobs and always looked tired. Back before Pepe told her he'd take care of her the way she did for him when he was little. I'd be going to the library and she'd pitch a fit. River never had that issue. Then again, maybe if her parents had paid more attention, River wouldn't have gotten into so much trouble over the years.

My mom didn't need to tell me to stay away from boys. I got that all on my own from watching the tears my mom shed every day over my father's infidelities. Still, she didn't let a day pass without insinuating that I was doing everything except studying. Back then, the worst thing that could have happened to me was getting pregnant. Why has that changed only ten years later? Why is the absence of a man and the promise of that same baby also bad, only in a different way?

"I'm not in a hurry. We've just been here for hours. These sandals are giving me blisters. It's hot as balls, even in the AC, and you're driving me crazy."

"*No me hables así*, Sky Magdalena Lopez. I gave birth to you."

That "I gave birth to you" argument is going to follow me around forever. Why do Latin mothers, or maybe all mothers, like to hold that over our heads?

I gave birth to you, wash the dishes.
I gave birth to you, get a 4.0 GPA.

I gave birth to you, I'm not going to die without being a grandma.

"That's not my fault," I say, and receive an old-fashioned smack on the back of the head. Fine, I deserve that. But being around her makes me revert back to a teenager, and those were the worst years of my life.

"Are you seeing someone we don't know about?"

"What? No." Hayden's face, his impossibly beautiful face, flashes in my mind's eye, and I'm sure a blush spreads across my body.

"Sky, I'm worried about you." She pinches the bridge of her nose.

The tension goes out of my body because I hate when she's upset. I put a hand on her shoulder. "I know, Ma."

"Are you sure you can't work things out with Bradley?"

I snatch back my hand from her shoulder like she's made of acid.

"Don't be dramatic, Sky. You know what I mean. Men are weak. You can't always blame them. Sometimes, they can't get everything they need from you, so they have to—"

"Don't even finish that sentence, Ma."

"I want you to have financial stability. If you won't give Bradley another chance, then I know a nice young doctor. You might remember him—"

"Can you stop?" I want to tear my hair from my skull. "I can take care of myself. I don't need someone else's checkbook."

"Sky." She tries to reach for me but I take a step back, sending a delicate vase full of soft pink flowers shattering to the ground. "Listen to me."

"No. I don't care how much Bradley is worth on paper. I'd rather not have a dime to my name than let him touch me ever again. I'm not like you."

I turn away from her, pushing away the tears that swell in my eyes and put on a smile that I don't feel. The front door jingles.

A sales lady comes running from some storage room with a crease on her forehead.

"I'm so sorry," I say, choking on the sorry. "I'm here for the Vargas-Antonucci wedding. We'll take a mix of the white and blush tea roses for the aisle. Sunflowers for the centerpieces. White and sunflower mixes for the four bouquets. And I'll pay for that vase separately."

The sales lady's frown quickly disappears when I hand her my credit card.

No amount of money will fix my broken heart, but at least it'll pay for this broken vase.

. . .

After we get home from the florist, I sit on my balcony sipping a bottle of water, and my heart does a little flip when I see Hayden standing in the center of the lawn, towards the line of trees, hammering a platform together. I suddenly realize that almost every guy I've ever dated has been blond.

My dad was short, but muscular. He never shaved his mustache, and it was always a glossy black. His skin was darker than mine and he never smiled. He wasn't the kind of man who chased after skirts. He was that angry, silent man who made women want to know why he was so serious. It made them come to him.

I've made sure that every guy I've dated is nothing like my father physically, and somehow I still ended up in the same situation as my mom. Maybe it has nothing to do with race or culture. Maybe my mom's right, men are weak. That doesn't mean I have to be weak as well.

The only couple I've ever looked up to is Pepe and Tony.

I watch Hayden stand up and stretch. He works out the shoulder that was injured. The afternoon sun does wonderful things to highlight his biceps.

My aunt Cecy is making her way across the pool, towards the lawn where Hayden works. She's got a tall glass of lemonade in her hand. Aunt Cecy recently got a new facelift, boob job, and tummy tuck. Who knew that a few snaps here and there would give her the sex drive of a twenty year-old sorority girl?

She wags her new ass over to Hayden and offers him the lemonade. I kind of want to shout across the way and tell him there might be a rufie in it, but no one but me (and maybe my girls) would think it's funny.

Hayden is all smiles and thank you's. He drinks it and says something that makes Aunt Cecy giggle loudly. I've never met someone as good-natured as him. It's like a beacon of light.

Bradley also pulled me in when he smiled at me.

My heart tells me to pull back. But I stay at my balcony and watch Aunt Cecy put her hand on Hayden's shoulder and Hayden wiggle his way out of her cougar claws by taking one step away.

When she doesn't seem to be getting anywhere, she saunters back past the pool where her husband, Peter, is passed out on a chair with a towel over his hairy belly and a beer in his hand.

I can almost hear the way she snarls at him on her way back into the house.

Who needs reality TV? I've got more than enough drama right in my own backyard.

When I look back to where Hayden was working I realize he's gone.

"Hey, Rapunzel," a voice comes from below me.

My heart seizes and my skin gets hot. I feel like I've been caught, even though I haven't done anything. Well, snooping isn't *nothing*.

"Building me a castle?" I ask Hayden. I lean over the balcony to get a better look at him.

His tan is deeper, which makes his eyes that much bluer, even from up here. And yep, he's still shirtless. God bless Hamptons summers.

"You're already in the castle," he says. "Actually, I'm building your uncles a wedding gazebo."

"What? That's news to me."

"Yeah it's part of my labor to pay back the dress and the hole I put through the roof."

"That wasn't your fault."

He shrugs, and for the first time since I met him, he doesn't smile. Okay, he does, but it's the fake polite kind that really shouldn't count.

"My old man doesn't seem to think so. Either way, I'm not just a roofer."

"You surf, too?"

From the corner of my eye I can see someone watching us from the kitchen window. The blinds open partway, and when they see me looking they snap shut.

"That too," he says. "But I'm also really great with a hammer."

I cough my water down the wrong hole. "You should let other people tell you that."

"Why do you think your uncles hired me?" he chuckles. "I've got layers."

"I'm sure you do."

"But really," he says, "I like building things in my spare time. Makes me feel good, you know, having something tangible to look at."

"Roofs aren't tangible?"

"They are," he says thoughtfully, "but they aren't solely me. It's half a dozen dudes tramping around a house. When I build small projects like this, it makes me feel good. Useful."

"I think I get it. It's like your own kind of art, only with hammers and saws and nails."

He looks over his shoulder to where Uncle Peter is starting to snore. He scratches the back of his head. "So, do I call you Rapunzel now, or should I stick with Nurse?"

My heart skips a few beats. It's either because of Hayden or an uncommon case of AFib.

It's not like he's asking me if I want to get married. But I can feel him edging towards something else. Maybe to getting a coffee sometime, though he doesn't seem like the coffee drinking type. Bradley drank a gallon almost every day.

"Rapunzel is less accurate," I say. "My hair isn't nearly long enough."

"Juliet?" he suggests.

I shake my head. "My cousin's already named that. You wouldn't want to get us confused."

"That couldn't happen," he says.

Over at the kitchen window the blinds open again. Don't they have a telenovela to watch?

"We have an audience," Hayden says.

"Welcome to my life."

"I feel like I should dance for them or something."

"Don't get Aunt Cecy riled up."

He laughs, and I could listen to his laugh over and over. I press a hand against my stomach to stop this feeling from spreading.

"I've got to get to work," he tells me.

I want to tell him to stay. That his eyes and his smile and him...just him...are my favorite things to look at.

"Okay." I wave, starting to retreat back into my room. "Sorry you got stuck with this."

He shrugs. "It's not so bad. There's one upside."

"The lemonade?"

He walks backward, keeping his eyes on me. "I was going to say that at least I get to see you from far away. But the lemonade's good, too."

CHAPTER 5

Leti, River, and I skip family dinner and head out to the end of Dune Road for a free concert. Everyone pretty much goes to bed after dinner, and considering breakfast, there's no way I'm sticking around for another round of Point-out-Sky's-Life Choices.

"Ignore it," River says, regarding Maria and my mother. She drives with her knee while she lights a cigarette. "Maria just tries to get under everyone's skin to make it seem like her life is more perfect. I'm pretty sure her fiancé is gay."

Leti barks a laugh. "Not the way he was looking at these girls over Christmas." She shimmies her breasts, which are pushed up with the help of a fuchsia bikini top. In the setting sun, the light catches the bit of gold on her tooth, and I wish I could remember the last time I laughed like that.

It almost feels like I spent more time trying to *fix* things with Bradley, and such a short time doing the beginning stuff. The happy stuff. The wooing and courting and dancing stuff. I don't remember when it changed. All I know is that no one should be unhappy for that long. If it had been River or Leti, I would have advised them to get out quickly. It's easier to see the flaw in other people's relationships because you don't believe that could actually happen to you.

I don't want to be that girl again.

When we get to the parking lot, we flash our resident pass and the bored girl on her phone waves us in from her booth. We park and polish off champagne splits that are *technically* supposed to be for the wedding toast. I swiped half a dozen that won't really be missed.

The rush of the waves and the tuning of strings fill the late summer air. They're my favorite sounds.

"Okay," River says, throwing her cigarette on the ground and crushing it with her flip-flop. "It's been a pretty shit year. What with my little trouble with the law, Leti's accidental deportation back from Sweden, and Sky's love life, we've had enough bad luck to last us a damn fucking good while."

She raises her champagne split and Leti and I follow.

"This is a toast to not letting life get us down. We are young and we are going to grab life by the hairy balls and refuse to be anything short of fantastic."

"Amen, sister," Leti clinks her glass.

"And to getting laid!" River hollers, catching the attention of some surfer-looking types around our age. She throws her golden curls over her shoulder in that wild, carefree way of hers, and they take notice.

I down my champagne and enjoy the fizz that goes down my throat. I know better than to contradict a toast. And I get it, I know it's time to move on. As we polish off our champagne and walk up the ramp to the beach, I take a freeing breath and promise to reclaim my happy.

• • •

Happy comes with a side of fries and a super cold Long Ireland, a local beer. We were lucky to snatch up a table before the crowds came in.

"Are you going to talk to her or am I?" Leti says quietly. She dips five fries at a time in mayo, then ketchup before eating them. She's talking about River.

"Look, I don't care if she smokes," I say. "Smoking means she's not doing *other* things. Let her have that for now. When the summer's up, I'm getting her on the patch."

Leti doesn't agree, but we leave River smoking her loosies in the corner of shame. All I can think is that this gorgeous girl doesn't belong in that group of weathered old men and women who look ten years older than they actually are.

When River rejoins us, she hooks her thin but strong arms

around our necks and tells us how much she loves us.

I shush them. "It's starting."

The summer concerts are pretty chill. Mostly old indie bands that play small beach shows and even smaller towns, but they're pretty kickass. Growing up, the three of us gravitated more to old rock and folk music. I could listen to Joni Mitchell and Stevie Nicks all day and night.

I'm so lost in the music, in the cool night sea breeze, in the sway of a melody that makes me sing along even though I don't know the words, that I almost don't notice Hayden staring at me.

A jolt, like electricity, hits me and makes me sit up straight. River gives me an inquisitive look and I grin and point at my beer. I hide my face behind the plastic rim and glance around the place.

Couples dance and sway to the easy strum of a guitar. Kids play with the sand that piles up between the floorboards. Leti gazes dreamily at the bassist who could be a Clooney clone if Clooney was cloned as a hippie.

When I look at him again, he's still staring at me. He's shirtless. Why, in the name of sweet, sweet, Mary, does he have to be shirtless? Right, we're at the beach. Minimal clothes are okay in this social environment. His smile is brilliant even in the night. His blond hair is thick from salt water. His board shorts are black, covered with pink and blue Hawaiian flowers.

His legs are straddled around a bar stool, and for the first time I notice how thick and powerful his calves are, like a runner or a soccer player.

My face is still buried in my cup, the beer slowly but surely making its way down my throat, metabolizing into a pleasant buzz across my skin.

Then I remember he's shirtless, and my eyes trace him from his extremely happy trail up his abs. His abs. They're something carved out of gold. Can you even carve gold? No. Diamond. Rock-hard crystal formed from coal and pressure and oh my god my beer is spilling down my chin.

He waves at me, still smiling in that goofy way of his.

I wipe my chin and dab at my chest with a napkin. Leti looks at what has me so flustered and nearly jumps out of her seat.

She tries to whisper. "That guy is staring at you."

River turns around, a hundred times less subtle than me. "He looks familiar."

Where was I? The abs. Right. Then there's his chest. It's not over-inflated like those guys who spend hours downing protein shakes and bench pressing. It's like every pec and ab and bicep was carefully built from physical work. They're muscles I've never seen on any guy I've ever dated. Bradley wouldn't know manual labor if it hit him over the head with a hammer.

Stop thinking of Bradley.

Then the music stops and everyone applauds. While the first band unplugs and the next band sets up, Hayden hops off his bar stool and starts walking towards us.

Leti jumps up and flails her hands towards me. "Ohmigod he's coming to talk to us. To you!"

River squints at him. "Doesn't he look familiar? Is he an actor? Wait…was he in Magic Mike?"

"The last time you saw him he was falling through a roof."

Leti squeals and River sucks her teeth and says, "I *knew* I'd seen those abs before."

"*Shhh,*" I tell them. "Don't be weird."

"When are we ever weird?" River says.

It would take way too long to recall high school right now.

"Hey, ladies," Hayden says. He's got a bounce in his step.

"You look good without plaster and blood all over you," River says.

Hayden laughs. "Thank you for noticing. This is my fancy suit after all."

Leti beams at him. "Are you here all alone? I'm Leti, by the way. Sky's incredibly available cousin."

River holds her cup to cheers his in greeting. "River. Yes that's my real name. No jokes. I'm sure you remember Sky."

He claps his hands and practically fist pumps the air in triumph. "I *knew* I'd find out your name."

I give River my death glare.

Hayden holds his hands out victoriously and points at

me. "Sky."

"What?" She shrugs. "I didn't know you were keeping it a secret."

"I wasn't." If I were wearing pants, I would smooth them out. But since I'm not, I smooth out the imaginary wrinkles on my legs.

Hayden looks at my empty cup. "Can I get you ladies another round?"

Leti and River hold up their cups with their most charming smiles. "Please and thank you, handsome stranger."

"Please, no strangers here," he says. When he speaks it's hard to take my eyes off him. "Sky?"

"I'm good," I say.

"Don't listen to her," Leti says. "She's drinking the Long Ireland."

Hayden winks at me. "Good. So am I."

He walks up to the wooden bar, and our eyes follow the muscles of his back.

"If he were covered in tattoos," Leti says, "he'd totally be my type."

"Hush," River says. "This one is for Sky. He's such a dork. A hot dork with rock solid buns, but still. He couldn't stop looking at you."

"Can we leave this alone?" I bury my face in my hands.

"You asked for this," Leti says. "Do *not* fuck with the Universe. You said the man you wanted wouldn't just drop down at your feet. And he *literally* did. Appropriate use of the word *literal*, thank you."

"This isn't life by committee over here," I say. "I'm not ready for a thing."

River winks a sultry blue eye. "How about a fling?"

I can feel my blood heating up from their suggestive glee, from Hayden looking back every chance he gets. "I came to the Hamptons to be alone and to have space to think before the wedding crazy started. What do I get? Nosy family members and friends who are supposed to *love* me shoving me towards the first erection they see."

"Technically," Leti says, "he doesn't have an erection. But if things work out, he could! And he could have friends for the friends that *you* love."

I roll my eyes.

River shakes her head. "Look, we're not saying marry him. We're not even saying to sleep with him, though I'm sure you could if you wanted to. All we're saying is that you are being presented with a super hot guy who clearly likes you so much he *bounced* when we told him your name. Don't let your shitty past shit all over your future. That's River's wisdom for the night. Now he's walking back here, so act like we haven't been talking about him this whole time."

Hayden takes a seat at our table. "Here you go, ladies."

"How do you figure we're ladies?" River asks him.

He shrugs. "Well, my mom raised me to treat all women like ladies."

River takes the beer he offers and smiles. It's hard to make River genuinely smile. It contradicts the badass persona she's cultivated over the years. "It's like you took a wrong turn from a fairy tale. Are you sure you're from New York?"

"Born and bred Long Island, with a small stint upstate," he says. "But this far out east, the Hamptons are an expensive fairytale for city folk."

"Oh my god, you just said *folk*," Leti says.

He sets my beer in front of me and clinks it, slightly bowing his head towards me.

"Thank you."

"My pleasure." He looks behind him when two guys shout his name. "If you'll excuse me, I'm going to get back to my friends."

I can see Leti's eyes go wide as telescopes. River swings her head at me and bats those thick dark lashes. She holds out her hands in a form of supplication.

Ugh, fine. Just because I want to brood and be alone for a whole summer doesn't mean I have to drag my friends through my funk. We made a toast. A pact.

"Sky," my best friends whine. I give in.

"Hayden! Wait," I say.

Hayden turns on his heel and that million-watt smile of his blinds me. "Yes?"

"You—you should stay," I say. I try not to wince as River's excited nails dig into my leg. "There's plenty of room here."

His smile quirks into the sweetest, most likable crooked smile. "I thought you'd never ask."

When he turns around to get them, Leti and River pull me into a giant bear hug. "You are the best. You are the queen. You rule. We owe you."

If I'm not ready to get some action, it doesn't mean I can't play the fairy godmother of summer sex to everyone else.

CHAPTER 6

As the night sets in, the bands get louder and so does the crowd. Leti is deep in conversation with Football Scholarship. He's tall and over-inflated in the chest, but has a kind smile and eyes made lazy by beer and the easiness of Leti's conversation. She can talk about almost any part of the world to anyone. Most of her stories start with, "So I was really bombed in…" This time it's Ireland. "I was with these UN people on this literary tour. Mostly James Joyce stuff. I was the American that everyone hated because I was loud and I knew all the right answers."

River scoffs. "I was there, and if I recall, we had the help of our super smart phones."

Hayden's arm brushes closer to me. There are so many people around us that our big table suddenly feels tiny. It seems that no matter how much I want to avoid his stare, it's right there, waiting for me to look back.

"Do we even still have that t-shirt?" I ask, wetting my lips with my warming beer.

"You won a t-shirt?" Hayden asks.

"Yep!" Leti says, pumping her fist in the air. "Literary Champs! With a clover on it. We were going to do one of those Sisterhood of the Traveling Clothes thing, but I think it's in my hamper back home."

"I never even got to wear it," River says.

"Same," I say.

Football Scholarship holds his hands out to Leti and asks her to dance. The song is sexy, all bass and sultry siren vocals. She doesn't even look at us before taking his hand and joining the other couples.

Hayden's other friend, Sgt. Pepper—and I only call him that

because that's actually his title in the Army—sees his chance in the empty space beside River. On the outside, it might seem that she isn't interested in the Army guy at all, but I know better. A telling sign of River's like is how disinterested she seems.

"Shit, Sam," Hayden says. "When was the last time you were home before now?"

Sgt. Pepper looks down at the beer can in his hands, then glances at River, who is busy licking the rim of her margarita cup.

"A while. Good to be home though."

"Sam was supposed to be in finance," Hayden says. "But one day he shocked us all when he picked up his shit and announced he'd enlisted."

"I think everyone was shocked but me and this guy," he says. "You weren't, were you Tripp?"

"I would have been surprised if you hadn't," Hayden says. "Then again, there's the war, and then there's your dad."

Sgt. Pepper's eyebrow twitches a tiny bit when he hears that. "Both are a war in their own way."

Something about the way he says that makes River look up. It's almost like a part of her was starting to wander off and just came back.

"I think the next band is a Blink 182 cover band," Hayden says. "Do you want to take a walk on the beach?"

"How do you know I wouldn't enjoy Blink 182?" I take a sip of my beer.

He rests his chin on his fist looking more and more like a storybook prince. The part of me that is so jaded she can't see straight tells me to say no. To go hide in the bathroom or wait in the car or just walk back home even though it's dark and unsafe. Anything is safer than getting your heart crushed into millions of microscopic pieces and then set on fire. Again.

But something nudges me in the ribs. Or should I say, River nudges me in the ribs.

"Are you going for a walk?" River asks in that way that's so obvious I'm getting set up.

Who needs enemies when you have friends who will shove you into an unforgiving sense of embarrassment?

Hayden laughs his beautiful laugh. "I'm waiting for Sky to give me the pleasure of her company. Not that you lot aren't great."

"We'll all go," River says, pinching me between my shoulder blades.

I keep smiling and sling my arm around her. I pinch her in the tender spot in her side just to see how she likes it.

"What about Leti?" I ask.

Hayden points to the couple happily making out among other dancing-kissing couples.

"Right," I say following the others down the beach steps.

It's not that I don't like kissing. It's not like I'm swearing off men forever and pretending that I'd rather try being a lesbian. It's just that I want time to myself. The problem with needing a mental health break is that everyone takes it upon themselves to try and fix something that isn't so easily fixed.

Still, Hayden is a nice guy, and he hasn't actually done anything to suggest that he's actively trying to get inside my bikini. All he's doing is looking at me. There's nothing wrong with looking I guess.

• • •

The wet sand is cold. River and Sgt. Pepper walk ahead of us. He points out some constellations, and she pretends like she's listening when she's actually staring at his lips.

"Don't tell your friend," Hayden tells me in a hushed voice, "but Sam doesn't actually know if the constellations he's pointing at are the right ones."

"What?" I ask in mock-distress. "A boy lying to impress a girl? Never heard of that before."

This far out on Long Island, where the light pollution fades, there are so many stars. It's easy to forget you're surrounded by beautiful things when you don't even bother to look up.

"I don't know them either," he says. "But at least I don't pretend. Sometimes if I think I see a shape I name them all after myself."

"What's the point of discovering things if we can't name them after ourselves, right?"

"I wish I'd been alive back in Christopher Columbus's day."

"So you could get in early on the pillaging and spreading of smallpox?"

"No." He grazes his arm against mine. I suck in a breath at the warmth of his skin. "So I could name everything after me. Haydenland, a place for all to come."

"That's very generous of you."

"What about you?" he asks, walking closer to where the waves crash and the surf spumes like champagne around our ankles. "Sky World? Skylandia? The Mysterious Island of Sky?"

"Not so mysterious," I say. "And I wouldn't need a whole country. Just a little piece of land with a castle and a taco truck open twenty-four hours a day."

"I'd let you live in Haydenland if I could get in on that food truck action."

"Okay. But I'd need a break on my taxes."

"Taxes? This is Haydenland. It's like paradise. Taxes don't exist in paradise. Only good things."

I tuck my hair back into its ponytail. I want to think of something witty to say because I want him to think I'm so smart and so funny. Instead, a part of my brain shuts off. Maybe it's self-preservation. Maybe I'm just exhausted. But I stand there with the champagne sea crashing at my feet and a beautiful guy waiting for my next words, which have floated away like lost messages in proverbial bottles.

"Don't take this the wrong way," I say. I brace myself for what I'm going to tell him, because a small part of me doesn't want to. But this is how I feel right now. "You're really nice...but I'd just really like to be alone."

You'd think that would make him stop smiling, but it doesn't. It's a smaller smile, sad.

He bends down and sifts through the wet sand. It's a perfect half clamshell. I have a jar full of them in my dresser.

"Here," he says.

"What's this for?"

He scratches the back of his head. "Well, I want you to have something to think of me by that doesn't involve roof tiles or rusty nails sticking out of my back. Plus, I'm pretty sure it's worth a million dollars."

"I'd like to think that seashell patterns are as individual as snowflakes, but I don't know if that's a real fact."

"It can be a Sky fact. Those are all the facts I need."

"Thanks, Hayden."

I start walking back the way we came and break into a run until I reach the car. I'm not playing hard to get. That's the thing—I'm not playing at all. I'm on the verge of being twenty-four, and I'm starting over. I'm unsure of so many things, except that I do want Hayden. I think of his beautiful eyes, his daydream smile, and the way he warms when he talks to me. It makes sense to run away before I let myself get swept away into the arms of another heartbreak.

CHAPTER 7

"Sky Lopez," River groans. I pull back the curtain in her room. "It is an ungodly hour of the morning, so what the fuck do you think you're doing?"

"It's 1 PM," I tell her. "I've gone for a swim, had breakfast with the family. Also, Ass Grabber Greg is here, and he asked if you were coming to the wedding."

"Ugh," she says, rolling over and tangling herself more in her cigarette-scented sheets. "He's my least favorite of your cousins."

"I want to go talk to the caterers today. They haven't returned my emails. Uncle Tony has all these phone calls lined up and Pepe has this showcase."

"You would think that with throwing a two hundred plus person wedding, that doesn't include local crashers, they'd take time off work. I don't get it. They're too perfect. It hurts my jaded soul."

"Maybe that's why it works. Both of them are workaholics, so the time they do get to see each other is precious."

"Or maybe they both have really big—"

I plug my fingers in my ears and shout "laalalalala" at the top of my lungs.

Her laugh is like a crackling fire, and it's followed by a whooping cough.

"Let's go," I say. "If you don't come to the caterer with me, my mom is going to force me to let her tag along. If I tell her you're coming, she'll stay home."

"Your mom's hated me since high school. I should win an award."

It's a sad part of our relationship, but yeah, my mom thinks that River is (how does a nice Catholic Ecuadorian put it?) loose and immoral. And she thought that even before River lost her virginity.

"She'll come around," I say.

"My own mother doesn't like me, I don't expect other mothers to. Besides, I did crash my car into her kitchen that one time. And set her drapes on fire when I fell asleep with my cigarette."

"Smoking is a hazard."

She lifts her head from her pillow, but it's like it's too heavy. "Take Leti."

I wiggle an eyebrow at her. "Leti didn't come home last night, and if I point that out Las Viejas are going to have strokes. So, sorry champ. Help me, Obi-Wan. You're my only hope."

"Fine, I'll get up. This means you owe me right?"

I shake my head and slap her thigh as her eyes flutter back to sleep. "Nope. You still owe me from the other twenty times."

"Jesus, you're keeping track?"

I shrug. "Someone has to."

. . .

We drive to Deep Blue Sea, a fish market near Riverhead that doubles as a no-frills restaurant. They have two-for-one lobsters that rival some of my favorite lobster spots in Boston.

"I love being out here," River says. "Reminds me of when we were kids."

River's an honorary member of my family. I remember her being there for more of my Christmases than hers.

"What happened to that last guy you were dating?"

She shrugs and turns the wheel to make a right. "Loser. Not that you're surprised. He didn't like that I quit gambling cold turkey."

I bite a broken cuticle. "Are you still okay with that?"

"Sometimes my mind gets restless, you know. The first few days I felt like if I didn't at least bet on the weather, my head would explode."

"If you want," I say, "I know people you could talk to. There are retreats…"

"No, Sky," she says firmly. "The only people I need are you and Leti. Don't be tricksy, you little hobbit, I know that retreat is a nice way of saying *rehab center*."

"I'm not a hobbit," I say, "I'm taller than you."

She reaches out and musses my hair. "Now for the real question. Why the fuck did you steal my car and leave sweet sexy Hayden high and dry?"

I roll my eyes. "Rule #1: If one River Thomas is too intoxicated to drive, take the keys."

She shakes her head, and her medusa curls dance with a life of their own. "Whatever. Hayden was super sad when you left, by the way. I think he really likes you."

"He doesn't know me."

"That's the point," she says, flicking her turn signal on to cut off a guy driving too slowly. "He gets to know you, and then you do the kissing and baby-making parts without the actual babies."

"I feel like between you guys and my mother, I'm talking to a fucking wall." I cross my arms over my chest so she knows I mean business. "When I *want* to be with someone, I will be."

"So tell me straight up that you haven't been salivating over that boy since he fell at your feet? Tell me you two don't make eyes at each other from your balcony and the lawn."

"Fuck," I say. "That was you peeking through the blinds?"

She smirks with her pink lips. "I know attraction, and you two have it. Don't lie."

"I think this is the turn." I point to the exit, and she makes a hard left.

"We came here last month and it was so good," I say, forcing the subject to change. "We should get one lobster mac-and-cheese to go."

When I get out of the car, my heart hammers in my throat and my legs go a little weak. They're closed.

"When was the last time you spoke to them?" River asks, leaning on the hood of her car.

"July! They catered Pepe's Fourth of July party! That's

when we hired them and put down a deposit. Someone called me three weeks ago to confirm, and we sent in the check. Oh my God, this is horrible…what am I going to tell the uncles? They're so busy as it is. How am I going to find a new place?"

River holds her hand against the glass. "Maybe they're just closed for today?"

I point at the glaring sign that says "Closed for the rest of the summer."

"This is horrible!" I start pacing. "What do we do? Most places require months in advance to fill orders that big."

"Sky, chill," River says.

"Chill? That's easy for you to say."

"Because I hate responsibility? True, but also because we'll find something."

"What?" I ask, smacking my hands at my sides. "The wedding's in three weeks. What am I going to tell Pepe and Tony?"

River lights her cigarette and shrugs. "Have you considered not telling them?"

"What?"

She blows smoke and the wind carries it away from us. "Before you blow that pretty little head of yours into smithereens, let's go into town and ask around."

"But—"

"I know it sucks, but trust me. Okay? No need to get the uncles upset if it's not necessary."

I nod and follow her back into the car.

That's the thing about River—she might shy away from responsibility, but she'll never leave you hanging.

⁎ ⁎ ⁎

We drive around town and stop at our favorite restaurants. Each manager I speak to gives me a sympathetic face with a notice that they're booked solid. The reason Pepe and Tony picked Deep Blue Sea was because they love seafood. The only other seafood place in town is solidly booked for every other wedding

ZORAIDA CÓRDOVA

in the Hamptons.

"What about this place?" River drives past Margarita Grill. "Don't you come here to eat alone?"

Side-eye, side-eye, side-eye.

"I come here for lunch," I say.

"Alone."

"You know," I say, "you go out alone, too. There's nothing wrong with that."

"I never leave alone," she says, salaciously.

"You're impossible."

She leans over and kisses my cheek. "What's wrong with this place?"

"There's nothing wrong with it, but it's one-note."

"You're kidding me, Lopez. Is this your wedding or theirs? I'm sure the uncles will be happy with whatever as long as *someone* cooks for two hundred."

I look down at my lap. She's right. Maybe I have been treating this like my wedding. It's not like I *want* to get married now. It's not like Bradley and I were engaged.

"It's hard to explain," I say. "It's like everything I've been doing has been *leading* to this. Now that it's gone, I've lost more than my path. I lost my endgame. Holy shit, I don't have an endgame."

"Look," she says, "we'll find something. Let's go online and make a list of places nearby and then hit them up this week."

River turns the key and revs the engine. Nice families run across the street. Cars drive slowly enough that no one bothers to look both ways. Then, my heart nearly jumps out of my chest when I see a silver Mercedes zoom down the street. It almost clips a woman with a stroller, which makes everyone shout after the car. I sit up and try to catch the license plate number, but it's long gone.

"What's wrong?"

"Nothing," I say. Actually, everything. Everything is wrong. "I think I just saw a ghost."

Maybe not a ghost. Maybe just my ex-boyfriend.

CHAPTER 8

River steps on it, but we drive around and around without a sign of the silver Mercedes. She glances at me with a worried look on her face. I looked at her like that the last time she was in trouble.

"Everyone here has that car, Sky. Doesn't his family go up to Cape Cod during the summer?"

I nod, clutching my purse in my hand. "You're right. It's like relationship PTSD or something."

"When was the last time you spoke to him?"

"The day I left Boston."

"Sky…" she takes her eyes off the road long enough to make me look at her. "I wouldn't judge you."

"Last month," I say. "He called just to talk. To ask me back. I said no. He calls every now and then but I don't pick up. I don't get it. He can flash his smile and his Amex and get any girl. I just want him to leave me alone."

When she pulls up in front of our house she flashes me a smile. "That's the thing. You aren't just any girl, Sky."

Before I have the chance to thank her for keeping me sane, my mom comes running out the front door. She pulls me out of the car before River even hits the parking brake.

Ma's wearing her nice silk blouse, the kind she only puts on when we have company so they won't see her in velour pants and at-home t-shirts.

"Ma, what are you doing?"

She pulls me into the house, past the foyer, through the kitchen, and into the dining room where everyone is having lunch.

Leti looks up and gives me a warning glare as she bites into a BLT. She shakes her head. I've seen this look before, when we were at her quinceañera and her mom made us dance with "nice boys from her church." Leti looked at me sideways and muttered, "Run," under her breath.

I can see her mouth the same thing right now. "Run."

Except I can't. Everyone's staring at me. Aunt Cecy's fanning herself with a tacky metallic fan, Maria and Ass Grabber Greg look up smugly from their sodas, Uncle Peter pops the top off his beer with his teeth, and Las Viejas press their hands to their hearts and sigh like schoolgirls.

Nope. Nope. Nope. Nope.

There's a stranger sitting at the table. He isn't eating. He's tall, dark, and devilishly handsome in that manicured way. His facial hair is trimmed so neatly, I bet he has to get it shaped professionally. His hair has the right amount of lift at the front, his eyebrows are thick and long, and there's not a stray hair for miles on that glistening, smooth forehead.

He looks over his shoulder, and I can feel his rich brown eyes check me out. He starts with my toes. I haven't gotten my nails done in a couple of weeks, but the color hasn't chipped. Pink and happy, the color I get when I want to make myself smile.

I remember my mom's warning this morning. "Wear something nice today. I'm tired of seeing you in a bikini top and sandy shorts."

She knew.

Run.

It's a trap.

Then he looks at my legs, freshly scrubbed, shaved, and oiled after my morning run. I threw on a blue dress the color of Hayden's eyes.

Wait, what? The color of periwinkle flowers.

Because my mom yanked out my ponytail band when she rushed me out of the car, my hair has that weird crease in it. I can feel her smoothing it, raking my hair back like I'm a prized poodle.

"Xandro," my mom says. "You remember Sky. She's a nurse. I was telling you before."

Xandro gets up from the table, and I hear someone call him a gentleman. He's tall and muscular. His blazer is so white it reminds me of the time I left my whitening strips on my teeth too long. His tank underneath is the color of medium-rare salmon, which makes me think of seafood, which makes me think of Deep Blue Sea, which reminds me that the restaurant is closed and that I have to tell everyone.

I take a deep breath.

"Look at her," Grandma Gloria whispers. "She's nervous. *Que linda.*"

I vomit a little in my head.

Xandro extends his long, thin fingers out to me. They could be a piano player's or a violinist's fingers. Bradley had long, strong fingers, but he sucked at any of the fancy musical training he had received over the years. His hands were good for beer pong, and well...other things.

I shake Xandro's hand, wishing I could shield myself from his dark stare, and, oh yeah, the other dozen creeps in my family watching our exchange.

"Sky," I say, "but I'm sure you already know my blood type with this crowd."

He laughs. How is it possible to hate someone's laugh instantly? It is. There's something about it that makes my skin crawl. It's like he's humoring me, like "oh, you're cute."

My mom presses her hands on my back. I can hear keys jingle in the entrance and feet scurry upstairs. River, that lucky bitch. My mom ushers me two steps closer to Xandro so I can smell his saccharine cologne.

"Xandro is Jimena's son," she tells me. "You remember don't you? They used to live next door to us in Queens?"

I vaguely remember a primping little boy who got picked up and dropped off in a special school bus. Special because it wasn't the yellow public school ones I had to get on. The neighborhood kids picked on him every chance they got because of his freshly pressed uniform, the careful sweep of his hair. A nickname comes to my lips and slips out, "Strawberry."

Xandro's polite smile snarls for a moment. "No one's called me that in forever."

My cheeks are red, but not for the reason everyone suspects.

"I'm sorry, I just—"

He corrects his frown and smiles again. "It's fine. That was a long time ago. I'm actually renting a house in the neighborhood."

What a nice way to say how rich he is without actually saying so.

My mom's face is beaming, surely hoping I'll fall madly in love and pick out curtains for the rental. "Go wash your hands and join us for lunch."

I take a step back, smiling politely. "River and I just had lunch. Thanks."

My mom gives me a look that tells me I'd better shut up if I know what's good for me.

"But there's always room for roast beef," I say, running off to the guest bathroom. I splash water on my sweaty face. My mind is already a carousel of thoughts, and I don't need to add Xandro to it. Then again, living with my family already feels like being at a never-ending circus, so why not.

When I come back into the dining room, I see a couple of bills exchange between Leti and my cousins Yunior and Mike. Yunior sees me first and shoves the money in his pockets. They're taking bets! With family like this...

"I don't remember you from the hood," Yunior tells Xandro.

"That's because you're too young, *mijo*," my mom says. I haven't seen her smile this much in years. "Xandro, tell us about your practice."

Xandro takes a napkin and drapes it over his knee. He doesn't take his eyes off me as he tells us about Gonzalez and Gold, the nip/tuck operation out of South Beach.

"I was thinking of getting a little bit done here," Aunt Cecy says, pulling at her already stretched out face.

Xandro leans forward and says, "You should wait at least six months for this operation to heal."

My cousins snicker and giggle as Aunt Cecy's face turns red.

"Ay, Cecilia," my mom tells her. "You don't need that stuff."

Xandro realizes the mistake he made, too late. "She's right. You don't need any more work. Beauty runs in your family."

Oh sweet Christ. I pile a bunch of roast beef on my bread.

My mom reaches over and takes a few slices off. She glances at Xandro. God forbid he sees me eating. I take the jar of mayo and spread on a healthy helping.

"Xandro," my mom says. I hate the way she says his name, like he's halfway to becoming a god and she's looking for his supplication. Please, Xandro, please take my hopeless daughter in exchange for this sandwich! "Would you like something else besides the salad?"

"Sure," he says. "That roast beef looks great."

I take a bite and speak with my mouth full. "It's really good."

Yunior shoves a bill into Leti's hand under the table. Normally, I have better table manners, but this is what they get for ambushing me like this.

"Sky," my mom motions to the spread. Oh *hell* no.

I laugh. "Oh, you want me to make the sandwich?"

Leti cough-laughs into her hand. I shoot her a look that should kill.

I take a knife from the table and cut my sandwich in half. I have a flashback of family parties where the women would be in the kitchen and the men in the living room. Even as a little girl I was taught to fix a plate for my father, my male cousins, my uncle. Like they couldn't get off their lazy hides and make one for themselves. So now, I cut my sandwich and drop half on Xandro's plate.

"Sky!" Maria scolds me.

I smile at our guest. "I hope you like mayo."

He chuckles, like I'm the funniest girl in the world. Then, much to everyone's surprise, he eats it. Cousin Mike hands Leti some more money. I'd better see half of that cash since they're betting on my humiliation.

"So," I say, "how come you're in town?"

"I'm looking at some property. We want to expand to New York."

"Sky's not working right now," Maria says. "Maybe she can work for you. If not, I'm sure she'd appreciate some references."

"It's okay." I say. "I'm not going back to the hospital."

"When did you decide this?" my mom asks through polite,

gritted teeth.

I shrug. "Just now. I'm going to get my masters in Psychology and Children's Development."

Xandro looks overwhelmed. "Well, if you change your mind—"

"I'll let you know." I take the open bottle of wine chilling in a bowl and pour myself a glass. I can practically feel the steam blowing out of my mother's ears.

"You know what would be nice?" Aunt Salomé asks. "If we all went on a family dinner before the wedding. What's the place that's doing the catering?"

I cough wine onto Xandro's blazer. "Oh, God. I'm so sorry. Hiccups."

He smiles through his teeth, but the little vein on his forehead throbs. He takes the dozen napkins getting shoved in his direction. "It's fine. I have to go to the cleaners tomorrow anyway."

"Why don't we have a barbeque instead?" I suggest. "You know how loud we can get, and they're not really equipped for a big group. Or better yet, a wine tasting!"

"Count me in," Leti says.

"Great." How is it possible that my heart feels like it's pumping in every part of my body at once?

"Of course you're invited, Xandro. You and Sky should catch up over lunch."

"We're having lunch now," I point out.

Xandro checks his watch—a sleek silver Movado. "Actually, that would be great. I really have to go, but I'll pick you up tomorrow at noon."

"I can't—" I start to say, but my mother cuts me off.

"She'd love to."

Xandro takes my hand and presses it to his lips. "I can't wait to see you again, Sky."

When he leaves, I sink into my chair. Las Viejas talk amongst themselves and wonder what our children will look like. They comment on what a nice young man he is, and isn't it nice what he made of himself. No one, not a single person asks for my opinion.

Leti comes over and takes a seat beside me. "They bet you would agree to go out with him."

Yunior smiles smugly and holds his hand out to Leti. She slaps a couple of twenties into his open palm. I snatch them up.

"Hey!"

"Easy now. Leti still won." I count a hundred bucks and divide them between her and me. "Technically, *technically*, I wasn't the one who agreed."

CHAPTER 9

Later that night, my phone rings. When I see the number, I get one of those hot flashes that covers your body from your toes to the crown of your head. I hate that his name has that effect on me still.

Bradley.

Well, it's just his number. Even though I deleted it, I still know it by heart.

I changed the old song that was attached to it—"Born to be My Baby." I know, cheese much? But that was our song. The first time he sang it for me was on a drive to his parents' New Hampshire cabin. The road was rainy, and all we had was a gray sky and a staticky radio. So he turned it off and looked at me with those baby blue eyes and started singing.

Now his number plays the generic phone chirping.

Sometimes, I want to be a little weak. I want to pick up the phone or return the text message. There's nothing wrong with a little weakness. It means my heart's still working even though I'd like to think I'm dead inside, that I'm made of steel. I'm not. I'm flesh and blood, and a little part of me will always want Bradley because the hurt can't completely erase the good.

But tonight, I let the champagne wash away the weakness. I lean back in my chair and embrace the lonely night. I opt for a little bit of steel, and let the phone ring out.

CHAPTER 10

I skip breakfast and lie in bed with the sun streaming through my window, reliving the last couple of days. The one image that keeps resurfacing is Hayden's face when I left him on the beach. It could also be because the roofers are here. I can hear their boots on the roof, their hammers against nails. I know if I look out the window I'll see Hayden working on the gazebo. Every day, my aunts and cousins bring him lemonade in exchange for one of his brilliant smiles.

That's quickly replaced by Xandro's chemically white one when I remember we're having lunch today. If I was going to be forced to go on a date with someone I'm not interested in, then why don't I just go out with someone I'm extremely attracted to? *Sky Lopez, you did this to yourself,* I think. I roll over in my bed and shove my head in a pillow.

"Wakey wakey!"

I turn to catch a ball of blonde hair cannonballing on me.

"Ah, you dick." I roll over, holding my side.

"See, you don't like it when someone wakes you up, do you?" she asks. River climbs up the fluffy mattress and cuddles up to my side. Her long legs are golden and soft. River has a way of making herself comfortable really quickly.

"Your alarm isn't scheduled to go off for another five hours."

"I never actually went to sleep," she says. She presses her head in the pillow to avoid the question. That's when I smell the cigarettes and whiskey on her. "I did something you're going to love me for."

I groan and pull the cover over my head. "River," I say by way of warning. "What did you do?"

"Hey!" River takes her pillow and slams me over the head with it. "I do great things for you. I was hanging out at this house party and I met a guy who's a chef. I told him we'd go to his restaurant and check it out for the wedding."

"That's amazing. Damn, but I have lunch with Xandro. I just want to get it over with. Thanks for bailing on me yesterday, by the way."

River holds her hands up defensively. "Listen, there was no way I was getting involved in that mess. I'm already in the catering stuff. We'll go after your lunch."

I open my closet and pull out a maxi dress that requires no effort. Maxi dresses are basically muumuus with better fabric and colors.

River bats her sultry lashes at me. "I also happened to be outside when a strapping, shirtless man gave me this and asked me to deliver it to the Sleeping Beauty who slept so hard, she didn't hear the rocks tapping at her window last night."

"Wait, what?"

She grabs me by the shoulders. "Sky, don't be an idiot. I love you, but I'm not going to watch you torture yourself for the rest of the summer. You've helped me when I needed you most. Now I'm going to do the same for you, in a different way."

She shoves the round white thing in my hands, presses a kiss on my cheek, and runs before I have time to react. I hold the white disk in my hand and turn it over. It's a sand dollar. Smooth and white with black marker scrawled across the surface. At first, I'm not exactly sure what I'm looking at. But my heart reacts before my mind does. My stomach flutters and my chest gives a little squeeze. The black marker spells Hayden and his phone number.

CHAPTER 11

Margarita Grill is my favorite place off-season. They have bands come and play, and the locals come out of hiding after the Manhattenites and reality TV types leave. If the waitress didn't recognize me from my solitary lunches, we'd have to wait an hour for a table. She appraises Xandro and gives me two thumbs up.

I pull out my chair and sit across from where Xandro is already scanning the menu. Because of how crowded it gets during the summer, they add extra tables, which puts me back to back with the person sitting behind me.

"What's good here?" Xandro asks.

"The Mexican street corn is great. It's not *actually* street, but they try their best."

He smiles politely and nods. "I don't eat corn or cheese."

I laugh because I think he's joking, but when he looks confused, I realize he's not kidding. Not one bit. Instead, I'm the joke. I'm the girl ambushed into a "lunch date" with a guy who probably remembers me from my time with braces.

I order a glass of red wine and tap water.

Xandro asks for a skinny margarita and switches out tap water for bottled sparkling water.

"Red wine isn't very good for your teeth," he says playfully.

I lick the front of my teeth and take the fat red wine glass the waitress places in front of me. "None of it is actually good for you. That's not the point of drinking booze."

"What's the point?" He sits back, arms languishing on the armrests with his tall, skinny margarita in hand.

"The point is to get a buzz."

He shrugs, not agreeing or disagreeing. From the way he looks at his cuticles, then smoothes the wrinkles on his pants, to the way he settles his smoldering dark eyes back on me, I know there's something cooking in his carefully styled pompadour.

"So, how've you been since I saw you yesterday?" I say, placing the napkin across my legs and sitting back. "Are you liking the neighborhood?"

He smirks at my cheekiness. "I'm great, actually. I've always wanted to rent a house out here for the summer. I spend most summers at my place in Florida, but I gave it to my mom two years ago."

"Yeah, must be a pain to bring over girls when your mom's home."

He laughs into his drink, nearly snorting tequila. "You've gotten really blunt."

"How do you know I wasn't always?"

He turns his head from side to side. "I remember a little girl with braces that sparkled from across the hallway. She wore a long braid down her back, and the kids in the building called her Pocahontas. She wore men's t-shirts and leggings before it was cool to wear leggings."

So he does remember me. I take a long sip from my wine glass. "I still can't bring myself to watch Pocahontas because of those kids."

"I can't bring myself to eat strawberries," he says a little more quietly.

"Why did they call you that?" I ask. "I'm sorry I brought it up, but that's the first thing that came to my head."

"No, I've gotten over it," he says, not looking up from his lap for a few seconds. "My mom put something red in my uniform whites. They came out pink. You know the kind of kids we grew up with. They hounded me every day, calling me Strawberry. My mother couldn't afford new socks or pants until the next paycheck, but the damage was done."

"The kids in the building were pretty terrible."

"I hated that place," he tells me. "I promised myself that I'd never let my kids grow up like that."

"You turned out fine," I say. "So did I. Sometimes you can have all the money in the world, go to the best school, live in the best neighborhoods, and the people can be just as shitty as the poor side of town."

He shrugs. "Doesn't hurt to not go hungry."

I answer with a sip of wine. "Well, we're the adults now. It's our turn to take care of our mothers."

"Most of the women I meet don't understand that about me. Not you, though. We come from the same kind of place, and we got ourselves out of that. But enough of the past. Right now, I want you to tell me about yourself. You said you're a nurse."

I nod, fidgeting with the corner of the menu. "Yep. I did a year at Brigham and Women's Hospital in Boston."

I wonder what else my mother told him. The idea that this stranger, quasi-stranger, knows everything about my life makes me want to break into hives. I let the last drops of wine coat my tongue. The waitress comes around and takes our order.

Another round of drinks. I order guacamole and steak tacos with extra queso, and he orders a shrimp salad, hold the croutons and cheese, and the dressing on the side.

"I have a couple of classmates who went into medicine. It's the best kind of job security because there will always be sick people."

I try to be my polite date-self but can't help making a face. "Or, you know, it's a good way to *help* people."

He chuckles, and then I remember that I hate his laugh. "Oh, you're one of those."

"Excuse me?"

"Relax. I just mean everyone has their reasons for choosing a career in medicine. The hours are long, so long that it almost doesn't make sense to have a family because the chances are more likely in favor of divorce."

I think of Bradley's parents. They were both doctors. They might as well be divorced since they both have not-so-secret affairs and sleep in separate rooms. Did I really think Bradley and I could have something considering where he came from?

"You must love being a doctor."

He smirks. "I love being a plastic surgeon."

Because of course he does.

"I learned from the best doctors in Florida, but everyone wants to go to Florida to get their work done. At the beginning of the year, I decided to open up my own office in the city with my college roommate, Dr. Gold. Gonzales and Gold just had a good ring to it, don't you think? He specializes in implants for both sexes. I specialize in faces."

As gross as I find cosmetic surgery, I'm oddly interested in the way he talks about it. "That's the strangest thing I've heard all day."

The waitress sets down my guac on the table, and Xandro helps himself without asking. I want to remind him that the chips are made out of corn, but I decide not to.

"Ever since I was little I loved to draw perfect faces."

I shove a giant helping of creamy guacamole into my mouth.

"I'm not talking about the Golden Ratio or that symmetry bullshit, but more along the lines of helping people achieve the person they want to see when they look in a mirror. Everyone has that person. Though there are exceptions."

"What do you mean?"

"I mean, I turn people away when I think they don't need work. For instance, if you came into my office and wanted to change something about your face, I'd decline."

I've met surgeons who tell me I might want to shave a centimeter or so off the slight bump on the top of my nose, and maybe for a little while I believed it. In a weird way, Xandro is giving me a compliment.

"Well, thank you for not taking my hard-earned money for something so frivolous."

He smiles. "I mean it, Sky. You are exceptionally beautiful. I have clients who would kill for your eyes. It's a particular shade of green and gold. Your forehead is not too big or small. Your cheekbones are perfection and your jaw line is incredibly defined. Then there's your lips. I could try a thousand times and not get the exact fullness of your lips. Your mother was right, you're just as beautiful as I remember."

Part of me wants to take my face and put a paper bag over it. It's not that I don't think I'm attractive. It's that I hate being analyzed. Still, since I've deprived myself of a shred of romance all summer, I can't help but flutter all over. It has nothing to do with him. Words have a power all their own.

"Thank you," I say.

"I'm just speaking the truth. My eyes are fixed on you."

"Why?"

"You're gorgeous. We come from the same origins. We have similar families. It seems like fate."

"I'm not looking for anything right now."

He leans over and places his hand on top of mine. "You might think so now, but I think you'll change your mind."

Our food comes just in time because the fluttering just turned to panic. Xandro watches me eat with that infuriating smile across his face.

"At least you're doing something you like," I tell him, trying to bring the conversation back to careers.

"It's the best of both worlds."

I can't imagine how peeling back someone's skin and shaving down their bones or injecting ass fat into lips is something to love, but to each their own.

Then, he says the one thing I've been dreading since my mom shoved us into his red Maserati. "Your family tells me you're recently single."

I chew my steak taco extra long, imagining the ways I could get back at them. Diuretic in their breakfast mimosas?

"Yeah," I say, sitting up straighter, as if better posture is the thing that's going to make me look like I'm keeping my cool. I go through my catalogue of things to say, but this is a stranger. I don't care if we crossed paths back in the day. I don't care that my mother and family think he's the best thing since sliced bread. Sliced bread isn't even that good. "Things end."

"That's bleak. Well, now that we're neighbors again, we can go out and catch up again."

There's nothing to catch up on because we were never really friends. "I'm going to be really busy planning the wedding and all."

"I'm sure you'll have some downtime now that you're not

working," he says. His confidence in asking me out makes my skin crawl. "Besides, didn't you hear? I'm invited."

I want to order some more wine but I can feel the headache blooming at my temples, and that would only make him order another drink as well.

"Your mom says you don't have a plus one, so I'm offering my services. I'm not just a surgeon." His voice drops down an octave and his eyes get that lazy look, like he's ready to throw down in bed. "I'm an excellent date."

I signal the waitress for the check. It's like my brain is throwing up flares that write "nope-nope-nope" in the sky. I reach for my purse.

"Stop it," he says pulling out a shiny black card that clinks on the glass table. The waitress takes it and brings it back. He signs with a flourish of his pen. His letters are bold and, unlike every other doctor's signature I've seen, incredibly neat.

"I'll drive you home."

I shake my head. "I'm okay, I have some wedding things to take care of while I'm here."

"Do you need company?"

"Some of the other bridesmaids are joining me." I throw in as many wedding-related activities as possible to ensure that he won't want to stick around.

He pulls me into a hug and lets his hands slide down my waist. "I'm glad we're neighbors again, Sky. I can't wait to see more of your beautiful face."

CHAPTER 12

Leti and River pick me up. I'm holding a tray of black iced coffees. My phone buzzes with a text. It's Lucky Pierce telling me she's in town. My hands are too occupied to respond so I make a mental note to text her later.

"How was your hot date?" Leti asks saucily.

"He said he'd never cut up my face because I'm *so* gorgeous." I hand them their coffees.

River pulls out and starts driving. "Well if that isn't romance, then I don't know what is."

I shake the ice in my coffee before I take a sip. "Where is this restaurant?"

We take a turn off the highway and drive for about five miles. We pass an old RV and nothing but trees.

"River?"

She pulls up her phone and holds the screen up to Leti's face. "Read that."

"We passed it."

River makes a sharp right at the next exit and we turn around. We drive in a circle and still there's nothing.

"That's not an address, River," I say, panic starting to flood through my veins.

We do another round, this time slowing down a bit. I realize something.

"What's the name of the restaurant?"

"Just his name. Luke's."

"You mean, Luke's *HOT DOGS*?" I point to the RV parked off the highway. There are a few cars parked beside it and a bunch of beachgoers making a line at a window.

"That's Luke!" River shouts.

"What were you doing when he told you he was a chef?"

River shrugs. "I don't know...he asked for my number or something."

"River!"

"I'm sorry! He doesn't *look* like he sells hot dogs off the side of the road." River steps on the gas and we drive past the stand. With the windows down, we burst into a fit of laughter.

When we're quiet except for the sound of wind blowing through the car, I realize that we still don't have a solution to the catering problem.

"I'd just like to point out," I say, "that this would only happen to us."

"Come on," Leti says. "We have better luck than that. You have to put your desires into the Universe and the Universe will answer. You just have to be specific. Like with Hayden. Have you called him yet?"

River catches my eyes in the rearview mirror. "I'm sorry, Sky. I tried."

"I know, baby." I stare out the window. The wind makes my eyes feel dry, but even our failed mission raises my spirits in a way lunch with Xandro could not. "I'll figure something out."

"Let me see the shell," Leti says.

I put up my feet on the armrest between them and wiggle my toes. "It's a sand dollar, and I'm not saying a word."

"What are you going to do about it?"

I take a sip of my bitter coffee. "That's between me and the Universe."

• • •

After River's catering lead failed epically, we returned home to join my family around the pool. River tells me to stay calm. We're going to find something, even if it means buying two hundred TV dinners at Costco. It's reassuring, really.

Uncle Tony is at the grill turning burgers and hot dogs while everyone else takes in the last of the day's rays. He's wearing Pepe's men's beachwear. The neon board shorts don't really go

LOVE ON THE LEDGE

with the Wall Street vibe he still can't shake off. That's how you know it's True Love.

"How was your date with Nip/Tuck?" cousin Steve asks. He's grown a foot since the last time I saw him. As much as I complain about my family, I really do love seeing them all at once. That is, until they start to pick on me.

I throw my bottle of sunscreen at him. It hits him right in the gut, and he moans and almost rolls off his lounge chair.

"Leave Sky alone," Uncle Tony says, using metal tongs to poke a juicy burger.

I step into the pool and shiver as the cold water envelops me all the way to my waist. I grab onto a purple pool noodle and float over to the deep end where no one else goes. Out of my whole family, I'm the only one who knows how to properly swim, something I have to thank Bradley for.

I realize there are so many little things that Bradley taught me or showed me while we were together. Things like swimming and learning to like the taste of whiskey and how to tie a proper fisherman's knot and how to deliver a killer serve. I wonder if I'll every truly learn to forget him.

"How long has my mom had Xandro up her sleeve?" I ask, leaning my face towards the delicious sun.

"You always think the worst of people," Maria says. "He stopped by to give your mother a message from his mother. Apparently, Xandro just got out of a five-year relationship, and he's *looking*."

"Well, you can save your money," I tell my cousins, leveling my eyes at each one of them. "This is one pony you won't be betting on."

Leti and River act all innocent, as if I didn't see money pass through Leti's hand. Surely she's gotten River in on it, which is the last thing that River needs.

"I say they end up dating by the end of the summer," Maria says. "You've never *not* been in a relationship, Sky. You're a serial monogamist. It's like you *have* to be with someone or you can't function."

Hearing that come from Maria of all people makes me

pretty ticked off. "Considering I spent all my college years away at school, I don't see how you can know that."

She purses her lips and brings her sunglasses down back over her eyes even though the sun is setting.

"Well, I've got my money on someone *else*," Leti says.

I widen my eyes in her direction. She just can't help herself when she's around everyone. My cousins are a mini gossip mill. When our cousin Margie got knocked up it was like a round of telephone that, by the time it got to me, had exploded into a story of how Margie was pregnant with triplets and one of them was Asian.

"Who?" Yunior asks. "I hope he's not a doctor, because Nip/Tuck is going to have some serious competition."

He screams as the purple pool noodle hits him in the face.

"You guys need to get your own lives," I tell them, splashing everyone within distance.

There's a chant of "Aww, come back, Sky."

But I'm already walking away, my wet feet smacking on the warm blue tiles that create a path back to the house. I grab a half empty bottle of prosecco from the fridge and a plastic cup. That's how classy I feel. I open the door to my balcony and let in the breeze that announces sunset.

They've got me all wrong. But that's okay. I've decided this summer I might surprise everyone, including myself.

I turn the lock on my door and set the sand dollar on my bed. I pace back and forth weighing my options. What do I say? I'm not looking for a one-night stand, but I don't want a relationship either. Sure, that doesn't sound psychotic at all. After all, the boy just wanted to walk with me on the beach and I turned around and ran away.

I wish I had Leti's sweetness, River's charm, and Lucky's gusto.

What do I have? A wishy-washy attempt at friendship. A broken heart that I have to work on before I let anyone else put their grubby hands on it—figuratively of course.

I have a sand dollar, that's what I have.

I punch in the number, and wait.

"Hello?" he says.

CHAPTER 13

Naturally, I hang up.

My heart hammers in my chest, and I throw myself on my bed like the big, brave girl that I am.

When he calls back I nearly jump out of my skin. Of course he's calling back. If I don't answer, he's going to think I'm a creep. I'm not a creep, just a coward.

"Hi!" I say, too high-pitched.

"Hello? I just got a missed call from this number."

I'm a little disappointed that he doesn't recognize my voice. But I plow through my embarrassment.

"Hey, Hayden. It's Sky—you gave River a sand dollar—" There's a sentence I never thought I'd ever say out loud.

He laughs. "I'm just kidding, Sky, I know it's you."

I choke on my words. "How?"

"River actually came up to me this morning while I worked on the gazebo. She gave me your number."

That bitch. "How come you didn't call?"

"I got the feeling you wouldn't want that."

I let myself slide down my bed. My heart slips and slides inside my chest. No, no, no. "I'm sorry."

"You don't have to apologize. It's cool. I just figured if you wanted to talk to me you would call when you wanted to. I'm pleasantly surprised it only took twelve hours."

"You were counting?"

I can hear a couch creak with his weight. The noise of the television goes away completely. He's settling in to talk to me.

"Oh, I've been staring at my phone all day. I even had my friend call me and make sure my phone was still in service. But enough about me. How was your day, Sky?"

I'm glad he can't see the smile plastered on my face. I like the way he says my name. Like the way he repeats it over and over, even though there's no one else he could be talking to but me.

"I prevented a potential calamity from happening."

"Did another hole appear on the roof?" he chuckles. "This time it wasn't me, I swear."

I tell him about River and Luke's Hot Dogs and the catering problem. "It's one more thing I have to worry about."

"What else is there?"

"Well, now there's the gazebo that this guy is taking forever to build."

"Hey, now. That is excellent craftsmanship. It'll get done before you know it."

I settle back into my bed, the voices from the living room filtering upstairs every now and them.

"How did you end up working with wood?" I realize the way that sounds instantly, but it's too late to take it back. "You know, building stuff. You know, carpentry."

There's that laugh again. "When I was a kid we lived near a lumber yard. That was upstate before we moved out to the Island. This old man that worked there used to see me walk around by myself. He thought I was lazy and a vagabond, naturally. I just wanted out of the house when my folks fought. So he put me to work, shaving wood into pencils. I can make pencils, if you ever need them. I'm not just a roofer who builds gazebos and has great hair."

"No," I say, "you're all of that *and* also carry sand dollars in your pocket."

"I forget to change out of my shorts from the beach sometimes. My dad hates that. I'm sure it's a safety hazard, but I crossed that line when I—" He whistles and it sounds like a cartoon elevator plummeting. "Fell right at your feet, Sky. Plus, sand dollars are the perfect way to make new friends. That's how dolphins pay for everything they need."

"You're crazy," I say.

"Thank you. That means a lot."

No, really. Hayden is nuts. How does he manage to be so innocent and sexy all at once? "How are you so happy?"

He's quiet for a bit and I feel like I botched it. Who likes to hear that they're too happy?

"Listen, if you knew the shit in my life.... Let's just say that if I don't make myself look at something positive—like falling through a roof and opening my eyes to find the most perfect human I've ever seen, or getting fired by my dad only to have him rehire me to build a gazebo where I can see your balcony and get a peek at your sad smile when you drink your coffee."

I shut my eyes. My body does lots of strange things. My heart leaps and falls. My tear ducts ache, but stay dry. My stomach flutters, and my skin shivers from his words and the cool breeze coming from the open balcony.

"I try to look at the glass half full side of things. Otherwise, what's the point of being miserable?"

"You're not part of some cult, are you?"

I picture him shaking his head. Those blue, blue eyes. That full, full mouth. "Believe me, I'm no boy scout. I mean, I literally was a Boy Scout, with the badges to prove I can tie knots and light fires and all. But I'm not just happy for the sake of it. I'm tired of seeing the sad parts of life. Aren't you?"

"Yeah," I say honestly. "I really am."

We fall into silence, but it isn't uncomfortable. I imagine myself sitting beside him, watching each of us find comfort in a little bit of quiet.

"Why did you call me, Sky?"

Then the comfortable part goes away and a million things rush through my head again. Wedding. Cake. Photographer. Bradley. Stella. Bradley and Stella. Maria rolling her eyes. River smoking. Xandro's skinny margarita. Centerpieces. Hayden. Hayden. Hayden.

"I honestly don't know," I laugh nervously.

"Hey, that's okay, too. I don't need a reason. I just ...wondered."

I push away all the thoughts that aren't about Hayden and me and the present. I focus on this moment and his phone call and stop myself from trekking through the past or freaking about the future.

Don't be an idiot, River told me.

"I just wanted to talk to you, I suppose."

"I suppose that'll do," he says, jokingly. In the moment of silence I imagine he licks his lips, and then my thoughts focus on that—his perfect full lips. The fullest, most kissable lips I've ever seen on a guy. "I know someone hurt you real bad, Sky."

My heart runs laps around the room.

"No one told me, I just know. I don't want to be the guy who chases after a girl with a broken heart."

My disappointment tells me that's exactly what I wanted, and I feel a little bit selfish. "Okay."

"So, let me be your friend."

I sink into the pillows, comforted by the softness of his voice. "My friend?"

"Yeah, like two people who are totally not attracted to each other being friends."

"Oh."

"Just kidding. I'm completely attracted to you."

This is the part where I tell him that so am I. "Hayden…"

"Look, I do want to get to know you. I can't deny that you're the most beautiful person I've seen in my whole life. Including Adriana Lima and Giselle Bundchen, but they're folded up in catalogues under my mattress so it doesn't count."

"So you want to be my friend, but you also want to let me know that you think I'm pretty."

"Sky, pretty doesn't even begin to describe what you are," he says. I decide I love the sound of his voice. "So being friends seems simple enough. Plus, I heard the old ladies talking about you and they said you'd be going back to Boston at the end of the summer. I don't fancy getting my heart splattered. I'm a hazard to myself as it is. Simple, right?"

"I don't think simple is what I'd call it," I say. I dig my toes into my comforter. I don't know why I have a sudden urge to stretch, like my skin is too tight. I want to tell him that I'm not going back to Boston, but I'm still not sure. I have a job waiting for me if I want it. Or I can start over at a new place here in New York. I do want to go back to school, but so much is going on. I can even just say "fuck it" to everything and move to South Africa.

"You're a strange person," I tell him.

"Thank you. I like to think of myself as un-ordinary."

"Wouldn't that be extraordinary?"

"No, no. I'm not extraordinary. Not yet. I'm just not ordinary. I'd like to think there's a difference, but perhaps my brain is just fried."

I realize how late it is.

"Speaking of," he says. "I have to get up to be at work by five o'clock."

"It's midnight. I'll let you go."

"If you insist," he says. "But if I didn't have to sleep, believe me, I'd stay on the phone as long as you'd let me."

"Or," I say, "we could talk in person."

"You stole my line." He chuckles. I love the sound of it. "I wanted to invite you to a bonfire at Tiana Beach tomorrow night. You know, now that we're friends."

"I'd love that."

"Great. I'll see you."

"Goodnight, Hayden."

"See you at home, Sky."

Tonight, I don't need champagne. I already feel drunk on his words.

CHAPTER 14

But I don't see him in the morning.

I forgot to set my alarm clock and slept through all of their hammering on the other side of the house. I locked the door so that no one (ahem, River Thomas) would jump on me in the morning. I quickly check my email and see a new message from the DJ. He's been pestering me for a bigger deposit after getting a mostly '80s playlist. I mark it as important and decide to answer it after I've had coffee.

When I get downstairs, my mom corners me by the coffee machine. My head is still fuzzy with sleep.

"Sky," she says. "Cousin Felipe and his wife are here with their daughter, Daisy. I told them Daisy could stay in your room until the guest room roof is patched up."

"Excuse me?"

Cornered isn't the word I'd use anymore. Ambushed is more like it. I take the coffee cup and put it in the machine slot. It lights up and asks for water. Of course, six hundred people are in the house and no one can refill it. While my mom stares at me and the coffee machine makes all kinds of robotic sex noises, I rub the crud from my eye with the sleeve of my robe.

"Daisy can stay in your room."

"No," I say.

I take the steaming mug and hold it up to my nose.

"What do you mean, no?"

"Ma, Uncle Tony renovated the basement *just* so that people would have places to sleep. There are six beds downstairs."

"You can't ask a little girl to sleep in a basement by herself."

"She won't be by herself," I say. "All the kids are down there. Maybe if you get your mind out of the gutter, you'll see that this isn't about Daisy. You just don't want me to be alone for two seconds."

She gathers herself, holding her hands to her chest. "I don't see what the problem is."

"The problem is, if Daisy is there, I won't be able to entertain all the guys that come crawling through my window, *Ma*."

It's the wrong thing to say at the wrong time because that's when Maria and Yunior and Uncle Felipe and his wife and Daisy round the corner into the kitchen.

My mother is mortified. I'm still pretty okay.

"Good morning, everyone," I say, giving them my best smile. I shouldn't antagonize my family, but they make it so easy. "I'm going for a swim."

• • •

Before my swim, I leave a message for the photographer to call me back. I ask the baker to email us the final design of the cake. I get the shipping confirmation for the one of a kind, handmade wedding toppers, each modeled after the grooms.

I swim until all I can think about is the burn in my arms, as opposed to the fact that two of my younger cousins are over in the backyard trying to flirt their way into Hayden's pants with lemonade and ham and cheese sandwiches.

I push myself out of the pool and groan when I see that Xandro's here, deep in conversation with Uncle Felipe's wife. She's grabbing her fat at the waist, and I can imagine he's giving her a price quote. We have our own personal family butcher… how nice.

"If you want to be alone with the guy," Leti says from the pool chair behind me, "you only have to say so."

She thumbs a finger at the Sun God that is Hayden Robertson. My new friend.

I throw the pool noodle at her, and she spills her margarita on her top.

"Come on, Sky. Maria's bringing her fiancé to the wedding. He's going to be insufferable. Everyone else has dates. I'm getting pretty close, I just have to make sure he can handle his liquor."

I dive back into the pool. Even though I'm tired, I need a reprieve from them all. Even Leti. This pool isn't deep enough, though. I'm going to need to dive into the ocean.

When I surface again, brushing the chlorine water from my eyes, Hayden is sitting at the edge of the pool chatting with Leti. I swim to them, my breath more ragged than I'd like.

"Hey," I say.

His face lights up with a smile. He's red from the sun. His shirt is bunched up on his hands. He uses it like a towel.

"You should jump in and cool off," Leti says suggestively.

"I'd probably need a good shower to rinse off the grime," he laughs.

I pull myself out of the pool and sit beside him. I'm so aware of the way my body tenses up when he's near. I want to reach out and see how the five-o-clock shadow on his face feels against my hand.

"The gazebo looks really great," I say.

"Believe me," he says, "I've got a few surprises coming up. It's going to be my best work. Especially after ruining your dress."

"Don't worry about it!" Leti smacks him on the back. He nearly falls forward, but I put my hand on his chest. His pecs tense up. He stares at my hand plastered to his hard torso.

I let go and try to ignore the way he smiles at me.

"The good thing about having one of the grooms be a fancy designer is that he can sew up a new dress."

I wouldn't put it that lightly. Pepe was furious, but Tony calmed him down. Tony's a good balance for Pepe's riotous emotions.

"Am I still seeing you tonight at the bonfire?"

I can feel the heat of his stare on my face. It only flickers down to my boobs once. Friends do that right?

"We'll be there," Leti says.

Hayden pushes himself up, dusts off his jeans. "I can't wait."

• • •

While I put waterproof eyeliner on Leti's eyelids and River flips over her hair to get crazy volume, my cousins Maria, Elena, and Juliet stand at the door.

"When are you leaving for the bonfire?" Maria asks. She's wearing a black and red sundress.

River shifts her weight to one leg. "Why?"

"Because we're coming, too?" Elena says, rolling her eyes. Nineteen and already getting lip injections, Elena looks more ready to go to a nightclub than a casual bonfire.

"Who says you're going?" Leti asks.

"Um, Tripp did." Juliet says, pulling her sequin top up so you can see the tattoo on her hip. I'm betting that her mom has no clue that's there, mostly because she's still alive. Our mothers threaten us with murder when it comes to piercings, tattoos, and premarital sex. It's a miracle Leti's still alive since she's guilty of all three.

"Tripp?" I want to puke a little. Just the thought of my little cousins calling him that makes me itch all over.

"We're not all fitting in my car," River says. The subtext— you bitches aren't getting in my car.

"We know," Juliet says, smirking. "Xandro's driving us."

I hate this. I hate feeling like I'm in high school again with every single family member in my business. I hate that everything I do gets reported back to my mother, that I'm on the verge of a quarter-life crisis and it gets worse because, even in a mansion, I don't have any privacy.

"You know what?" I say, holding the edge of my bedroom door. "I don't care. Go with Xandro. We'll see you there."

I shut the door.

"Now that we're infiltrated with a bunch of rats," River says, "guess we'd better be on our best behavior."

Leti and River exchange a secret smile. One that says there's not a chance in hell that's going to happen.

CHAPTER 15

Tiana Beach is just an extension of the stretch of beaches on Dune Road. Behind us, a row of houses flanks the ocean. I've always wondered what it's like to live facing the beach like this. To see the storms rolling in, the rise and fall of the tide. I can imagine it gets lonely during the winter, but considering the summer months are the most hated for locals, it wouldn't be so bad.

The bonfire faces a house weathered by sea salt and strong winds. Silhouettes of people crowd at the porch with red plastic cups in hand. There's music, but it doesn't really reach the beach. Sergeant Sam Pepper is deep in conversation with Hayden and a bunch of other guys sitting around a huge fire. Over towards the water, people are playing volleyball. They wear glow-in-the-dark wristbands to tell the teams apart. The ball is a bright neon thing that bounces from fist to fist.

My cousins and Xandro sit on logs around the fire, way too over-dressed for their own good. Xandro is chatting up Maria when he sees me and cuts her off by standing up and walking towards me. His loafers kick up sand in Maria's direction.

"Sky, you made it."

Leti and River abandon me because they're terrible friends. River sits on Pepper's lap without asking, and Leti helps herself to the cooler of beer.

"Yep, I was invited."

I start to walk towards the bonfire, but he stays close to my arm. I wave at everyone. When Hayden sees me, I turn into a puddle of Sky. I don't want my heart to dance around like it has no control. I don't want my cheeks to blush and burn. I don't want my hands to be unable to lie still.

"Everyone, this is Sky," Hayden says. "Sky, everyone. You know your family, obviously."

"Unfortunately," Juliet says. Her top glitters in the firelight. She's already drunk. Great.

"Sit here, Sky," Xandro says, pushing Maria a little bit on the log. There isn't a lot of room. There's lots of room on the log that Hayden sits on.

I go to the cooler and grab a beer. "I'm okay for now. I've been sitting on the phone all day."

"Sky's planning her uncle's wedding," Hayden tells his friends.

"Sort of," I say.

"Yeah, she's not working right now," Maria tells them.

"I'm taking time off."

"What were you doing before?" one of the girls asks. Her hair is so long, I'm sure if she stood up it would go down past her hips.

"I'm a nurse. I used to live in Boston. I'm trying to decide between getting into hospitals there, or here, or going back to school. I keep going back and forth."

"That's awesome," the girl says.

"I have lots of friends at the medical centers on Long Island," Xandro says. "I could get you through the door."

I'm reminded of the way Bradley liked to show off his connections about everything—from his dad's practice to City Hall to his friend of a friend who knows one of the million Arab Emirate princes.

I take the empty seat beside Hayden. He clinks his beer to mine.

"Hey," he says.

"Hey."

I don't let go of his gaze as we both drink from our beers. Something about Hayden makes me want to smile forever.

"Whose house is this?" Leti asks.

"Ours," one of the guys says. His name is Jacob and he's married to the girl with the Rapunzel hair. "It used to be my parents'. They were lawyers. I almost became one, too, but then Suzy here introduced me to beer making. That's our beer you're drinking."

"It's really good," I say honestly. "I love beer."

"I don't really drink," Maria says, sipping on the mouth of the glass.

Leti and I exchange the same annoyed look.

"That's amazing that you guys have this operation," I tell Suzy. They're so young and free. She looks up at him and his eyes radiate with love. It's nice to know that there are still people out there who make it work.

"Before me, Jake drank nothing but Corona Light, bless his heart. I was making moonshine with my dad since I could walk. It's a different life, but it's fun. You have to do what you love, you know."

"I wish I'd grown up with that kind of thinking," I say. "Or had been a little bit more rebellious like this one over here."

Leti takes a bow and grabs another of the sweet lagers.

"There's nothing wrong with the way you grew up," Maria says. "Our mothers worked hard. We had everything."

"I know that," I say defensively. "But it would have been nice if, instead of forcing me to go to nursing school, my mom would have let me do what I liked. Look at Elena. She's such a fantastic artist, and she's miserable trying to become an accountant."

Elena sighs. She knows it's a losing battle and the sad part is that she doesn't even try. "Art doesn't pay the bills."

"What would you do differently?" Maria asks. "What's this passion that you have that makes you so resentful of your mother?"

One of the guys around the fire makes a cat noise.

"I think we've talked enough about me for one night," I say. "Who wants to go for a swim?"

The waves aren't that hard, and I really just want to get away from them all.

I stand, but Xandro's hand grabs my wrist. "You shouldn't. It's cold and dark."

"I won't go far." I pull away from him.

"I'm coming, too!" Elena shouts.

"Yeah, it'll be fun," Suzy says, taking off her sweater.

I pull my shirt over my head, and everyone gets down to their underwear. I jump in first, diving headfirst into a wave. The force of it pushes me back hard. It flips me over, and for a moment, I let myself float in the deep, dark of the ocean.

This is what it takes to be alone, I think. Diving into the sea. When I can't hold my breath anymore, I break the surface.

A blond head is swimming towards me. "Sky, come back. You're going too far."

"You scared?"

I lick the salt water from my lips. I can't touch the sand. That's my favorite feeling, floating in water. I grab him by his shoulders and he secures a hand around my waist.

He laughs. "I'm scared you're going to turn into a mermaid and swim away."

I push off him and dive back. I *am* a mermaid. I let my body float on the water. From here, there is nothing but open night sky and brilliant stars. Hayden's warm hand grabs me by my ankle, like my anchor.

"I have to apologize to your friends for my cousin," I say. "I don't know what it is. Every chance she gets she just digs into me."

"I'd say she's jealous."

"Jealous? She's just holier-than-thou. She's so self-righteous, I don't know why she didn't become a nun like she originally planned to."

Hayden's laugh fills the whole sky. Elena screams as her sister chases her along the beach. Maria is standing at the shore, probably watching us. The glow-in-the-dark ball zooms back and forth between fists. It's a pretty perfect night.

"I know what it's like to do something just because your parents want you to. But you, Sky, you still have a choice. You show your freedom by taking time off. You show it in giving yourself the chance to start over."

"I didn't think of it that way."

"And you don't have to apologize to my friends. None of

us are strangers to crazy families. Half of Jacob's is in his house right now. Believe me, you're perfect."

I rest my hands behind my head. He lets go of my foot and puts a hand on my back. It reminds me of my first swimming lesson. Bradley made me float while he stood in the pool and placed his hands under my back. *"Relax, don't you trust me?"*

I don't remember if I answered, but I did as he told me to. And he let me go, so I sank and then splashed around. *"Oh, come on, it's just a joke, baby. Don't be mad."*

I wasn't mad. That's the worst part. I smiled and I kissed him. Everything he did, even when he was being mean, I still felt the compulsion to kiss him.

Now, Hayden doesn't ask me to trust him. He holds onto me because he doesn't trust me not to swim away. I bob in the water and stretch my arms out.

"This is perfect," I say.

Hayden doesn't smile. He looks as torn as my heart feels. His finger touches my cheek and I swear it banishes the cold. He wets his lips.

"Sky."

I'm about to say his name. I'm about to say fuck it, to our being friends arrangement. I don't know where I'm going to be at the end of the summer, and I don't know what I want from him. At this moment, I don't care if our hearts get tangled and messy. I don't care that my family and Xandro are watching, or that I'll have to answer for the impulse of this moment.

I don't care.

I just want to taste the salt on his lips.

I put my arms around his neck and pull him closer. He comes easily, meeting my lips with his. I've imagined this from the moment I met him. I imagined kissing him as he lay there, fallen from the sky. I imagined kissing him when he handed me that seashell. I've imagined kissing him in every daydream. But kissing Hayden now is more wonderful than anything I dreamt up. He kisses with a confidence that tells me this is the right thing to do. He kisses like he's dreamt of me, too.

He secures an arm around me, and pulls me out of the

water and against his chest. I wrap my legs around his waist, my anchor in the still, dark sea. I feel a part of me float away. It's the part that's stopped me from doing this sooner. Something that's been too afraid to let go, but now, in the freedom of the night sea, it finally can. And in its place is Hayden.

Hayden. Now I can admit that I've wanted him from the beginning. Now I can let myself go and have him.

His lips are so warm, while the rest of our bodies shiver in the cool air. I want his lips to banish the cold from me. I pull back to catch my breath even though I wouldn't mind drowning with his mouth against mine. He's smiling. Of course he's smiling. It's a beautiful thing. He traces a wet thumb across my cheekbone.

"Sky," he says. I'll never get tired of my name on his lips.

But then someone screams our names. I jolt up, splashing. In the dark of the night, we don't see the wave—we just feel the force of it crash over our heads.

I don't have a chance to hold my breath. I breathe in saltwater. I thrash to get to the surface, but the wave presses over my head. I tumble once, twice in the dark. Something hits my head.

Then, his hand is wrapped around mine. He pulls me up, and I choke and cough and try to get some air. Hayden secures a hand around my waist and drags me to the sand.

"I know CPR," Xandro says, running over to us.

I hold my hands up and cough until my throat is raw so I can breathe properly. Hayden puts his hoodie around my shoulders while a chorus of concern rains down on me.

"I'm fine, guys," I say, voice hoarse. Hayden holds out his hand to help me stand, but Xandro swats it away.

"You've done enough," Xandro says.

"Whoa," I say. "Hold on a minute, Hayden didn't do anything."

"You let her go out there even though it wasn't safe," he says.

"I *let* her?" Hayden says. I realize this is the first time I've seen him not smile since the day I met him, and he had just fallen through a roof.

River and Leti come to my side. Suzy runs inside to get a blanket. How did everything turn so ugly so quickly?

I put my hands between Xandro and Hayden. "Back off, both of you. Nothing is Hayden's fault. If you're going to blame someone, blame the ocean. He's the one that pulled me out. I'm the one who wanted to swim. You got that? *I* wanted to swim."

"Typical," Maria mutters.

Suddenly, I'm too tired to argue. I let River pull me towards the fire and Suzy wrap a thick wool blanket around me.

"We're going," Xandro says. Elena and Juliet put their clothes back on and shiver with their hands close to the fire. They complain, but Maria quiets them with a single glare. "Sky?"

"I'm fine," I say. "I'm going with River."

"Don't be silly, Sky. You're going to catch a cold."

"Somehow," I say, smiling. "I think I'll manage to take care of myself."

CHAPTER 16

When they leave, the air gets a little lighter. Everyone still dotes on me. Jacob makes me a hot toddy with Suzy's family whiskey.

"Are you sure this won't make me go blind?" I ask him, grateful for the warm cup. The air isn't that cold, and the fire is almost as tall as I am, but the wave felt like it was trying to dig into my bones.

"That's moonshine," Suzy corrects me. "And you'll be fine."

Hayden doesn't come back to the fire. He plays volleyball and then stands at the shoreline. Now that they know I'm not in any danger, River and Leti challenge the boys to a game of "let's chase each other and make out." At least, that's what it looks like from here.

When Jacob goes into the house to make sure his friends aren't breaking anything, Suzy sits next to me.

"I'm really sorry about tonight," I tell her.

"Don't be!" She tucks her hair behind her ear. "It's just nice to have people around. No one visits us in the winter, except for Hayden. He's a really good friend."

That makes me smile. "I'm starting to see that."

"I've never seen him get so upset. He hates bossy men. Considering his relationship with his dad, I'm not surprised."

"Oh, I've seen it," I say, thinking about the way the old man seemed more concerned with losing a job prospect than his own son being hurt.

"I can tell you one thing," Suzy says. "I've known Hayden since I moved up here from Tennessee. He's fiercely loyal. There's not a malicious bone in that boy's body. He's eager to love, even if it means getting hurt."

"He told me he wants to be friends."

She shakes her head. "I said he was loyal, not smart. Not always. He just wants to be with you, Sky. I knew about you the second he got home from work after his little accident. And there was nothing in that kiss you two shared that said you're just friends."

It's weird when a stranger admits they know so much about you, but I like Suzy. Her accent is sweet-sounding, or maybe it's the whiskey.

"Why are you still sitting with me, girl? Go talk to that boy."

And I do. I guess all I need is a little push from a stranger to do something that feels entirely natural. Why is that?

I take his hand. He doesn't seem surprised. He looks down at me and smiles. The waves are tempestuous now. There's a bright white light at the end of the beach that makes me feel like I'm walking in a dream.

"Thanks for saving me," I say.

"Sky," he says, half smiling, half shaking his head. "You scared me. I could feel you getting pulled out of my hand."

"Well, the ocean got a taste of me and spit me back out."

He tucks my hair behind my ear and zips my/his hoodie up to the top, leaning in real close. "I doubt that. You taste amazing."

Fire. I close my eyes and think of the fire that lights inside of me.

"Friends don't say that to friends," I remind him. But I suppose we never had a chance. Not really. "They don't kiss either."

"That's very true. But before the wave crashed over us, I was going to kiss you until the tide pulled out."

His confident smile knows that I'm not going to correct him. Still, the moment is gone, and the idea of all the repercussions of my impulses come to the forefront of my mind.

"I think I'm still concussed," I say. "I don't know what you're talking about."

He laughs, and the warmth of it makes me want to bury myself in his arms. The only thing that's stopping me is me. I know that.

"We have to go," I say. "But I'll see you tomorrow."

"Actually, tomorrow's Sunday."

"You could still come over. You don't have to do any work."

"I have an idea. But we have to wait till it's dark out."

When he tucks my stubborn hair back one more time, I take his hand and hold it.

"Yeah? What's that?"

"It'll be a surprise," he says, smiling wide and bright and just for me. He leans his head down and lets his face linger in front of mine. He's waiting for me to decide what I want. He's giving me space. He presses a kiss on the tip of my nose. "Don't worry. We won't go far."

CHAPTER 17

The closer the wedding gets, the more deliveries arrive. Because everyone in the house is too busy filing their nails or roaming the Hampton shops and beaches, and because the grooms are equal workaholics, I sign for another package.

Dozens and dozens of boxes of alcohol. Leti is the only one who will get off her ass and help me take inventory. We have a giant walk-in fridge where the white wine and champagne boxes go.

Leti takes a bottle of the bubbly as payment for her services, and I take one to the newly converted office and former pool house. Half-naked mannequin bust-forms make me feel like I'm walking through a fairytale where all the women have gone bald and are frozen, but still wear their best dresses.

Two of Pepe's apprentices, girls fresh from FIT who desperately want to work in fashion, greet me with high-pitched squeals. I fork over the champagne and they pop it open. I wonder what it's like to work for Pepe. I had the opportunity to be one of these employees, but even though I love clothes, my heart was never in the world of designers. I can't get past the fake kisses and runway shows, the models who try as hard as they can to starve themselves thin. Especially after I've treated so many bulimic and anorexic girls at my old hospital. The only thing I made Pepe promise me was to use models that didn't look emaciated.

"Okay, *nena*," Pepe says, tugging on the measuring tape around his neck. His shirt is unbuttoned down the middle of his chest, and the sleeves are rolled up to his elbows. Somehow, it defies wrinkle-science. "Let's try this again."

I put on the slip of the dress and he pinches the fabric,

stabbing it with silver pins until it starts to take shape.

"I heard you had a little too much fun at the beach last night," he says.

I deflate, letting my hands drop. I regret it when a pin digs into my skin.

"Nothing terrible happened," I tell him. "Wait, what did Maria say?"

Pepe purses his lips and scratches his head. Even if he knows all the details, he's not going to tell me. Pepe is an excellent secret keeper. He didn't come out to the family until my senior year of high school, even though his clothing choices in the '80s were sort of a dead giveaway.

"Only that the *roofer boy* almost got you drowned, and you wouldn't listen to that guy who wears too much gel and suede boat shoes in the summer...."

"Xandro," I smirk.

It's not that Pepe judges people by their wardrobe choices... it's that...actually, yeah, that's what it is. But it definitely shows when he doesn't like someone, and I'm thrilled that he doesn't look at Xandro the way everyone else in the house does.

"That's not what happened," I say. "I decided to go swimming and a wave almost pulled me out." I can feel my skin warm at the memory of our kiss. "*Hayden* grabbed me just in time and pulled me back to shore. I don't know who Xandro thinks he is, but he's bossy as hell. He reminds me of—"

I don't say it. He reminds me of my dad. When he was around, the times he'd make it home instead of spending the night in a strange house, he'd boss us around. He told me when to go to bed. He made me change my clothes if he thought they were too provocative. Because nothing says provocative like jeans and t-shirts I'd outgrown, but had no replacements for. That's why I took to wearing Pepe's hand-me-downs. If my dad didn't like the food, he'd scrape his plate into the garbage and tell my mother he'd had better. If Pepe was watching TV, he'd berate him and call him lazy, even though he knew well that Pepe went to night school after his shifts at the restaurant.

Sure, Xandro is tall, handsome, polished. But there's

something in the undercutting tone of his words, the demand, the need to bend other people to his will. That was my father. I used to stay away from Latin guys for this reason exactly. But Bradley had some of the same qualities. It has nothing to do being brown or white, it's something that runs deep in their hearts.

"I'll tell you one thing," Pepe says. "Xandro's not going nowhere. Not the way he's got his eyes on you."

"If you don't want him," Emily, a petite, buxom girl, winks at me. "I'll take him."

"Have at it," I say, pulling the dress over my head. I switch back to my sundress and step out of the curtain.

"You don't want that," Vera tells Emily. "Men who take too long to get dressed are hiding something."

"Yeah," Pepe says, "their boyfriends."

"Pepe," I say, "how are you so calm right now?"

Pepe takes the stretch of fabric scrap and folds it neatly on the table. "Believe me, I'm not. I'm so nervous I could shit bricks."

"Please don't," Vera says, deadpan. "Ze carpet is white."

"Do you remember what I was like before I met Tony?"

"You certainly wore fewer jewel tones," I say.

Emily snickers and champagne comes out of her nose. Vera makes a face and shoves a box of tissues towards her.

"I was wound up. It was right after I had gotten the apprenticeship at Valerio Guzman."

"Ohmigod I love their purses," Emily says. "Not as much as yours, Pepe."

"That's my girl. Anyway, I was happy. I threw myself into my work. I fell into a routine of coming and going. But there was something missing. It was like a part of me was still sleeping, even though I was out, loud, and proud. When I saw him—I had no idea if he was gay or straight—suddenly I came awake. All of me. He'd dropped a bunch of files on the way out of the elevator, and I normally took the steps, but for some reason I decided not to that day. And he didn't usually take his lunch break at that time, but he got held up."

"Was it love at first sight?" Emily asks.

"Yes," Pepe says, "and no. I knew that I needed to know

more about that man. I needed him in my life. But I was too afraid that he wouldn't feel the same way. There's no such thing as gaydar. People like to think that it's real, but when so many men and women spend their lives trying to hide a precious part of themselves, there's no kind of radar that'll detect it if it doesn't want to be found."

"So what did you do?" Vera asks.

"I went into the elevator, of course. He apologized and we went our separate ways. But then…" Pepe smiles a mile wide. "I made sure to be downstairs at the elevator every day. It wasn't until we started dating that Tony told me he wasn't going anywhere. He'd just go downstairs to see me, then after I got in the elevator, he'd go back to his office."

"That's *so* sweet," Emily says.

It's my favorite story. Pepe and Tony are the only couple I know that really *fit* together. If anyone can convince me that love is a real thing and marriage isn't just an outdated tradition, it's them.

"Who made the first move?" Emily asks.

Pepe laughs, and his cool-as-a-cucumber persona is back. "He did, of course."

"When did you know?" I ask him after a long silence. "That Tony was the one?"

Pepe takes a needle from between his lips and stabs it in the pin cushion at his side.

"I didn't," he says. "I was in the closet for so long, I didn't think it was an option for me. It's a different time now. But back then, I thought I'd suffocate from feeling like I was alone. When I met Tony, when we went on our first date, I still didn't know. We were total opposites. He's a scotch on the rocks and I'm a Kir Royal. He smoked cigars and kept a little mustache comb in his suit jacket pocket. I had shaved the side of my head and was going through my pinstripe phase.

"Except there was the spark. The spark that goes beyond gender. It's like stars in your eyes, a great big galaxy in your body that knows something is changing, something is going to be different. There's a difference between love at first sight and enduring love. Sometimes one masquerades as the other. Enduring love, the kind that sneaks up on you. That's the kind of love I want for you, Sky."

I feel my eyes prickle with sad tears. I blink over and over until they go away and I'm left with a great twisting ball of uncertainty in my gut.

"Sky, I want you to do something for me. Think of it as a wedding present."

I choke laugh. "You mean, other than planning your wedding?"

"Bitch," he says.

"Okay, okay. What do you want?"

"As your present to us, I want you to do something nice for yourself. You've always done the right thing to make your mom happy. You're a good daughter, but you have to make choices just for you, not for everyone else. We aren't the ones that have to live with your decisions. You do."

I nod.

"Don't just nod and then ignore me. I mean it. For the rest of the summer, fuck everyone. I know what it's like to be at the shit end of their judgment, and look at them now, living in my house, eating my food, enjoying my life. The life they didn't want me to have. I'm not asking for anything in exchange, I'm not. But imagine if that part of me had never woken up?"

He shudders. I don't want to think of that either.

"Promise me, Sky."

"I promise."

I fall back into the comfort of the couch and he keeps sewing. When my phone buzzes, my heart jumps at Hayden's name.

Hayden: *Still on for your surprise?*
Me: *Sounds kind of fishy.*
Hayden: *It's a good thing you're a mermaid.*
Me: *Can I have a hint?*
Hayden: *Are you afraid of heights?*
Me: *Maybe. Are we falling out of airplanes?*
Hayden: *No....*
Hayden: *Tonight at midnight. Don't worry, I've got you.*

CHAPTER 18

When the clock hits midnight and Hayden hasn't shown up, I start to wallow in my disappointment. My hair is combed back into a ponytail. I brush on bronzer with glitter that makes my cheekbones pop. I brush mascara that extends my lashes to dramatic flirty wings. My lips, well, I leave my lips bare.

I lock my bedroom door and decline all invitations to go out from Xandro—his friends are having an A-list party and everyone in the house is invited. From River and Leti—they're catching a movie on the beach. My mom and Las Viejas—they want to watch a soap opera and keep an eye on me.

I wait, and wait, and wait. When I start to feel foolish, I let my hair down, not bothering to brush out the crease from the hairband. I forget about my lashes, and start to rub my eye.

I decide to check my phone and my heart jumps when I see three missed calls from Hayden, all time-stamped at 11:59, 12:00, and 12:01.

It's 12:15 am. I press down on the side and realize somehow I put it on silent.

When I call him back, he answers on the first ring.

"There you are," he says. Even through the phone, I can tell he's smiling.

"Sorry, technical difficulties. My phone is a jackass."

"My phone is a dinosaur, so I've got that going for me."

"Did you...er...leave?"

He chuckles. "Look out your window."

I open the door to the balcony and step into the cool summer night. The lights around the pool glow blue. Insects add their chorus to the distant sound of nighttime partners.

And then there's Hayden, standing below my balcony. He's

got a tote bag in hand. It's too dark to see the things poking out from it.

"I'll be right down," I say.

"No, wait." He steps forward and grabs onto a ladder that's been propped against the side of the house. It ends on the roof.

Are you afraid of heights, he had asked me.

Right now? Yes, I most certainly am.

"I'll hold it, you climb. The roof is flat, but don't stand. Just sit."

At my hesitation, He stands on the first step of the ladder and looks up. "I've got you, Sky. I promise."

Even if I did believe him, it's hard for me to relinquish that control. I switch out of my sandals, and into Keds that feel a little more secure. The last time I climbed up a ladder, I was trying to change a lightbulb in my apartment. The only downside to high ceilings. It's not so much that I'm afraid of heights as I am afraid of falling. The feel of having so much space between me and solid ground makes my stomach flip, and a sense of vertigo overcomes me. After the first light bulb change, I decided to get a bunch of lamps.

I grab the side of the balcony and step onto the ladder one foot at a time. When it rattles, I squeal. A light flicks on in the house. I *shhh* in Hayden's direction.

When the light goes off, I go up one step at a time.

"I'm right behind you," Hayden says.

When I turn around, there he is. I keep going until I get to the roof. I'm so floored, I almost let go and fall back.

"Easy, now," Hayden says.

There's a huge blanket laid out. A portable camping lamp rests in the corner and illuminates our little midnight picnic patch. There's bread, cheeses, and a bottle of wine.

I half crawl, half crouch my way to a sitting position. Hayden chuckles behind me. He stands up, very much the king of Haydenland, because right now we are in Haydenland.

"What's in the bag?" I ask.

He takes a seat beside me. Much like when I was floating with him on the beach, he feels like an anchor.

LOVE ON THE LEDGE

"I forgot cups." He hands me one of the clear plastic ones. "When you weren't picking up, I thought you either changed your mind or fell asleep, I figured I wouldn't need them. But on the *chance* that you would come through, I decided to go ahead with this plan."

He twists the top off the wine and pours some for me first.

"I don't know how I put my phone on silent. I was feeling very stood up, while I was the one who was late."

He clinks his cup against mine. "Well, you're here now."

I drink the sweet red, let it coat my tongue before swallowing. "This is delicious."

"It's from the Goose Walk Vineyards over here. I'm not much of a wine guy, but I did a job for them last summer. They gave me a case of this stuff to take home with me."

"You have a lot of cool friends," I tell him.

"I'm an only child, but I didn't want to be. Making friends came naturally to me because I didn't want to play by myself. Right now, my friends are the only people in my life that I feel like I can really count on."

"More than family?"

He takes a roll and breaks it in half, giving me the bigger half. "Yeah. When I was a kid I did everything to stay away from home because of the way my folks fought. They split last year. Wish they hadn't waited so long. Growing up, the people that were there for me weren't related by blood. Sometimes it's the family you choose that makes you feel like you belong."

"I kind of get that." I take a triangle of cheese. I have no idea what it is or what animal it came from, but it's salty and melts in my mouth. "In families, people have certain roles to play. The mother, the father, the aunts and uncles and cousins. But for me, my mother was both parents. My uncle, Pepe, he's ten years older than me. But when my dad left, even before that, he took care of me more than my dad ever did."

"That's why you're the maid of honor."

I laugh softly. "And because I'm the first one he came out to."

I've never told anyone that, not even Leti. Everyone

95

just assumed that Pepe came out to us all on the same night, at the same dinner. He brought Tony over and said, "This is my boyfriend."

No one batted an eye; they just welcomed Tony and made him eat three helpings of food. When I look at Hayden, I want to tell him everything that I'm thinking. I want to tell him that his blue eyes remind me of stars. That his hair is the softest hair I've ever touched, and I'm equally as jealous as I am in awe of it. I want to tell him that I like his shirt, even if it's just about the first time since we met that he hasn't been topless.

I want to tell him that it's not the wine, it's something else that makes me lie back and feel at total ease with someone I've only known for a handful of days.

But I don't say any of those things.

For a little while, we're quiet. It's a similar silence from our phone call. Except now, my body is alive with his nearness.

I can smell his detergent and soap, and beneath that the scent I've come to identify as *him*. I can't keep pretending that I don't know what this feeling means. It means that I like Hayden, despite any reason I can give myself, with him this near, I can't stop.

"Where'd you go, Sky?" he asks me, refilling his cup. He starts to reach for my face, to tuck my hair back but stops himself.

"I was thinking that this isn't what friends do."

"You don't drink wine and cheese with your friends?" He's coy, as if he doesn't already know that this dance we're doing is for one reason only—to figure out where we go from here.

"Yes, but—"

"But?" He eases back onto the blanket with a hand behind his head. "Sky, there's a huge but in our way."

"It's a necessary but."

"Are you sure?"

"That's what I'm trying to figure out."

"Alright, you explain your but, and I'll explain mine." He smiles, and that smile is so fucking gorgeous, I want to pounce on his face and make it mine.

He's letting me drive this car, and that is terrifying and

freeing in new ways.

"But," I've lost all the reasons. "Friends shouldn't be attracted to each other."

"Friends shouldn't have moonlit picnics on rooftops."

"Friends shouldn't look at each other the way you look at me."

"In my defense, I have to look at you that way. It's the way people are supposed to look at beautiful women."

Beautiful. It seems cheesy, but it warms my insides. It's the most obvious thing to say, but some guys never say it. Bradley never called me beautiful. Hot. Sexy. Smoking. On the days he felt that dating a brown girl gave him swagger he called me "fine." I reach for a memory in which my boyfriend of so many years called me beautiful, and I can't find it.

Suddenly, the roof feels too high, my feet too close to dangling off the ledge. I jump up and my cup slips from my hand. The plastic clatters all the way down and lands with a crack.

Hayden puts a secure hand around my waist and holds on tight.

I ease back into him, right against his chest. I can feel his heart thump through my body. Or maybe mine through his.

"If you're going to jump into the ocean and off roofs when I give you a compliment, I'm going to have to stop."

I look up and over my shoulder. His face is so close.

"It's not that. I'm in my head a lot."

"I'm not. Perhaps I should be. I'd probably get into a lot less trouble."

"Hayden, I'm just scared. My last relationship was for three years, and it didn't end well. I don't want you to be the rebound guy. I don't want a summer fling. I also don't think I'm ready to even think about something long-term."

"Whoa, whoa," he jokes. "What's with all the pressure?"

"Come on, Hayden."

"I get it. I don't want any of those things either. I'm careless with my body, but I'm pretty protective of my insides. I've been the rebound and I've been the doormat boyfriend. I've been the friend. And believe me, I would be glad to be your friend.

Friendship isn't a consolation prize for not being able to get in your pants."

I shake my head, unable to keep a smile from my face. "Hayden."

"See? That. I blame this on you. When you say my name— it's like you're calling for me from far away and only I can reach you. I hear everything you're saying. I'm the Nice Guy, Sky. I'm used to the territory that comes with it."

"The Nice Guy?"

"Yeah. Every girl that's ever broken my heart has told me that I'm *just so nice*. It sucks when girls prefer the guys that act like they don't give a shit, or treat them like crap, or are the opposite of nice. My dad was one of those guys. My friends have married those guys. That's just not who I want to be."

I look down at my hands holding his, and his hands holding me. Bradley was a bad guy. Sometimes he'd turn mean, and it always felt like he did it so I knew where our places stood. But when he smiled at me, it was like a spell. I'd just forget, and chalk it up to a bad day.

"So where do we go from here?" Hayden asks. "We've established that we are more than friends. But it's too soon for the long-term thing. Plus you're moving—"

"Maybe."

"Plus the unknown status of location. That leaves us with friends with benefits. Only that sounds smarmy. I can't do that."

He gives me a little squeeze.

"You could never be smarmy."

"In my experience, some girls want that."

"I don't."

"Then let's just agree that we're going to put a hold on defining or labeling anything."

"That's a shame. I've got a really great label maker for the wedding invitations."

His strong fingers dig playfully into my stomach. With my cup long gone, he gives me his.

"I just know that I want to spend time with you and possibly know what it feels like to kiss your perfect mouth again."

I have the urge to jump out of my skin. But he holds me tighter. The top of my head rests under his chin, in the nook between his neck and shoulder. I never fit in Bradley's nook. He was too tall and despite all the sports he did, he had a hard time building muscles on his shoulders. Not Hayden. Hayden is all muscle, and when I lean back, it's like his body was made to contour mine.

"I don't think I'm ready to get involved."

"We're not getting involved, Sky. That sounds too much like a label. We're exploring. When people explore it's about the journey, the need to travel."

His hands travel along my arms, brushing the chill on my skin.

"The need to discover the possibility of something life-changing."

He presses a kiss on my temple. I shut my eyes and listen to the drum of my heart.

"You're saying a lot of nonsense right now," I say, sitting up from his hold. The breeze picks up and pushes my hair over my face. He leans on his elbow, and I take a mental picture of how he looks right here and now. Voices try to overpower my thoughts.

Don't be an idiot.

Make yourself happy.

It was just one time...

I know all of these things, but it's a lot to ask of yourself to take a chance on something new, when your past still has a grip on your present.

"All I ask is that if for some reason I'm not making you happy," he tells me, "or if you decide you aren't staying, be honest with me. People undervalue honesty these days."

I nod, leaning myself closer to him.

"Friends," I say.

"Friends," he says.

You don't kiss friends. You don't dream of them caressing the inside of your thighs. You don't imagine what your life would be like if they were *it*.

Hayden and I can't be friends. Friendship is not a consolation prize if a relationship doesn't work out.

But for now…I'm okay without the label, the definition. For now I want to sit under the starry night with a boy too good to be real.

"Sky."

I respond with a kiss. His lips are a whisper against mine. He doesn't move. He lets me kiss him, lets me set the pace of my mouth on his.

Kissing Hayden a second time is different than I thought it'd be. It's surprising. It's soft, softer still. Everything about him—his calloused, his pecs, the sharp jawline—is in direct contrast to his soft, beautiful lips.

He pulls me against his chest, a hand on my lower back. His skin against mine sets off a series of landmines in my mind. I'm aware of the underwear I put on this morning, the wine on my breath, I'm aware that I don't know where I should put my hands because I want to put them everywhere. All over him. I'm aware of the moan that escapes my lips when he kisses me back.

He turns me seamlessly so that I'm resting on the blanket, pressed against the roof. It's a good thing we're over my bedroom. My foot kicks the remnants of our feast to the ground.

"You're a mess," he says.

"You have no idea."

I pull him by his t-shirt back on top of me. I love the weight of him, how solid he feels. He tickles my lips with his tongue and I open up for him. He tastes like sweet, red wine.

I lift my hips to meet his and grin when I feel his dick harden against my thigh. With quick raspy breaths, he says my name, like a prayer, a wish.

The heat of his body answers mine. I move my leg to allow him to press into me, my hands lift his shirt at the waist, tracing the ripple of his taut muscles. I want to get lost in the feeling of him.

He moans against my mouth.

"Sorry," I whisper.

"Don't be." He licks his lip where I bit him. In the golden

light of our lamp, they're red and swollen.

Hayden gets up on his knees, and I wish he wouldn't. The cold night fills the empty space he just left. I pull at the belt loops on his jeans, but he doesn't budge. He smiles, a wicked and beautiful thing. He lifts his shirt over his head, and my breath hitches. It's like he fills the entire sky, haloed by a dreamy light. He returns to me. I press my hands on his shoulders, but he takes my hands and secures them against the roof, over my head.

I kiss his jaw, every inch of it, the way I've wanted to from the beginning. I wrap my legs around his trim waist. My dress is all the way at my hips, giving him complete access to my soaking wet panties.

He presses a hand between my legs. He presses his forehead against mine, and I can see the struggle that flits across his face.

My senses are on edge. I want him to move his hand. I want him to tear off my thong. I want him to bury himself inside of me and never come out.

He growls against the skin of my neck, our pulses racing to a finish line that we cannot see.

"Oh, God, Sky."

He lets go of my wetness. He takes my face up with both hands and looks at me. I feel so naked under his bright blue eyes. He kisses my cheeks, my nose, my jaw. He's about to kiss my lips again, but a car revs close by.

Doors slam and drunk singing makes its way up the driveway.

"Let's swim!" Juliet says.

Someone shushes her, and they do a terrible job of being quiet. Hayden and I stay perfectly still. He chuckles into my shoulder. From here, we can see my cousins make their way into the backyard. All they have to do is look up and they would see me with my legs wrapped around Hayden's waist, his shirtless body pressed against me.

I wish they would all just go away. I push my hips up to grind against him once.

Hayden sighs into my neck, pressing tiny kisses along the way. His voice is a whisper. *"You're bad news."*

"Come on," Yunior says. "We're going to wake everyone up."

"Sky is so lame that she didn't come."

Yes, Sky didn't come. And it's going to be all their fault.

"I don't know what Xandro sees in her," Maria says, stumbling around, getting closer to the pool.

I freeze and so does Hayden.

"Shut up," Elena says. "You're just jealous."

"Scuse me!" Maria loud whispers. "I am *engaged*. I don't need to be jealous. She's not doing something right if her man was stepping out on her like that. Now she's got Xandro strung along like a puppy dog."

"You're being a bitch," Elena says, and turns around and leaves them.

Hayden looks at me. I don't know what is more embarrassing. The fact that my cousin is airing out my dirty laundry behind my back, or the fact that Hayden is here to listen to it.

I can't stand the sadness, the questions in his stare so I turn my face. I'm about to throw the empty bottle of wine in the direction of the pool, but I don't have to.

"Guys!" Yunior says, fumbling over a potted plant. "Help me get Andrea upstairs. She's puking all over my car."

"You deal with it," Maria says. "That's what she gets for doing so many shots."

Part of me wants to go and help them, but the other part of me wants to go to my room and lick my wounds.

"Come on," Yunior hisses.

Juliet is the first to go help. Maria stands at the poolside and watches the blue water ripple. She picks up a ball bouncing on the surface, turns it in her hands, and throws it as hard as she can.

When they're gone, Hayden kisses my cheek. I want to ask him to come in, but I don't want to talk about what he just heard. That was for me to tell him when I felt ready.

Hayden folds the blanket and throws it over the roof onto the balcony. He puts the trash and lamp in the bag and heads down first. I concentrate on my feet on each step of the ladder until I get to my balcony. I decide to keep the bag of provisions for next time. I really want there to be a next time.

My heart hammers in my throat. I don't want him to go just yet. I lean over the side and kiss him.

"I had a nice time," I tell him, nuzzling my nose into his shoulder.

He traces his finger up and down my arm. "Sky."

I smile and collect myself. My lips feel swollen, my panties are most certainly uncomfortable, and I'm sure my mascara makes me look like a raccoon.

Hayden takes my hand and kisses it. "See you tomorrow."

I watch him go down the ladder with the ease of a cat. He props the weight of it on his shoulder, like he's picking up a stack of pillows. He has to get it back to the other side of the house where the construction is happening. The metal rattles, but after my family's racket, I'm sure no one will notice.

After I shower and as I drift off to sleep, I close my eyes and think only of his face. I don't know if it was love at first sight. But now I can't deny that it sure is something.

CHAPTER 19

The only thing that can bring me down from the Cloud Nine that is Hayden's lips is sitting down to breakfast with my family. My mother gives me a curious eye. I scroll through my emails and try to avoid it.

"When did you get to bed?" she asks.

"Way before these clowns got home," I tell her. You'd think that because I'm the one who stayed home, I'd be off the hook. You'd think wrong.

Las Viejas give me their side-eye, and Maria holds her hungover head with both hands. Her skin is a pale green, but not as green as Andrea and Juliet. The only one who doesn't look the worse for the wear is Elena. I remember her defending me, sort of, against Maria's words. She gets a smile from me.

Some of the roofers walk across the backyard, and my heart jumps when I wait for Hayden's blond head. Then I remember he's banished to building the wedding gazebo.

My mother watches me stare at them, and calls for my attention. "You have to stop being so rude to Xandro. He's an old family friend."

"Just because we lived in the same building together," I say, talking with my mouth full, "doesn't mean we're friends."

"*Escuchame*, Sky," my mother says. *Listen, Sky.* "I raised you better than to be so rude. Give the boy a chance. He's from a good family. He goes to church. He's handsome. He's a doctor."

Everyone is nodding.

"I'm sorry, I thought we were having breakfast, not discussing my love life. It's nobody's business."

"Don't talk to your mother that way," Maria says.

Anger fills my mouth and threatens to turn my fantastic

mood into kindling. Then I see him, Hayden, walking past the glass doors that lead to the backyard. He can't see me through the reflection in the glass. He looks at his own image and rakes his hair back. His body drips with sweat as he carries a stack of boards over his shoulder.

My mother follows my eyes to Hayden. He turns around and makes his way back to his station.

"Sky, give Maria some of your pills for her headache."

I have the good kind of painkillers. That's a benefit of being a nurse. None of that over-the-counter sugar-coated medicine. I look at Maria and remember her words. None of them are dying. They need a sports drink and some sleep. My family doesn't realize that being a nurse doesn't mean that I'm a pill factory. They also don't realize that treating a hangover isn't why I went into medicine.

I pick up my plate and decide to take my food to my room.

"Oh, I'm sorry," I say, my voice sickly sweet so they know I'm lying. "I ran out."

* * *

After I scarf down my breakfast, Leti knocks on my door.

"You look thoroughly fucked," I tell her.

She sits down next to me and eats the remnants of my toast. "You should try it."

"Where's River?"

"She didn't come home last night?"

I shake my head.

"Do you think she's getting into trouble again?"

Leti and I stare at each other like we're trying to convince ourselves that everything is all right. A bright orange leaf flies in from the balcony and lands at my feet. It's the first sign that the summer is going to come to an end soon, and for the first time in three months I'm not ready.

"No, I think she just wanted to get out of the house." The truth is, I *hope* River isn't getting into any trouble. The last time she hit rock bottom, it was hard to pull her out of it. I'll be there for her no matter what, but she's never been one to ask for help.

"Would she tell us if she was?"

I shake my head. "Probably not."

"Well," I say, picking up my empty plate. "We can't wait for her. We have to get the seashells for the centerpieces."

Leti rolls her eyes and mumbles, "I bet that's why River's not here. Hiding from your wedding chores."

"Shut up," I say. "It's nice."

"Why can't we just buy a bunch of seashells?"

"Because," I say, "this way they're special."

I don't tell her that when I conceived this idea, I was drowning myself in Pinterest. Nothing makes you wallow in the feeling of being dumped as much as looking at pretty things on the internet. Wedding things. Wedding things you'll never have with the guy who broke your heart. But wedding things you can gift to your favorite uncles.

I scroll through my email to find the picture I want, but my inbox is full of wedding stuff. I remember I flagged the email from the DJ and read it.

I stand up from the bed, forgetting that my plate's on my lap. It falls to the floor and smashes in half. I shut my eyes and hope that I'm reading correctly.

"Sky, you're freaking me out."

I give her my phone and wait for her to read the email.

"That little shit!" she shouts.

"Can he even do that?" I ask. "We paid the deposit."

Leti shakes her head. "I'm going to one-star his ass. Who names themselves DJ Dee Troyt?"

"I think I'm having a heart attack."

Leti looks at me, unconvinced. "No, you're not."

I press my hand on my racing heartbeat. I can hear my voice rise in pitch. "First, there's a hole in the guest room so everyone's getting shoved into one basement. Then, the caterer doesn't tell us they're going out of business. Now, the DJ is cancelling on us. I'm supposed to be putting this together, Leti. This is all on me! What am I going to do when Pepe and Tony find out? Oh, sweet Mother Mary, I'm going to have to tell them about the caterer right now, aren't I?"

"Sky?"

"This is horrible. I'm the world's worst wedding planner. No, I'm the *worst* niece in the world."

"Sky!"

Leti's hand smacks me across the face.

"Thanks, I needed that."

The floor creaks outside my door. I run over and stick my head out to see who it is, but the hallway is empty. I shut the door and press my body against it.

"Get a grip," Leti says. "We can't panic."

"That's easy for you to say. You get to come and go as you please."

She sasses me with a sway of her head and a purse of her lips. "Excuse me, Pepe and Tony are my uncles, too. Have you stopped to think that the reason why you ended up planning all of this by yourself is because you wouldn't let anyone really help?"

I let myself slide to the floor. "I've been pretty crazy, haven't I?"

Leti nods. "You're kind of like bridezilla, except you're not even the bride."

"You're right." I take a deep breath. "Know any DJs?"

"Actually, a few. They're all in Sweden though. I'm going to email my contacts because we all know that out of everyone in this house, I have the best taste in music. We'll fix everything. Have a little hope."

"Okay," I say, because in reality, there's not much else for me to do. I've always been the kind of person who needed to be able to fix things, and when I can't I get really down on myself. But now, I've got River and I've got Leti.

Leti's furiously typing messages into her phone. When she sees me staring, she snaps. "Come on, now. You get us a ride to the beach so that even if we don't have a catered dinner or music, at least we'll have the Hampton's most beautiful and cost-effective seashell centerpieces."

CHAPTER 20

Hayden: *I'm outside whenever you're ready.*

Me: *I'm coming!*

Hayden: *You have no idea what that just did to me…*

Leti gets a good look at the smirk on my face and gasps. "You bitch. You've been holding out on me."

"I don't kiss and tell."

She shakes her head. "Lies."

"I'm going to get some water bottles to go," I tell her.

"I'll go ogle your man in the car."

When I shove three bottles in my basket and shut the refrigerator door, my mom steps forward from the hallway. I put a hand on my chest. "Jesus."

"Where are you going?"

"Seashells. Beach. Centerpieces."

"With that boy, Sky?"

"Ma, his name is Hayden."

"I don't like it," she says, crossing her arms over her chest like she means business. "Boys like that only want to get in your bed."

I'm counting on it. Yes, I've decided. Probably.

"You always think the worst of people," I tell her. "And you're wrong. Just because a guy is shiny on the outside doesn't mean he's a good person."

"But," she grabs my hand to pull me back from the front door. She's not listening to a single word I'm saying. "Xandro is coming to visit today. You should give him a chance, Sky. You could still be a doctor's wife if you play your cards right."

I pull out of her grip so fast, I bump against a side table. One of the photos falls off and the glass cracks. It's my high school graduation picture. God, look at that hair. I set it right and keep heading for the front door. She calls and calls my name. My own mother doesn't care if a guy cheats on me or is controlling, as long as he's got MD plastered over his forehead.

"Fuck my life," I say.

I deflate when I see Xandro's shiny convertible parked in front. I love cars, but not when they're shaped like penis rockets. Xandro is already halfway up to the house wearing a thin blue t-shirt that hugs his slender muscles.

Behind him Leti and Hayden are waiting for me at his truck. If only I could get to them while avoiding the plastic surgeon in the white linen pants.

"Sky! Just the girl I was coming to see." He pulls me by my shoulders and scoops me into a bone-crushing hug.

"Ouch. Can't breathe."

He lets me go and smiles down at me. "You missed an amazing party last night."

"Yeah, I was beat." I shouldn't feel badly for missing his party. I loved being with Hayden. But even from out here I can feel my mother's pressure on me. Actually, that would be her eyes peeking through the curtains.

"Don't worry, babe. I'll be throwing my own shindig soon enough. I've already told my friends about you and your situation. I know Dr. Claremont, the head of trauma at Beth Israel."

"I'm in pediatrics."

He shrugs, throwing away something I specifically chose for myself. Bradley was the same way. He didn't understand why I cared about taking care of children. He wanted me to switch to the ER once he was done with medical school. To him, it didn't matter as long as he was going to get paid.

"I really have to go." I wave and duck to the right.

He grabs my hand and pulls me back so I'm facing him. For such a slender guy, he really is strong. I hear a car door open and boots hit the ground. Xandro looks over my shoulder, like he's daring Hayden to come over.

"Where you going?" he asks.

"Wedding errands."

"I can take you if you'd like. You won't ruin your dress in that dirty old truck."

It's not old. The only dirty part of Hayden's truck is along the bottom where it treads over mud and sand. But Xandro doesn't need an explanation.

He's the second person today to not listen to my words. To just keep talking as if I'm not even here.

"We're fine. Besides, you might get sand on your slippers," I tell him, motioning to the white leather boat shoes. I make a move to go again, but this time he stands in front of me as a barricade. Something in my belly twists in a warning sign. I do *not* like Xandro.

His smile is smug and his teeth are so straight and white. It's like an illusion and I don't want to see what's beneath that. "Come on, Sky. I'm sure your mother doesn't care for your choice of company lately."

I take several steps back. Who does he think he is? I smile and pat him on the shoulder. "Don't be so hard on yourself, Xan. I'm sure my mother cares for you a whole lot."

With that, I get in the passenger seat of the truck, and when we leave, Xandro is still at the front door, scratching his head.

CHAPTER 21

"This place is fantastic," Leti says, digging her feet into the sand. "How have we never been here?"

Hayden shoves his hands in his pockets. "There are lots of little beach strips like this. Most people don't bother because they're just out of the way."

I hold my arms out and let the sea breeze spin around me. After we walk up a sandy hill covered in tall grass and polished stones, we arrive at Hart Beach. No matter where I look, it's like we're the only people around. The exception is a tiny shack that looks too small for anyone to live in.

"Is that a house?" I ask.

"That's a bungalow," Hayden says. "I worked on it last summer. The Sanders had it built when they got married two years ago, but they divorced this summer. She took the house in South Beach and he bought a bachelor pad in Hell's Kitchen."

"Wow," I say. "A romance for the ages."

Leti is sprawled on the sand with her phone in the air, texting. "Gary's on his way. There's no way I'm going to third wheel with you two making mooney eyes at each other."

I kick sand in her direction. When I turn to Hayden, my breath hitches a little. He takes his shirt off. It's like the cut of his muscles are directional arrows pointing at his crotch. Watching Hayden get undressed is my new favorite pastime. He folds it haphazardly and sets it on a patch of grass. When he walks towards me, it feels like the space between us is getting longer. Like he's on one of those moving tarmacs and he's walking in the wrong direction, but I don't mind because I get to look at him a little longer.

"Are you okay?" he asks.

Me? I'm just drooling a little. No big deal.

He takes my basket. It's the most ridiculous and endearing thing, seeing Hayden hold a wicker basket.

"Ready?"

I nod, and we leave Leti's unhelpful ass lying on the beach waiting for Gary.

For a few minutes, we walk in silence. I pick the most obvious shells. The big ones that don't have many chips in them. Hayden gets closer to the water. He rolls up his pants to the ankles. Digs his hands in and pulls out a brilliant set of seashells. My favorite is a tiny blue one that twists on both ends. It's the color of his eyes.

"This guy doesn't belong here," Hayden says. He takes the shell and places it in my hand. "He came from a magical land, far, far away. Here."

I don't have any pockets so I slide it into one of his. It's a flimsy excuse to touch him, but no one seems to mind. "Hold it for me."

"Sky," Hayden says.

I drop a handful of white shells in the basket, and try to match the severity in his voice. "Hayden."

He sighs. "I need to ask you something without coming off like a dick."

My stomach fills with nervous knots. "Okay?"

"What's with Enrique Iglesias back there?"

I laugh so hard that it feels like I've expelled a demon. "Oh my God, he does look like Enrique Iglesias."

"It's glaring."

"He's an old family friend. My mom's got it in her head that we should date." I should say, my mom's got it in her head that we should get married in a huge church ceremony and have lots of babies that I can stay at home to raise.

"But you don't?"

I look at his face to make sure he's seriously asking me that. "Of course not!"

"I'm sorry," he says. "You can do whatever you want. I obviously don't own you. I just...don't like the way he looks at you. Like you're this prize instead of a person."

"Aw, you're jealous."

"Fifty percent jealous, fifty percent indignant for you."

I take Hayden's hand and cross my fingers with his. When our palms touch, it's like they were always meant to be touching, and even when I bend down to grab a shell he doesn't let go.

"I appreciate it. But I don't need another person worrying about what I'm doing."

"It's not that, sweet Sky." He kisses my knuckles. "It's that—oh, fuck it. I'm jealous. I am sixty-five percent jealous. I didn't expect to be. I want to be Mr. Cool Guy, but when he kept grabbing you, all I wanted to do was rip off his slick head and toss it in the back of my truck."

I laugh. "That'd be too messy. Besides, I've had eighteen years of taking care of myself."

"You'd been getting hit on since you were five?"

"Oh yeah. Little Elijah Stintson. He used to stand at the bottom of the steps and look up girls' skirts. After the parents complained, they made the girls wear slacks."

"That's one way to solve a problem. I don't doubt that you can take care of yourself, Sky. But if he does become a problem, just know that you can come to me."

I realize we've stopped walking. The basket is full of seashells in all colors and sizes. Down where we left Leti she's joined by the boy who will always be known to me as Football Scholarship.

I've spent a lot of the summer walking around the beach, and it's always felt lonely. Granted, I was more often than not literally alone. It was like the sound of the waves and the cry of the seagulls mimicked the sadness in my own heart.

Now, the waves crash and the birds flutter at a different rhythm, like my heart is changing.

"I really like you, Sky."

"You don't even know me." I don't let go of his hand.

"I know stuff," he says indignantly. "I may not know what you were like in high school or the whole story about the guy who broke your heart. But I know that you love your family. That you've been working hard on this wedding when everyone else is treating it like a vacation. You pick up the slack because you know that no one else will. You don't fall for cheap tricks and flashy smiles. Which I guess is good for me."

I did fall for cheap tricks and a flashy smile. That was a very succinct way to sum up Bradley. But it wasn't his car or his clothes or the restaurants he took me to. It was that he looked at me like I was the only one in the world.

And then it stopped.

"Where did you go?" Hayden traces his finger along my cheek.

"I'm here," I assure him.

"Do you want to see the breakup bungalow?"

"Can you get in?"

"When he left, Mr. S. gave me the keys. He wants me to buy it from him, but it's worth more than my own house."

"You have a house?"

Hayden smiles. "It was the only thing my Nana ever had, and she left it to me. My dad was pretty pissed. I was eighteen and I didn't have to work for it. Doesn't mean I don't work hard."

"I know you do." Then my face turns scarlet from admitting that I watch him work. Stop blushing, Sky. You've already kissed and felt each other up a little.

Still, Hayden is more than blush inducing. If I'm not careful, I might set myself on fire from how hot my body turns at his touch.

"Yeah."

He takes me through an overgrown patch of grass. I can imagine what this would look like if it was taken care off. The bungalow is a rectangle box. The front is a huge window that faces the ocean. The door is out back. Hayden pulls out his key ring. There are a dozen silver and gold keys. I wonder how he keeps track of what opens what. Or maybe he doesn't and tries each one at a time.

He grabs one from the middle and opens the door.

The house is cool, even though it bakes in the sun all day long. There's a tiny kitchen. The counter holds a coffee machine and a bag of chips. How can a guy, with a body like that, survive on coffee and chips?

A small bed faces the window. Other than that and a side table with an old-fashioned green lamp, the house is bare. There are hooks and nails on the wall where pictures might have hung. It's like they took everything that mattered and fled.

That's what my apartment looked like after I tossed my things in the back of River's car and hightailed it back to New York.

"It's like a little hobbit house," I say, running my hand on the counter.

"Isn't it? Part of the appeal I think is to make you feel like a giant."

I walk around the bed and stand in front of the glass window. My brain is screaming: *bedbedbed*.

My heart is screaming: *HaydenHaydenHayden*.

"I don't know," I say. "This view is attraction enough. Do you stay here a lot?"

He nods. He's on the other side of the bed. Too far, I think.

"My mom's been living with me since the divorce."

"Ah," I say.

"I just want to give her space. Besides, I don't think I help. I offered her this place, but the window scares her."

"Staring at the ocean when you're depressed is a huge no."

"Any suggestions on how to help a divorced woman smile?"

I shake my head. "It happened to my mom, and I don't think she's smiled since. Not really."

"I never want to be that way."

"You can't be." I sit on the bed.

He sits down beside me. The sea breeze clings to his skin. His hair waves more at the top.

"Why are you smiling?" I ask him.

"I was just thinking that you look beautiful surrounded by the sea."

I wish someone had told me a long time ago that boys like Hayden exist. Maybe I always knew. Maybe somewhere between Disney princes and broken hearts I forgot about this boy. This boy with his golden hair and brilliant blue eyes whose single touch makes me want to jump out of my skin and run for cover because I'm afraid of what it would mean if I stayed.

I'm tired of being sad. I'm tired of being lonely. Most of all, I'm tired of being afraid. I excommunicated myself to the beach. It was the timeout I needed. But right now what I need more than that is to kiss Hayden Robertson again.

But he beats me to it.

His lips, salty and full, cover mine. He holds my face and pulls me to him. I close the distance by throwing myself on him and knocking us both to the bed. I don't care if it's desperate. I don't care if it's a dead giveaway of how much I'm attracted to him. I've decided that the best way to deal with my feelings for Hayden is to act on them.

He laughs softly against my lips. I can feel the vibration of his laugh across my body.

"I'm glad your reaction wasn't to run away."

I silence him with a kiss. No thinking. Just kissing. That should be everyone's life motto. If it were, there would be fewer problems in the world. Or maybe more, who knows.

I straddle him. The bed is plush and molds to my knees. His hands pull at the hem of my dress, raking his nails along my thighs. He stops to cup my ass and squeeze.

His penis throbs against his jeans.

"Oh, God," he says.

Thank you, Pilates.

I press quick kisses on his mouth. I have a desperate urge to touch all of him at once. So I do. I kiss his neck. I trail kisses down his chest, licking my way down to his abs. Oh, dear, God. His abs. They should be a monument. They should be hologrammed against the sky. They should never ever be hidden by clothes ever again.

I undo his button.

I hold the tip of his zipper.

Hayden grunts, and it is so sexy that my panties are soaked right through.

He takes my hands and stops me. He sits up and flips me on my back so quickly I bounce a couple of times.

"Sky," he says. "Sweet Sky."

He presses his hands against my knees and pushes my legs apart. It's the most demanding he's ever been with me. My heart races. I sit up on my elbows to watch him.

He kisses each knee, then presses a wet kiss on the inside of my thigh. He licks a circle and sucks the skin. A thrill runs up and down my body, concentrating in my center. I'm sure I'm going to have a hickey there and I really don't care if I do.

I can't remember if I shaved this morning. But suddenly Hayden does something so delicious, it makes me forget everything else.

He scoops his arms under my legs. I secure them over his shoulders. He looks up at me with those gorgeous blue eyes. And then he kisses me. He presses his lips between my legs, against the wet fabric of my thong.

One, two, three kisses that send sparks on my skin.

I moan and grab hold of his hair. He smiles in response, pleased with himself. He knows that it's driving me crazy. He knows that I want more.

Hayden pushes my thong to the side. His breath is cool against my heat. He teases a lick on my clit. When he presses his mouth against me, my body goes up in delicious flames.

Leti was right, it's been a while since anyone's touched me this way. But it's been even longer since a guy has gone down on me like Hayden. Like he wants to be there. Like he's savoring my wetness. Like he wants to feel my insides tighten for him.

I answer all of Hayden's licks with a moan. When he alternates between licking and sucking, I lift my pelvis up right against his face. He grabs my ass and pulls me closer still. My thighs pulse to the rapid beat of my heart. I arch my back. I pull at his hair. I want to get lost in the moment of Hayden and the sea and sky that surrounds us.

When I come, it's like a wave crashing over me. It's raw and intense and keeps rushing through me until there's nothing left of me to give and I collapse on the bed.

Hayden kisses the tingling skin on my hips. He sits up on his knees. He licks his lips. Stares at me as if he'll devour me again. And I want him to.

I push my dress back down. I beckon him with my index finger. He lies back and pulls me into the nook. I press my hand on his chest. His heart beats faster than mine.

I throw a leg over him, and push myself up to kiss him. I can taste myself on him.

"You're incredible," he tells me.

Whatever I'm about to say is lost as I scream. I jump out of the bed so quickly that I fall off. Hayden reaches out and grabs me just before I go over the side.

Leti bangs on the window of the bungalow.

Hayden laughs.

"Oh, God. What if they saw?" I hiss.

"Not a chance. We can see them, they can't see us. I would never put you in that position, Sky. Not when there are so many other positions I'd rather have you in."

He kisses me, hard and deep. I know he's still aroused.

"I know you guys are in there!" Leti shouts.

Hayden collapses on top of me. He chuckles. "You should go out first. I need a minute."

I kiss him. "Okay. But just a minute."

CHAPTER 22

Hayden adjusts himself on the ride back to the house. Gary and Leti ended up collecting more seashells than we did. He promises to see Leti that night and goes off in his own car. I know that if I return home without her, we'll both never hear the end of it.

"So," Leti says in the car, "did Sky ask you to the wedding yet?"

I turn in my seat and smack her.

Hayden laughs. "Be careful now, ladies. I'm having a hard enough time focusing on the road."

Leti bursts into a giddy laugh. "Gary already said yes. I think River will eventually get around to asking Sgt. Pepper. That just leaves the maid of honor."

Hayden makes the turn to our house. When we're on the right side of the lane he turns his gaze back to me.

"I'm sure if and when Sky wants to take me to the wedding, she will ask me. No pressure though. My tux from Jake and Suzy's wedding still fits."

But when we get to the house and Xandro's car is still in the driveway, Hayden's beautiful smile falls.

Leti gets out of the car first and takes the seashells with her. I unbuckle my seatbelt and turn to him, readying myself for a goodbye kiss.

"Thanks for today."

He nods. "No need to thank me."

I should tell him that today was amazing, that I haven't felt that way in so long. But all he does is glare at Xandro's car.

"Where did you go, Hayden?" I try to use his words back on him. I trace my finger along his jaw. Turn his face so he sees

119

only me.

Whatever it is, he doesn't want to say.

"Do you want to go to the beach tomorrow?" I ask.

"I'll be here actually," he says. "Gazebo time."

"Then I'll wait. We can get dinner or something."

It's like something switched in his brain between our blissful moments on the beach and now.

"Maybe, Sky. I just—" He looks down at his lap, at Xandro's car, at me. "That guy's still in your house."

"Hayden, it's not my house. I have no control of who my family invites over."

"Look, I've been in this situation before, and in the end, I'm the one who loses."

"What are you losing, Hayden? There's nothing to lose. Xandro is just—" I hesitate.

"He's the guy your mother would rather see you with. I'm the guy who put a hole in your uncle's roof."

It hurts to hear those words coming from him. Hayden is beautiful from the inside out and I want everyone to see that.

Xandro's the guy my family is pushing on me because they don't trust my judgment. Because they don't think I'm capable of finding someone who will fit their laundry list. But I am. I think I have.

"He's nobody."

"I'm sorry." He grips the wheel and shakes his head. "You don't owe me an explanation. I've gotta go."

The abruptness of it leaves me speechless. There are no kisses or longing stares. There's just a goodbye, the rev of his engine, and his taillights turning on my street.

• • •

In the house, Leti jumps in front of me and starts to push me back out the door.

"Abort, abort, abort. Turn around."

I grab my keys and start to head back out but my mother rushes from the living room.

"Sky, get in here."

My emotional roller coaster is killing me. I just want to crawl into my bed and try to figure out what just happened with Hayden. How did we go from the best oral sex of my life to awkward jealousy?

"What?" I stand at the doorway to the living room where my younger cousins are piled up on top of each other watching a movie.

"Sky," my mom says, pulling me into a corner. "What took you so long?"

I turn away from her and she follows me into the kitchen. I'm red with anger. Red with the thrill that comes with the memory of Hayden's mouth between my legs.

"I already told you."

"Xandro's been waiting here to take you out."

"Ma, I don't want to go out with him. I'm sure he's a perfectly nice person, but it's not going to happen. Please, please respect my wishes."

My mom crosses her arms. Her frown deepens. When I told Hayden that my mom hasn't smiled in a long time, I wasn't exaggerating. Maybe that's why she manages to look so young and wrinkle-free.

I can see bodies shift in the doorway of the kitchen where half of my family is eavesdropping.

"You're not thinking straight, *nena*. You're not thinking about your future. You've spent the last three months lazing around the house. Now you're doing God knows what with that boy."

"That boy? Do you mean Hayden?"

"Don't be stupid, Sky."

Don't be an idiot, Sky. Don't be stupid, Sky. Don't let your past shit on your present, Sky. My head throbs with a serious headache.

"I can't deal with this right now." I turn to walk past her, but she doesn't budge.

"When are you going to decide to get your life together? You quit your job. You haven't even tried to look for a new one."

"Is this about me not wanting to date Xandro, or me not

trying to find a new job?"

"It's all of it. I didn't come to this country to have you end up with nothing."

There is it. The first generation pressure. My mother had to work on assembly lines, in dirty kitchens, and cleaning filthy homes to put food on the table. I got to go to school so that I would never have to have that life. I have to have a job that pays well. That is until I find a husband that makes even more money than I do.

I get to have my whole life planned out for me because she didn't come to this country so I could squander my opportunities. It's too much pressure.

"Stop!" I shout. I've never shouted at my mother. Not even when I thought I'd burst at the seams from being so angry. "Stop trying to fix me, Ma. I'm not broken. There is nothing wrong with my choices. This is my life, my life, not yours."

She stands so still, I want to shake her to make sure she's okay. She looks small and sad and on any other day I would wrap my arms around her and tell her to stop worrying about me. But this goes beyond worry.

Finally, my family stops pretending not to eavesdrop and they all stand at the doorway. Some of them stare at me with looks that say, "Damn, girl, you in trouble." Then there's Maria's face that tells me how much she disapproves of my tone.

Let them disapprove.

"What are you guys looking at?" I snap.

Yunior and Elena do the smart thing and walk away.

"Isn't it enough that you're ruining your own life?" Maria asks. "Now you have to drag the wedding through it?"

"What do you mean?" my mom asks.

My heart seizes. Maria's eyes are trained on me as she says, "Tell them, Sky. Tell everyone how there's no caterer or DJ. God knows what else is wrong. She's been keeping it all to herself. Don't you dare lie. I heard you and Leti."

"I bet that made you real happy didn't it?" I ask. I *knew* I heard someone outside my door.

"What am I going to do with you?" my mom asks, like I'm

a lost cause.

"Maybe for once, you're all going to leave me alone."

Xandro stands at the front of them all. "Sky, I think you should apologize to your mother."

I laugh. Leti comes forward as if to hold me back. Do I look that far gone? When did my summer of reflection become my summer of judgment?

"It's a good thing I give zero fucks about what you think."

Las Viejas gasp so hard, I think they've collectively absorbed all of the oxygen in the room. Even Aunt Salomé crosses herself, and Grandma Gloria shakes her head at me. I think this is the very first time they've looked at me this way.

I grab a set of car keys from the door and turn around. For the first time in my life, I'm going to turn my back on my family, and on some level it's liberating. On another level, I feel like I've started to cross a line from which I might not come back.

CHAPTER 23

"Was I wrong?" I ask Leti.

We huddle in the dimly lit crowded bar off Montauk Highway. On the outside it looks like a shack that's about to fall down. On the inside, well, it still looks about the same. But it's the only true dive bar around that isn't infiltrated with summer tourists.

Harleys line the front like a barricade. It's not the most welcoming bar, but the bartender doesn't ask questions or fake a smile. She slams beers in front of you and throws a bag of salt and vinegar chips in your direction.

"I've never seen you so mad," Leti says. "You're usually the good one."

"It's just too much. They're shoving Xandro in my face. And then Maria. Why is she *so*—and why is *he* so—"

"I know," Leti says. "I should throttle one and you throttle the other."

"Now Pepe and Tony are going to know that I fucked up."

Leti tilts her head back and drinks deeply. "Yeah, and they're still going to love you. There is nothing you can do that'll make that change. Even if you set the place on fire."

I shake my head. "I can't go back. Not until I fix it."

"We've been *trying* to fix it. Me, you, and River. What do you call that?"

I laugh. "The Lost Girls. We're like a girl grunge band."

"We're more than that."

"I know we are. But I've been so wrapped up in my own mess lately, that I've put the wedding stuff on the backburner."

Leti smiles, and the hanging bulb over her head makes the gold star on her tooth shine. "It's okay that you have a life."

'Leti, tell me the truth. Do you think I'm making a mistake taking so much time from work?"

She drinks her beer and gets a layer of foam on her upper lip.

"I think that you need to do whatever you need to do to get your head sorted out."

"That's not what Maria thinks."

"She's a hypocrite. Virgin my ass."

We cheers to that.

"Look," she says. "Everything is going to blow over. Xandro is going to go back to Miami or join a boy band or whatever he wants to do with himself. You're going to apply somewhere. We're going to get Pepe and Tony married with the best wedding they'll ever have, because we might fuck up along the way, but we always come through. And you're going to tell me what you and Hayden were doing in that cozy little beach box."

She wiggles her eyebrows and shakes her double Ds.

I tell her exactly what Hayden and I did. She fans herself when I get to the part of the earth-shattering orgasm.

"Bradley never made me come when he went down on me. He'd close his eyes and lick everything except for my clit for ten minutes, then he'd go to town."

"If I ever see that guy again..." she says.

I shush her. "You're going to Bloody Mary him into existence."

I don't tell her that he's called me a dozen times in the past few weeks.

"With Hayden it was amazing. I always thought I had to be, you know, in love with someone to have that kind of feeling. But I was in love with, you know who, and on the occasions I came, I thought that's as good as it got."

"My sweet, sexually-deprived girl."

"I've only had sex with three guys. There was Sir-Humps-A-Lot Smith, Jack-Rabbit-Jeff, and Bradley..."

"Well, if and when you make sweet, sweet love with Hayden, I hope he's better than expected."

"That fucking sucks, you know. Sex should be better for women. It's like guys get in there as quickly as they can and get out. They don't care if you climax or even feel good."

The barmaid, who's been cleaning her glass during our entire conversation, smirks at me. She refills my beer without even asking and I take it gratefully.

"Honey," she says, tossing her 1980s blonde mane over her shoulder. "If you wait for a man to please you, you'd best be ready to wait for a long time."

An old biker beside us thumbs in the bartender's direction. "Mad's got a point. My old lady uses me like a walking talking dildo, and I lie there and take it."

Then he goes back to his whiskey and television.

I giggle into my beer. "I'm going to do it. With Hayden, I mean."

Leti slaps me on my back so hard that I choke on my beer a little. "Atta girl."

"Thing is, I think Hayden's mad at me."

Leti looks confused. "How can he be mad when he got to touch your mostly pristine kitty cat?"

"Leti!" She knows I hate when she calls it a kitty. It's so weird.

"When he saw Xandro's car, he just shut down. It was the weirdest thing."

Leti rolls her eyes. "I hate when guys get jealous. It's not his fault that we're fucking hot and everyone wants a piece of this."

"Bradley was never jealous," I say. Mad places another beer in front of me. Each frothy sip melts away my tension and dissolves the angry knots in my chest.

Leti smacks me on the head. "Do you know what you're doing?"

"What?"

"You're comparing the most promising guy you've met this summer to the creep who cheated on you."

I stare at the amber liquid in my tall glass. "That's what you do, right?"

"That's what you do when you're not over someone."

"I am."

Leti shrugs. "Tell yourself that until you believe it, because that's a kind of heartache you don't want again, baby girl."

All of this revolves around my heart. Is it still broken? The day I found out Bradley was cheating on me was at a nightclub. He'd been gone for so long that I went to go get him. Then I saw him coming out of a stairwell with his arm around her waist, and everything inside of me shattered all at once. I ran, and he didn't chase after me. Not until the next day when he was sober.

"You know when you know that your relationship is over but part of you is still holding on?"

Leti shakes her head. She's never had a long-term relationship. She's never wanted to. It's hard to run across the globe when you've got your heart anchored to a person who doesn't want to join you.

"Well, that's what it was like. I was trying to hold on because I didn't know what it would mean if I let go. I don't want Bradley back. Not even a little bit. But I want what he took from me. He took my love."

I burp, loud and long. A cute guy at the other end of the bar looks at me like he can't believe that just came from me. I shrug. What do I care?

"Don't say that," Leti says. "No one can take your love away. That's yours, wholly and truly yours. Fuck Bradley. Fuck Xandro. Fuck anyone who thinks they can have a piece of you without earning it first."

"You're right. You have to earn love."

"Why can't we have relationships like Pepe and Tony? They're perfect. What do they do differently than we do?"

I snort beer. "They're gay?"

"They're honest."

"They accept their crazy."

"They love each other."

"They don't try to upstage one another."

"Yeah," Leti says. "I hate when guys are like, 'Look at all my gold and rubies. Be blinded and impressed.'"

I laugh. "I should call Hayden."

"Listen, I like him for you. He's a cool dude. But if he starts pulling that jealous crap you need to get out of there."

"I love you," I tell her.

"I love you."

Leti has earned my love. From the moment she beat up the girls who tormented me in school, to the time she explained to me that I was not dying, I was just getting my period, Leti has been more than family. She's my soul sister.

She's family, and even if she wasn't blood, I would still choose her. Like River.

River, who stumbles out of an unmarked door in the back corner of the bar.

I blink hard to make sure that it's her. That I'm not just drunk hallucinating the people that I love.

But that's most definitely her blonde curls, her tiny denim shorts, her favorite Coney Island tank top. She was wearing that when I saw her two days ago.

She stumbles out from the back with a huge guy at her heels. He grabs her around the waist. She can't support her own weight so he holds onto her, groping her wherever his large hands will reach.

"Hey!" I jump out of my seat and rush to her. I grab River and pull her out of the guy's hold.

"Sky! It's my Sky!" The stench of cigarettes and booze hits me hard. Her eyes are ringed with dark circles. Her nose is red at the nostrils. Her pupils are dilated.

Oh, God. River.

"Get out of here." The guy tries to push me to the side.

"You get out of here," Leti says, appearing on the other side of him.

Fear sparks in the pit of my belly. This guy is huge. He's got the kind of hands that could snap a neck in half. There's a pearly scar along his jaw, the only spot where hair won't grow in his patchy beard.

His teeth are rotting, and they smile at me. "I'm just collecting."

Collecting. River. She's gambling again.

"Sky," River says, "I'm sorry. I lost all of it."

"She doesn't have any money," I tell him.

He shrugs. "There's other ways to collect payment."

He traces that fat finger on River's creamy skin. She bats him away, but she barely has any strength to get up.

Adrenaline runs through my veins, sobering me up. All of my senses are on alert with warning signs pointing at this guy.

I take River's hand and pull her. "Get the fuck away from her."

My body trembles from top to bottom. I don't sound menacing or convincing. I sound scared. It makes him smile. It makes him grab for me instead.

I take several steps back. "I'm going to call the cops."

"Try it," he dares me. "Your friend's got a couple of treats in her pockets."

He leers down my shirt. His eyes grow wide and unfocused. His meaty hands reach for me. Leti jumps between us and pushes him back.

He hits the wall and grunts. He means to come at us, to hurt us, to put us in our place.

Then, the old biker who was sitting next to me appears at our side. He stands there, watching us. He doesn't make a move to help. His small dark eyes peek from behind bushy white brows. He turns his head from side to side.

"Told you not to come back here, Will."

Will stands straighter. "She owes me three bills."

"Should think twice about your clients."

Will wants to snarl. The bar's gone quiet. The TV runs on a sports channel, and the tap drips heavy fat beads of beer onto the bar.

When I turn around, every biker and patron is standing. Hands reaching at back pockets or the inside of jean jackets.

"Go on, get," the old biker says. "I don't even want to see you on a postcard, we clear?"

Will nods once and exits the bar.

Leti and I help River stand. Her head hangs back. I take her face in my hand and look at her eyes. It's like the lights are on but no one's home.

She tries to talk, but her words are nonsense and her breath is acrid.

"You, too," the old man tells us.

But we're already heading out the door. The sun has already set. Our car is parked in the lot, but none of us are in any condition to drive.

"Should we take her to the hospital?" Leti asks. She can't decide where she wants to stand so she walks in circles.

If we take her to the hospital, they'll find drugs in her system.

"I'm fine," River says.

Drunk logic is a funny thing. Only a person using another human to support their weight could claim they're fine.

"She needs to sleep it off." River's body gets heavier by the second.

"No," she says. "No home."

She lets go of me and crawls on the cement floor. I don't know where she's going, but she's right. There's no way the three of us can show up at the house like this.

"Who are you calling?" Leti asks, chasing after River. She's given up her quest and turns on the ground. She falls on her back and shuts her eyes, mumbling something I can't understand.

I find his number quickly. It takes a few rings for him to answer. Please, please, answer.

"Hey," he says.

"I'm sorry. Something's wrong. I need you to pick me up."

I can hear him pushing away bed sheets. "I'll be there in five minutes."

I go over to River. She's out cold. I lift her head and place it on my lap and brace myself for the longest five minutes of my entire life.

CHAPTER 24

Hayden makes it in four minutes. When I see the black silhouette of his truck driving up the street, my heart flutters. Relief. Happiness. All the feelings Leti and I were talking about before we saw River.

"She's passed out," I tell him. "I just can't take her home. She's not to the point where we have to take her to the hospital."

River's pulse is strong, and she opens her eyes every now and then to tell us she's sorry. She loves us. She'll never do it again.

The same old song.

"It's fine," he tells me, placing a hand on my shoulder. He lifts my chin to look into my eyes. "I'm glad to help."

He picks up River like she's a baby. She cocoons herself against his chest. I open the back door to his truck. Leti gets in on one side and we place River's head on her lap. It's like a contortionist's worst nightmare, but it'll do.

I hop into the passenger seat and look at Hayden. He doesn't smile, but he takes my hand and kisses my knuckles. I lean my head back, dizzy from alcohol and shaking from Will's threats. Between the parking lot and Hayden's house, dozens of scenarios worm their ways to my thoughts. What if we hadn't been there? What if Will had hurt River? What if River had never made it home? It's all too familiar, and I have to shut my eyes and take deep breaths to calm myself down.

In the back seat, River is awake and crying into Leti's lap. Leti brushes her hair back and soothes her.

When we get to his house, Hayden releases my hand to turn the wheel and park. It's a two-story home painted in all white with blue shutters. The grass is manicured neatly compared to the hulking mansions on each side.

We park out back. There's a long wooden picnic table and a grill. That's all I can see in the dark before Hayden shoves his keys in my hands. I open the back door and we follow him up creaking wooden floors.

He sets her down in what must be the guest bedroom. It's unused and the bed is made up perfectly.

"I'll get a garbage can," he whispers.

Leti huddles behind me, examining every inch of the room. "Does he live alone?"

I shake my head. "His mom lives here, too."

River's passed out. I take this opportunity to dig into her pockets. I find two little clear plastic bags, a crushed pack of cigarettes, and two hundred dollar chips. Leti sighs and swears under her breath.

"Fuck, fuck, fuck."

I set everything else on the nightstand, but I take the plastic bags into the adjoining bathroom and dump the contents in the toilet. That's three hundred dollars worth of blow.

When I come back in the room, Hayden's juggling three Gatorades, a bottle of pain killers, and a bucket. "Not the first time I've taken care of a wasted friend. You should ask Gary about last summer's fiasco," he tells Leti.

"Is it okay we're here?" I ask. "Your mom…"

"She's seen worse." He doesn't explain and I don't pry. "There's some t-shirts and pajamas in the dresser."

"I'll stay with her," Leti says. "It's my turn."

I can't help but chuckle. "Right."

"I can drive you home if you want," Hayden tells me.

I shake my head. I know what this means. Leti and River are in the queen-sized guest bed. That leaves me with Hayden.

"I'm not going anywhere."

• • •

Hayden's room is nothing like I would have imagined. Of all the boys' rooms I've ever been in, his is the cleanest. There's a king-sized bed with tangled sheets, like he got up in a hurry. A stack of comic books on the nightstand. A metallic lamp.

The furniture is the most striking. The nightstand, the bed frame, even the computer desk in the corner all look special. I trace my finger along the carving in the wood.

"Did you make this?"

"How can you tell?" He stands right behind me, framing my body with his.

I shrug. "Same designs as the gazebo."

He walks around me to a tall dresser. Everything still has a sweet wood smell. He takes a t-shirt and hands it to me.

"All of my pants are probably too big for you."

He sticks his thumbs in the waistband of his pajama pants. At first I think he's going to take them off, then I realize they don't have any pockets and he doesn't know what to do with his hands.

Hayden is nervous, and it's the most adorable thing I've ever seen. I don't know why, but him being nervous makes me less so.

"Be right back." I take the shirt and head to the bathroom. I rake my hair back a couple of times. My nose is red from a spot I forgot to slather with sunscreen. My eyes are red from all the booze I drank today. I look through the medicine cabinet. Mostly anxiety pills with his mother's name: Regina Robertson. I grab the eye drops and put two in each eye. I tilt my head back and keep my eyes shut for a minute.

I splash water on my face and use some of his mom's face cream. It's the same kind my mom uses. I draw a line of toothpaste on my finger for the walk-of-shame-tooth-brush. I give myself one last glance in the mirror. Hayden's t-shirt is the same blue of his eyes. It's like wearing a tent, and it feels wonderful.

I hurry back to his room where he's in a tank and pajama pants. He's flipping through a comic, but drops it when he sees me come back in.

"Wow," he says, his eyes taking their time from my toes, up my legs, and settle on my face. "Um, I can take the couch. I just wanted to make sure you didn't need anything else."

My heart goes into panic-preservation mode. What excuse can I give for him to stay? Oh, I know. "Don't go."

When his smile returns, I feel myself relax.

"Are you sure?"

"Hayden, today feels like it's gone on for a hundred years. I just want to lie down. Please, lie down with me."

He holds his arms out to me and I climb into his bed. "Two beds with you in one day. I'm either the luckiest guy alive, or I'm dreaming."

I tuck my legs into the covers and lean up against his chest. Maybe I'm the lucky one. "Thank you for coming."

"You don't have to thank me. Does this happen a lot with her?"

I nod. "Not in a long time. River's had a rough past. Her mom left when she was little. Her dad couldn't stand to look at River because she's the spitting image of her mom. That's what he told her once."

"My mom told me that same thing once. Why do parents say that, like it's our fault we get stuck with their genes?"

My mom's never said that to me, even though I have the same eyes as my dad. I can feel it in the way she looks at me though, like she has to look away eventually.

"I wonder what set her off," I say. "She's been clean for a year. I checked her into rehab after her dad died. She didn't talk to me for months, but then she called me when she wanted Oreos. That's how I know she forgives me. She asks me to bring her Oreos and we share."

"You're a really great friend. That's an important part of someone."

"I just hope I can help as much this time. River's like blood." I sink into the comfort of his body. It's like we've been doing this for so long. I wonder why sometimes it's easier to find that sense of familiarity with some more than others. When I started dating Bradley, it took us a solid month before I felt at ease in his place.

Stop, I tell myself. My self sounds strangely like Leti telling me to stop comparing Hayden and Bradley together. But I can't help it. They have the same coloring. Blond hair and blue eyes, even though I swear I don't have a type. Where Bradley is entitled, Hayden works hard. Where Bradley is undercutting and hurtful, Hayden is understanding and sweet. Where Bradley never cared who I went out with or if I didn't call for twenty-four hours, Hayden is already jealous of a guy I don't care for. That's the only problem. Jealousy destroys. I know this first-hand. It eats away at your heart.

"I'm glad you called," Hayden says. "I wanted to make a U-turn as soon as I left, but I wasn't sure how to explain myself. I feel like an idiot for the way I left you."

"My Uncle Tony says the best way to explain yourself is to start from the beginning." I look up at him. His skin is a magnet for my hand. I trace the slopes of his arm muscles, loving the way his skin warms to my touch. "What happened?"

He leans back against the headboard and sighs. "This might be too soon, but I feel like the summer ending is this ticking time bomb. So here goes. My last girlfriend and I ended on really bad terms. See this scar?" He points to the tiny nick on his forehead. It's covered by the flop of his hair. "She threw a hammer at my head."

"What the fuck?"

He chuckles. "Right? I'd been working non-stop for a few weeks. I wanted to save up some money to take her on one of those Europe backpacking trips. But I was an idiot. I wanted it to be a surprise. Then she started acting really weird for a while. She wouldn't return my calls or she'd just straight up stand me up when we did make plans. It was Gary that told me he'd seen her getting into some guy's radiation-orange Camaro. When I asked her about it she went ballistic. She said I didn't trust her. I didn't love her. I didn't put her feelings first."

I press my hand on his chest to feel the way his heart races.

"I told her we were through. She grabbed the closest thing she could find."

"Your hammer."

"Yep. Good thing she's a terrible shot or I'd be horribly disfigured by now."

"Hayden." I know he's trying to joke, but I've been there. I know he's hiding his hurt behind that smile. "You don't have to do that."

"That was in the spring."

"Did you go on the backpacking trip?"

He shakes his head. "I never told her about it either. It wouldn't have changed anything. She kept seeing that guy. Sometimes I see them zooming around town in that stupid car. Who paints a car orange?"

"Someone who really like oranges," I say.

This time he laughs for real. "So when I saw that guy still at your house, it just brought all of that back. My forehead still throbs. I'm like fuckin' Harry Potter and shit."

I sit up to get a better look at him. His hair is soft and smells like shampoo. It's still damp in the front. I kiss the tiny scar. I kiss his forehead. His nose. His lips.

"I'm sorry I was a dick. I'm just more protective of my feelings than I'd thought."

"You know," I say. "You're the first guy I've wanted to kiss since my last relationship."

His smile quirks up some more. "Wait, does that mean I'm not the first?"

I cover his face with my hand and push him back. "Don't be an idiot."

"I'd hate to break it to you, but having a penis comes with instant idiocy. It's in there waiting to burst. That's why we jerk off so much, but there's an infinite supply."

"Gross."

"This is happening really fast," he says. "But every time I look at you, I just find it harder to stay away."

I don't know what to say to him. Today's been full of so many ups and downs that all I want to do is crawl into a ball and sleep. "Can you just hold me?"

"For as long as you ask me to."

CHAPTER 25

We sneak into the house at dawn, before anyone is up. Hayden stays in order to finish up the gazebo. He pulls me into a soft, sweet kiss that threatens to curl my toes. I slept curled against his chest the entire night, and probably only drooled on him a little bit. If his alarm hadn't woken me up, I'm sure I would have stayed in the bliss of dreamless sleep.

"Can I take you to lunch later?"

"I can't," I say. "I have a lot of cleaning up to do."

"Tomorrow?"

"We're taking the family out to the vineyards."

"Which one?"

"Goose Walk and then the Long Ireland distillery." Before he gets a chance to look disappointed, I ask, "Do you want to come?"

He makes a face, half embarrassment, half trepidation. "I don't think your family likes me. I'm sure they'd rather see you with someone like Xandro. Not being jealous. Just stating a fact."

I roll my eyes. "I don't care. I want you to come. It'll probably help the female faction if you're shirtless. Probably half of the male faction as well, actually."

He squeezes my waist and it makes me tingle all over. "Shirts are so cumbersome, but I'll clean up."

"I have no doubt." I welcome the kiss he presses on my hand and want to pull him back to me, take him up to my room.

Instead, I leave him to work and find myself in River's room, where she and Leti are sprawled on the bed.

"I'm not ready for a lecture," River tells me.

"I wasn't going to lecture you. But I did bring cookies."

She sits up instantly. I throw the pack of Oreos. It's my last sleeve, but she needs it more than I do.

"Milk?"

I sigh and go to the kitchen to grab milk and three cups. They make room for me. River dips her Oreo, waits a few seconds, and then eats it. Leti likes her cookie dry, then washes it down with milk. I like to eat the cream first, the cookie last.

"River," I say. I don't care if I'm pushing her a little bit. She needs a good push. "River, please."

She finishes her milk. She sits up with her legs drawn to her chest. "I don't know what happened. It's something inside of me that sometimes just snaps. I met this guy at the beach the other night and he wanted to party. So I did. He took me to the back room behind Smitty's."

"Were you there all night when we found you?"

She nods. "I wanted to leave, but then I got a really great hand. And I just kept getting better and better until I lost it all. I was up ten grand. Ten grand, Sky. Do you know what I could do with that?"

I nod. She'd get a new car. She'd stop waitressing. She'd do something with her life. It's the same old River song.

"River," Leti says. "Can you just for a second stop and think what would have happened if we hadn't been there?"

She shakes her head. River always gets close to the edge of situations. So close that I think she wants to feel what it might be like to go all the way. I've been in the car when she'd step on the gas until she was at top speed, just to see what it would feel like. When we were in Ireland, she stood on the edge of a cliff with her arms and face tilted to the open sky. I was afraid she'd jump. But that's River. She likes living on the edge. My worry is that even if she doesn't want to, one day she'll get so close that there might not be a coming back.

She digs into her pockets but can't find what she's looking for.

"It's not there," I tell her. "It's gone."

"Sky! I owe Will money."

"Turn in the chips. I'll spot you the rest."

"I can't keep taking money from you."

"Yeah well," I say, turning angry. "You have to. You won't always have to but you have to for right now. I'd rather lose a buck than lose you, okay?"

She leans back. With the last smudges of her makeup, her pouty swollen lips, and her unwashed hair, she looks like a little kid trying to be a grown up. I feel for her. We're twenty-three, but even though high school and college are long gone, we're not finished becoming who we're supposed to be. I know I'm not.

"I'll get help," she says. "Just—after the wedding. I want to enjoy the summer with you guys. I'll be good."

That's the thing with River, I can't be mad at her. I can't say no to her. All I want is to wrap my arms around her and make the world better for her, but that's enabling.

"Okay, bitch," Leti says good-naturedly. "But you can't come to the tasting tomorrow."

River rolls her eyes. "Alcohol isn't the problem. It's everything else. Once the chips are down, I don't know how to quit."

"River…"

"You can't just leave me alone in this house. Everyone gives me dirty looks. Why can't it just be us?"

I rub her leg. "Okay."

"Okay," she says, feeling as if she's won.

"Listen," Leti says. "If you aren't going to take care of yourself for you, then do it for us. You know we love you no matter what, but that's what we're here for. For you."

River nods, but she doesn't look at either of us. She shuts her eyes. She squeezes both of our hands, and eventually, we all fall asleep. Still, I know what a false promise looks like, and River doesn't mean to keep hers.

CHAPTER 26

I leave before anyone in the house can notice I'm gone.

I roll down the windows of River's car to try to get the cigarette stench out, then finally stop at the gas station to pick up an air freshener. Someone honks behind me, but I ignore it and keep driving into town where I'm going to knock on the door of La Vie est Belle until they say yes to cooking for me.

My phone rings and I send it to voicemail. I park and grab a coffee. The restaurant isn't going to open for another hour so I've got time to kill.

My phone starts going off with a series of chimes, which tells me my family knows I'm not home.

Pepe: *Nena... please come home.*

Maria: *You're being selfish.*

Mom: *No me hables.*

Yunior: *Can you pick me up a large iced latte and a bagel?*

Tony: *Sky, whatever happened, we can talk about it. We should never have put this burden on you.*

That's the message that breaks my heart. It's not a burden. It's something I wanted. I start to type back, but my phone rings with a name I wasn't expecting.

"Lucky?" I answer.

"Holy crap are you hard to pin down," she says. "I texted you a few days ago to let you know I was in town. Are you freezing me out because of my mom and Bradley? I thought we were starting to be besties."

"I never got it, I swear!" I take a sip of my coffee. It's better than telling her I completely forgot about her text. "Wait, was that you honking at me this morning?"

She answers with a laugh. "Are you busy? I kind of have to

talk to you."

There is only one thing—or person—that Lucky and I have in common. I swallow the dryness on my tongue. "What's going on?"

"It's about Bradley."

• • •

My mom used to tell me that no matter what I was afraid of in life, I had to confront it. Back then she was talking about Heaven Moreno, a girl with a piggish nose who believed her parents when they told her she was the most beautiful girl in the entire world. Heaven was the fifth grade mean girl before mean girls wore pink on Wednesdays, and for some reason she hated me. She pulled my hair when the teachers weren't looking. She spilled her chocolate milk on my white shirt. She started a rumor that I didn't wear a training bra (not so much a rumor as the truth).

I tried my best to avoid her, but she found me. When I asked my mom to change my class, she refused. "You have to confront her," my mom told me. And on the day she put glue on my chair (our uniform pants were navy blue), I snapped.

"What's your problem?" I asked. Not so much asked, but whispered to the floor.

She sucked her teeth, fueled by the confidence of having every girl in class stand behind her. "You're my problem."

I didn't know what to say to that and everyone just snickered.

"You think you're hot shit." For a ten year-old, cursing in school made you a badass. She was a princess, but she wanted to be a badass. I was quiet and wanted to be left alone. "Well, you're not."

"Neither are you."

That was it. That was the first time I'm sure anyone had told her that. Tears brimmed to her eyes and as soon as the teacher walked in, she let loose with the waterworks.

Suddenly, I wasn't *the* mean girl, just *a* mean girl. I made the princess cry. My mom still had to come to school because I was accused of picking on another student. Meanwhile, I was still wearing pants with the ass covered in glue, and that was when I realized that the world wasn't fair. Sometimes confronting problems wasn't the best solution, but at least Heaven left me alone for the rest of the year.

Now that I've got River's car stalled in front of a house that belongs to a woman who ended my relationship, I remind myself that as you get older, you have different kinds of fears and problems to confront. This fear is that I'll never be able to get over Bradley. That I'm not strong enough to move on. That my little bit of steel is diminishing with every second the past is in neutral, and I'll end up being the kind of person I hate.

My knuckles are white around the steering wheel. I swallow a deep breath and release it slowly. It's just a house, I tell myself.

"Don't be an idiot," River had told me.

Maybe the advice I'm searching for isn't "face your fear." Instead it's "don't be an idiot."

Maybe life would be a lot simpler if everyone collectively stopped being idiots. Wouldn't that be grand?

I turn off the engine and dig into my purse. I find the blue seashell Hayden found for me at the beach. I trace the sea-polished surface, like it's a talisman of good luck. In a way it is. Just looking at it brings a smile to my face. I set it on the dashboard and walk up the driveway.

It's not the biggest house in the Hamptons, but it's pretty damn nice. Miniature palms line the front path to a house with the kind of modern designs that make it look more like it belongs in Mars circa 3199. I don't know why, but that gives me a little bit of pleasure knowing that the owner of the house and I are polar opposites.

"I was wondering how long you were going to stay in the car," Lucky says. Lucky stands a bit shorter than me. Her long dark hair is tied up in a messy bun. Her cool gray eyes are hidden behind a pair of shades. Her shoulders are red where her skin rebels against the summer sun.

"That obvious?" I ask.

She pulls me into a hug. Her black bikini is warm, like she

just got up from her lounge chair. If you had told me a few months ago that I'd be hugging Lucky Pierce and actually be happy to see her, I'd have called you crazy.

"You look good," I tell her.

"Yeah, all the restaurant stress leaves me with zero time to eat." She leads me around back, past a gate that takes us to the giant kidney-shaped pool. There's a giant hot tub and, of course, more than one grill—a propane one and a brick oven with a slab on it. Hedges block the view from the neighbors on either side. I wonder if Bradley ever stayed here.

I torture myself with that train of thought, then force myself to let it go when James Hughes, chef extraordinaire, finishes swimming his lap. The man who surfaces from the water occupies my entire brain. From the strong muscles that glisten with water, to the abs that ripple as he pushes himself out of the pool. He rakes his black hair back, and even from a distance I can see how green his eyes are.

I glance at Lucky, who stares at him. I recognize the look of love in her eyes. Lucky looks at James with complete and total adoration. When she sees me staring at her with a grin on my face she tries to cover it with a scowl. Why are people so eager to hide how happy love makes them?

"Shut up."

I hold my hands up innocently. "I didn't say anything."

But she doesn't stop that look from returning to her face. James brings his wet body over to us. He takes Lucky by her face and pulls her into a wet kiss. She doesn't complain as his hands wrap around her petite frame and grab her sizable derrière. When they pull apart, they take a minute to smile at each other. Something inside of me aches.

"You guys are gross," I tell them.

James goes off to dig in the beer cooler and Lucky gives me the finger. I grab her hand.

"Is he converting you to the tattoo-side of life?" I rub my finger across the skin of her hand, over a bright four-leaf clover that's inked just under her thumb.

She pulls her hand back and takes the beer James offers her.

I take one, too.

"I was trying to convince her to get, 'yes, chef' on her forehead, but it didn't go over so well."

Lucky makes a face. "I don't think forehead was the original place you suggested."

I twist off the beer—a Boston Lager, of course—and follow them to a plush lounge area beside the pool. A large palm creates the perfect amount of shade. The water ripples a perfect shade of blue, and for a moment I think of the sand dollar on my dashboard and the boy whose number is written on it.

"What's new, Sky?" Lucky says politely. I can sense she wants to get to the core of why she asked me here, but she seems nervous about it. "You up and left me when I finally had a friend in Boston."

"Hey," James says, taking umbrage to that.

"You're my boyfriend," she says. "It's different. I can't talk to you about the stupid shit you say."

"Why not?" He pinches her thigh. "How else am I supposed to know not to say it again?"

"The man has a point." I say, allowing myself to relax into the high comfy back of the wicker couch. There's a spread of cheeses, toast points, and homemade spreads.

"How's the wedding stuff going?" Lucky asks.

I do a shit job at hiding my stress. "It pretty much sucks."

"Why?" Lucky leans forward and James looks like he doesn't know if he wants to stay or run.

"It's kind of the small things that started going wrong. The roof caved in on one of the guest rooms."

"What the fuck?" James says.

"Everyone was okay," I tell them. I can feel my cheeks warm up. My head is thinking *HaydenHaydenHayden*, but I stop myself from going further in the story.

Mostly.

"One of the roofers fell through."

"Oh my God," Lucky says. "Was he okay?"

"Mostly. I patched up one of his cuts. He's, um, interesting." I chug my beer and shove some spicy hummus into my mouth to give myself a reprieve. "Anyway, the DJ bailed, and the caterer forgot to tell us that they're going out of business."

Lucky places her hand over her mouth. "Get the fuck out. It's—"

"Less than two weeks away?" I press my hand on my stomach and set down the toast point I'm about to eat. I really dropped the ball. "The worst part is that I tried to keep it secret because I didn't want anyone to worry. Only, I haven't been able to *find* anyone. Oh…Oh, I think I'm going to be sick. It's my own fault, not your food, James. I'm so sorry."

James and Lucky exchange a worried look.

"What?"

"If you don't tell her," James says. "I will."

"Tell me what?" I say.

Lucky looks at me with her big gray eyes. "Bradley's in town."

The queasiness in my stomach comes to a peak. I run into the house and I can hear Lucky shout, "Make a left!" I push through the first door I see and thank the gods that there's a sink. I throw up my morning coffee. My stomach heaves painfully. I almost forgot how much I drank last night.

I sit in the cool porcelain bathroom and replay what Lucky said. It shouldn't be a surprise. I *knew* that was his silver Mercedes I saw the other day. I can hear Lucky and James arguing in the kitchen. Well, technically even their regular conversations sound like arguing, so it's good to know that they're still going strong.

When I decide I'm ready to compose myself, I rinse my mouth out, clean up my mess, and head back outside.

"Sorry about that," I say, joining Lucky back outside.

We sit in silence, enjoying the bright sun and the warm breeze.

"I thought you should know," Lucky tells me. "Bradley is a total wreck. I haven't actually seen him, and he hasn't come near my family since James knocked him out, but he leaves crazed messages asking me to help win you back. He told me he was going to come here."

"Why are you telling me this?"

"Because you need to know. You also need to know that there's no way in hell I'd ever help that. That's a one-and-done kind of betrayal."

"Agreed." I think of my mom and every time she took my dad back. "Thanks Lucky."

She shrugs like it's no big deal. "I feel shitty about the way it all went down, but at least you and I got to be friends."

James returns with a bottle of seltzer and some ice. He nods at Lucky once. It's amazing the way they communicate. He's not much of a talker, but with a single look, Lucky seems to know just what he means to say. I think I'll add them to my list of favorite couples after Pepe and Tony.

"While you were puking," Lucky says.

"Thanks," I mumble.

"We were talking about how instead of going back to Boston we could stay here in the Hamptons for a little while."

James leans forward. It's hard not to look at his biceps, but it's even harder to hold the fierce green of his stare. "We were only going to stay for the weekend after the Foodie TV filming."

"But now!" Lucky says, impatient with the leisurely way in which James speaks. "We want to cater the wedding."

"What?" I almost spill seltzer all over myself. "Are you serious?"

"It won't be too complicated a menu," James says. He runs his hand through his hair and I can see him trying to do some sort of math. "But I guarantee it'll get done and done well."

"I don't know what to say."

"James and I have been there," Lucky says. "Everything was falling apart around us. It's our karmic duty to help."

"How many guests?" James asks.

"Two hundred."

"Give me a second," he says. "I'm trying to think."

Lucky turns to me. "This'll take a while."

He pinches her again and she squeals. I've never seen Lucky this relaxed and playful with someone. It's like the dark cloud over her head is long gone.

My stomach twists into knots as we wait for James to do

this thinking. Lucky stretches her feet out and lands them across his thighs. He massages a foot with one hand and scrolls through his phone with the other.

"I'm not gonna lie, Sky," he says, "I'm going to need to bring in some friends. Can I see the original menu you had planned?"

I pull it up on my phone and let him read it. His face ranges from a frown to a pleasant head nod, to a surprising, "That sounds good, actually." When he's done, he gives the menu to Lucky.

"Okay so here's the deal," he says. "I would 100% do this, give or take a few things. It'll be more pared down. There are too many pasta dishes."

"This wedding's half Italian," I say.

"That's the biggest issue since I won't have my kitchen. I have a buddy who has a restaurant, but it's in the city. They're not equipped for such a huge transport."

"I'll rent a van," I say. Tony and Pepe have done so much for me over the years. They paid for my braces. They paid for nursing school. They sent me on a summer backpacking trip with River and Leti all over Europe. The least I can do is put some of that back into this wedding.

Lucky squeezes his hand, and he looks at her, really looks at her. James doesn't know me from a hole in the wall. He's doing this for Lucky, because he doesn't want to see her upset. If someone had told me Lucky Pierce would be saving my skin right about now, I wouldn't have believed them. But she's full of surprises and I wish I'd given her more of a chance from the beginning.

"I'd better go make a few phone calls," James says.

"James——" I'm about to start kissing the ground at his feet. It's like a thousand pounds lifting from my shoulders.

"Don't you dare fuckin' thank me," he says. "I'm happy to do this."

He goes off into the house to make his phone calls.

"You have no idea how relieved I feel right now," I tell her. "Pepe and Tony are going to love it. They love watching his new spotlight on TV."

She brings us more seltzer. "Hello, I opened a restaurant with only a minor emotional meltdown. I *think* I know what you're going through."

As I let the relief wash over me, my brain starts to remind me of other things I have to get done. The DJ. Finish the centerpieces. *Tell* my family that everything is going to be okay.

"So," Lucky says. "Who's the guy?"

I sit up. All of my anxious thoughts of wedding planning get replaced by a single thought. The guy. "What guy?"

"Don't play dumb. I know that look. The one you called *interesting*. Spill."

Lucky sits back in her chair facing me. She means business. If I try to make a run for it, I wonder if she'll push me in the pool.

So I tell her. I tell her his name is Hayden Robertson the Third, and some people call him Tripp. She has the same disgusted reaction as I did and agrees she'd never call him that. I tell her that his perfect body fell at my feet and saw me in nothing but a thong and a form-adjusting bra. I tell her that every time I turn in his direction, I find his forget-me-not blue eyes watching me. Not just watching—admiring. I tell her about the number on the sand dollar and our rooftop date. About the bungalow, and saving River.

"That's so gross it's actually cute. He doesn't sound real."

"I don't think he is. I think that my mind is so desperate to think there are good guys in the world that it fabricated him, and the illusion is so strong that everyone sees him, too."

She takes a gulp of her beer and wipes her lips with the back of her hand. "You're preaching to the choir, Sky. I mean, you know my love life just as well as I do."

Bradley always kept me updated with Lucky's latest. I don't have to tell her. I'm sure she already knows.

"James isn't perfect," she says. "He's stubborn as fuck, and so am I. God knows he has his share of demons. The difference is that for the first time in my life, I'm with someone I completely trust, not just with my body but with my heart."

"I thought I had that," I say. I hate the way my voice sounds, but it feels good to say it out loud. When I'm at home I have to hide that hurt. I have to put on a face that tells my world that I'm fine. But no one truly understands. They want me to be okay, they want me to be "over it" because it'll make them feel like they can stop walking on eggshells. I guess it's harder to let people who know you see you this way out of fear of being judged.

Lucky won't judge me, I know that much.

"You'll have that again," Lucky says. "Maybe it'll take a while, but there is nothing stopping you."

"You know what the worst part about this is?" I say. "I actually like Hayden. I mean, I'm attracted to him. A blind person would be attracted to him. It's not just him. He's beautiful. He has this hair that's soft to the touch and always golden. His body alone makes me want to take a cold shower. But it's the stuff beneath that. He's got this feeling about him that tells me he's just *good*, you know."

"What's so terrible about that?" Lucky says. "Sounds like cake to me."

Yes, delicious cake with honey drizzled on top.

"I don't want to like him as much as I do. It feels too fast and too soon. I'm not ready, but knowing he's so close makes me want to forget that I'm not ready and let him look at me in that way—the way James looks at you."

Lucky pops a cheese cube in her mouth. She washes it down with her beer, the whole time studying me with those gray eyes.

"You're fucked," she says.

"Thanks."

"I mean it, Sky. You're going to lose yourself in your thoughts. It's not good. I know you're afraid of getting hurt. I'm the last person to urge you on to rebound fuck a guy just because. That's not good, and neither is getting involved with someone while you've got feelings for your ex."

"I don't have feelings for Bradley anymore."

She cocks an eyebrow, like she doesn't believe me. Do I believe me?

"Okay," she says. "But you're not the only one who's still

messed up. You shouldn't be ashamed because you *feel*. You're a real human person with real human feelings."

"Thank you, Lucky."

"Oh, I'm not done," she says. "Don't deny yourself that good feeling just because you're afraid to get hurt again."

"You know," I say. "The one good thing about my ex-boyfriend cheating on me with your mom is that now you and I get to be friends for real."

She half smiles. "I will confess I secretly hated you for being so fucking beautiful. It's disgusting."

"Shut up."

"Let's get down to business. Now that James is catering the wedding, it means I'm invited. What should I wear?"

"Hang on," James comes back in with his phone in hand. "Before you get started with the estrogen. We can do a tasting for your family in two days."

"That's perfect."

James gets back on the phone and starts ticking off a list for the person on the other line.

"Everything's happening so fast," I say.

Lucky leans back into her cushions. "Yep. You've got to enjoy it while you can."

CHAPTER 27

"Where have you been?" My mom looks like she could faint. Never did I ever even leave the apartment unless it was to school or the library. Now that I'm in my twenties, with a degree, and no longer living at home, she freaks out.

"Out." I say. I'm starting to feel the dread that comes with trying to keep secrets.

"Sky," Pepe and Tony rush into the living room from the kitchen.

Leti and River come out of their rooms. Maria and Yunior and all one thousand of my cousins turn from the TV.

"Okay, I have a few things to say."

"You really—" Maria starts to say.

"And you, most of all, need to be quiet." I hold my finger up to silence her. "I know that I should have told you guys about the caterer, I just really didn't want to upset you. I wanted these next few weeks to be perfect, but it seems like every time I turn around something is going wrong."

"Oh, *nena*," Pepe says, coming over to me. "You know you can share the workload. You don't have to do everything by yourself."

I look at my mom. I learned from the best. I don't mean that in a bad way, but growing up, she did everything by herself. She took care of me, Pepe, and even Aunt Salomé when Leti's father died.

"Ma, I'm sorry I yelled at you. But you have to let me make my own decisions."

She doesn't stay for the rest. She walks out of the living room and up the stairs to her room.

"I deserve that," I say.

"We'll just have to figure something out," Tony says, holding Pepe around the waist.

River raises her hands. "How do you feel about hotdogs?"

Tony just says, "Uh…."

"Guys," I hold my hands up. "It's done. I have someone."

"Who?" Pepe asks.

It's hard to hear them over Maria squawking something about how lucky I am, and Daisy crying about how her dress itches, and Grandma Gloria saying they'd better at least know how to make rice and beans, and River looking indignant like I just stole her thunder.

"It's a surprise," I say. Before they can riot and protest, I continue. "You'll find out in two days. It's going to be so worth it. I know I've been a little crazed the last few months, but you'll see. I will give you the perfect wedding."

"We have faith in you," Tony says. "We can't wait."

"What about the DJ?" Maria asks.

I bite my tongue.

"I've got that covered," Leti says. "Don't worry your bitchy little head off."

• • •

I step outside into the cool night air, leaving my family with something to gossip about. The evening is warm, and now that I can cross one thing off my list my mind wanders to last night. I picture myself in Hayden's arms, and my skin is instantly covered in a delicious warmth. I pull my phone from my back pocket to call him.

The call is interrupted before I can hit the little green phone symbol. I nearly drop the device out of my hands. It flip-flops like a fish trying to get out of my grip. But it's not a fish. It's a phone. And the person calling me is Bradley.

My heart thunders in my chest. I think about what Lucky said, that I might still have feelings for Bradley. I keep thinking about him, that's for sure. I know that when someone is part of your life, they leave a mark, whether bad or good. I know that

I can't keep comparing guys to Bradley forever. Sometimes the hurt has to fade, even if it doesn't disappear.

"Hello?" I answer.

"Sky!"

It's strange hearing his voice. I haven't even let myself listen to the voicemails he leaves me. It's like a memory that's fading, and I find myself straining to recall the details of his face.

"Bradley."

There's silence. He didn't think I'd pick up. I didn't think I would either. Now we aren't sure what to say because we're both surprised. At least I still know how his mind works.

"I heard you're in town."

"Guess Luck's still mad at me."

My eye twitches a little bit. I can picture him leaning back and smiling as he speaks.

"I guess so."

"Baby—"

"Don't." I sigh. Something inside of me hurts again. I know that men cheat. I know that women cheat. I know that there isn't a science, and that you're hoping that it doesn't happen to you. I know that when it does, you're more ashamed that you didn't notice, or you didn't want to notice. I'm ashamed that I'm ashamed. That I shouldn't feel that way because I did nothing wrong.

"I've missed you so much. I'm going nuts without you."

"I'm sure you've survived well enough." I chuckle. The first few weeks, I missed him so much I thought about making a U-turn on the Queensborough Bridge and going back to Boston. But I didn't.

"I need you—" I start to say.

"I need you too baby."

"No, Brad. I need you *to listen to me.*"

He scoffs.

"I need you to stop calling me. I need you to go back home."

"Sky, Sky, Sky. Why can't you just forgive me? Why can't we go back to the way things were?"

"Because I saw you! Because I *saw* the way you were with

her. For weeks I couldn't figure out what was wrong with you. I thought that I wasn't making you happy. Do you know what that's like? And sure enough you were happy. It just wasn't with me."

I can hear the frustration in his voice. "I made a mistake. You and I belong together, Sky. I know it. We've invested too much time in our relationship to throw it away."

"You're talking about us like we're stocks."

"You're different, Sky."

Maybe I am. I stayed with him for that reason...the investment. I didn't stay for love. And I'm not staying now.

"I am different," I say. I'm leaving a career behind. I'm not afraid of not knowing my next step. Just kidding, I'm terrified. But at least I'm confident that I want whatever my next steps bring me. "But you know what? I'm the only one out of the two of us who needs to be okay with that."

"We're not finished," he says. "I love you. I still love you."

"Don't you get it? We were over long before I left. You ended us."

"But—"

I've had enough. Something in my chest starts to swell and I know I have to let go. "Goodbye, Bradley."

I hang up and hold my phone to my chest. I nearly jump out of my skin when I feel someone standing behind me. River pulls a drag on her cigarette. She doesn't say anything, just nods, like she's proud of me.

I'm proud of me, too. I run up to my room and make myself comfortable. I find the number I was looking for before I got interrupted. Watching the phone ring gives me butterflies, and I decide that I love the feel of it.

He picks up on the second ring. "I was just thinking about you..."

CHAPTER 28

When everyone is packed away in Pepe and Tony's SUVs, Hayden pulls up to the driveway. He washed his truck so you can see the bottom half of it. Leti and River both whistle as he steps out of the car and walks towards us.

He's wearing a crisp white shirt and dark blue jeans. The spice of his aftershave tickles my nose when he kisses my cheek. He rakes his hair back over and over again.

"Damn boy," Leti says. "You clean up real good."

"So do you," he tells her.

She picks up the hem of her flower print dress and curtsies. River feels left out. "What about me?"

"You, River Thomas, are stunning."

She gives him a sardonic smile, like she doesn't believe him. River is River, and will never not wear a black band shirt and ripped shorts. Her aviators hide the dark circles under her eyes, and a thick leather wristlet hides a bruise where that brute Will grabbed her.

"Sky," Hayden turns to me. "You look—"

The cars, stuffed with my family, honk at us. "Hurry it up!"

"The wine isn't going anywhere," Leti shouts back.

We file into Hayden's truck. He backs up and, because he's more of a local than any of us, leads the way. I watch his face the whole time. It's disappointing to see him wearing a shirt, but the fabric does beautiful things to his muscles. He's like candy waiting to be unwrapped and licked down to the core.

"God, you're sick in love," River says, watching me watch him.

"Shut up." It's the best comeback I have, because she's right. I am sick. Sick in the head with feelings for a boy who is too good to be true. A boy I might not see after this summer.

At the vineyard there are, surprisingly, zero cars in the lot. It's a perfectly beautiful summer day and it's still tourist season.

"Is it open?" Leti runs up the driveway to the main door.

Pepe and Tony walk up holding hands.

"I called last night," Tony says, "to tell them we have a large group coming."

Hayden heads to the front of where my family looks like a mob ready to storm the vineyard. I don't miss the way Maria's eyes linger on Hayden's ass. Can't really blame her. All of his body parts should be immortalized in a statue. In my room.

"Hey," Hayden tells them, standing directly in front of the double doors. "Hey guys. I'm Hayden. Most of you remember me from falling through the roof."

Half of the family laughs.

Pepe gives me a side eye and winks.

"Is he actively trying to die?" River whispers.

"What are you doing?" I hiss at him.

Then an older couple comes out. They hug Hayden like old friends. The lady hangs a sign on the door that says. "Closed for private event."

"You're here!" the old man says. "Welcome…come in. We're all set up for you. You must be Tony and Pepe."

He walks up to my uncles and shakes their hands. "Hayden told me you're the party that placed the wedding order. This is Clara, my wife. We're happy to have you, even on such short notice. Hayden's like the son I never had. We'd do anything for this boy."

Uncle Tony has never looked so perplexed in his whole life. "Thank you so much, but I'm confused."

Hayden is right at their side. "Sorry, Sean. I wanted it to be a surprise."

Sean's eyes widen. "So you all have no idea what's happening."

Tony wraps an arm around Pepe. The two of them chuckle. "No, but we do love surprises."

"Hayden, do you want to tell them?"

Hayden smiles. The wind plays with his hair. The sky frames him perfectly, and in this moment I feel like falling.

"Happy Wedding Week," Hayden tells them. The he looks at me when he says, "I know it hasn't been as smooth as you wanted it to be, but I hope this helps. You have the place for the next two hours."

Tony and Pepe pull Hayden into a massive hug. Everyone claps a little, even Maria.

One by one, they follow Sean and Clara into the house. River and Leti bring up the rear, holding their thumbs up to Hayden.

"I can't believe you did that," I tell him, reaching for him. "How did you make this happen?"

He shrugs, like it's not a big deal. "I know everyone, and they love me."

"I can see that."

"No, really. Sean's hired my dad's company for years. Over that time, he and Clara took a liking to me."

"You're amazing." I land a kiss on his cheek. He presses me closer to him so I can feel him get a semi against my hip.

"*You're* amazing." He takes my hand and leads me inside. "Shall we?"

. . .

For two hours we drink wine. Pepe and Tony are showered with champagne (literally) when the girl behind the counter accidentally shakes it too much and loses her grip on the cork. It goes flying into the air and Yunior catches it, prompting him to shout, "I'm next!" like he just caught the bouquet.

Hayden doesn't drink and stays close to River, who has her arms crossed over her shoulder because she has to sip on water.

"If I have a sip," she says. "I might just puke. But I deserve it."

Hayden takes a bottle of sparkling water and fills her cup. "At least we get a little bit of bubbles."

Maria takes a seat with Las Viejas along the counter. They question everything, even though none of them know anything about wine. I might just die when Aunt Cecy asks for a little bit of sugar to put in their vintage rosé.

"Keeping it classy in 2014," I say, holding my glass to Leti's. She clinks.

"I think they're great," Hayden says.

"You don't have to spend every day with them," Leti says. "Well, you sort of do. But you get to have all the girls try to bring you snacks 'round the clock."

"Everyone except for your mom," he whispers in my ear.

Now that it's not a secret that there's something going on with Hayden and me, I walk him over to where my mom is perched making a face at a dry glass of cabernet.

"Ma, this is Hayden. You already know him, but I just wanted to re-introduce you."

He holds his hand out. I dare my mother to look into his eyes and not be smitten. *I dare her.*

She smiles despite herself. "Thank you for doing this. It wasn't necessary."

"No, I think it was," he says.

"*Lindo,*" Aunt Salomé says, pinching his cheek, then fans herself. "*Esos ojos.*"

"Right?" I say in agreement.

Hayden looks confused so I translate for him. *Those eyes.*

"Oh, *muchas gracias.*" He nods at her, and when I feel like we've spent too much time standing awkwardly in front of them, I pull him away.

"Don't worry about her," I tell him. "She'll come around."

He bites his lip. It bothers him that my mom isn't fawning over him the way everyone else does, but my mother's a tough nut to crack. I'm pretty sure the only person she'd like instantly is the Pope, and only because she'd be afraid to go to Hell if she didn't.

"We have a very untraditional arrangement," he says. "So I suppose I'll have to wait."

"Look at my family," I say. "As much as they try to hold onto tradition, it doesn't last for long. You have Leti, who travels the world and has teeth bling. You have Elena and Juliet, who'll be the first in their family to go to school out of state. You have my uncle marrying his long-time partner. Then you have me…"

He reaches for me and I stare at his hand like it moves in slow-mo. Hayden's big, calloused hands are everything I want right now. He twirls a lock of my hair around a finger.

"Yeah," he says. "I have you."

The way he looks at me makes me want to forget that I'm surrounded by my family. But then I realize my mom is looking at us. I give him my most charming smile.

"We're the modern family," I say.

A burst of laughter draws our attention to the great window facing the vineyard. The younger cousins have made their way out to the rows and rows of grapes. They're warned not to pluck any, but I'm sure one or two of them have stolen a grape from the vine. The nasty surprise will be when they bite into it and get nothing but sour fruit.

Over on the lawn, Steven and Elena take selfies, then take turns balancing full glasses on their heads.

"You can't take us anywhere," I say.

As much as I want to be embarrassed of them, as much as I want to be mad at them most of the time, I love them. All of them. Even Maria. Well, sometimes Maria.

"I'm glad you're having a good time," he says, brushing my cheek. He hasn't stopped touching me since we got in the car. I've never been so PDA in front of anyone, let alone my relatives.

"We're having an excellent time," Uncle Tony tells him. He and Pepe come in from their tour of the vineyard outside. His cheeks are pink from the various reds he's tried. He holds Pepe around the waist. Seeing them together always warms my heart.

Pepe takes Hayden's hand. "You're a different person when you're not covered in sweat. I don't know which one I prefer."

"*Pepe*," I say.

"If you ever want to try your hand at some modeling, you'd be perfect for next year's spring line. Very construction-worker-meets-surfer cool."

I look up at Hayden. When did we go from hiding on a roof to holding hands in front of my family? Part of me is warning me that this is too fast. But a bigger part of me, the hermit side that hid all summer, is happy to stand in the sun. No matter how long it lasts.

"I'm okay," he says. "I like working with my hands."

"I hope you continue to do more woodwork," Tony says. "The gazebo is coming out beautifully."

"Just wait. It's almost done. I want to make it perfect."

Tony and Pepe look at each other and share a small kiss. "Well, we're glad you came into our lives, even if you had to fall through the roof to do it."

"I'd do it all over again." He squeezes my hand.

"I'm just happy to see our Sky smile like that." They toast to Hayden.

I feel like I'm in a dream. And if I am, I don't ever want to wake up.

The two hours fly by. It's strange introducing a guy who isn't my boyfriend to my family, but he gets the boyfriend treatment, which is confusing. Or it *would* be confusing if Hayden didn't look like he was enjoying himself so much. There isn't any of that awkwardness because he knows just what to say. He talks Yankees with my cousins and offers Uncle Felix advice on the best way to get siding on his house in Florida. He lets my aunts feel his hair. He's doing everything he humanly can to please my family. The truth is, though, he doesn't have to. I told him that. But he's doing it anyway, and that makes my feelings for him deepen hard and fast.

When our two hours are up, and Sean and Clara load us up with an extra case of bubbly for the wedding toast (they're invited now), River and Leti and I pile into Hayden's car.

"Dude," Leti tells him. "You've gotten everyone in the family to like you in two hours. No boyfriend or girlfriend has ever done that in the history of our family."

"A little wine goes a long way," he says.

"That," Leti says, "and I'm pretty sure everyone has been mentally undressing you for weeks. That helps. Wow, our family is terrible. Right, River?"

Leti nudges River in the ribs. She didn't have a drop to

drink. She didn't even smoke once. She smiles weakly and looks out the window.

"A pretty face helps, too." Her smile is forced and meant to placate us. She'll talk when she's ready. She always does.

Before I go inside, Hayden kisses me. He holds my face in his hands and explores my lips with his. His fingers find their way through a tangle of my hair. He tugs and pulls me even closer. I answer his kisses with a flick of my tongue. I let my hands slide from his chest to his crotch. His dick strains through his jeans.

If we turn the car around and go to his place, everyone will notice. My family might like him now, but sex is *not* a topic we bring up—unless we're gossiping.

I pull myself away from him. It's the hardest thing I've done all day. "Thank you again."

"You don't have to thank me, Sky. I don't know how long we have together, so I just want to make every moment last."

"If you're not watching your calories," I tell him, "tomorrow the chef is going to do a little tasting for the family."

He leans into my neck and kisses me over and over. "There is one thing I've had a craving for since I got a taste."

I reach for his pants. The pulse in his dick answers to the wetness between my legs. "Or…can you come over tonight?"

"Sneak in?" He winks. He takes my hand and crosses his fingers with mine.

"Yeah."

He sighs, long and hard. "I have to be on a job tomorrow. It's a little far out on the Island. But I'll be back by the evening."

I try not to pout. He kisses my lips softly. He leaves me floating so high on clouds that I'm sure nothing can make me come down. Not even Maria's jealous puss or my Mom's still disapproving glare. Not the young ones screaming as they run around the pool, or Leti's complaining that Gary hasn't called her in twenty-four hours.

Not even the single text from Bradley that says: *You don't mean what you said. I miss you.*

CHAPTER 29

"I don't think I made enough food," James whispers to Lucky and me.

All thirty members of my family staying in the house stare in James's direction. In his white chef's jacket, with Lucky as a stand in sous chef by his side, he looks like the miracle he is.

"It's fine," I say. "They'll share."

"Tony, Pepe, this is Chef James Hughes."

They shake his hand enthusiastically.

"Of course we know that already," Pepe says, squeezing his own cheeks. "I can't believe you're doing this! Sky, this is the best wedding gift."

When I told them that James Hughes had agreed to cater the wedding, it was like I jolted them with a defibrillator. Now that they're staring at James, I think I might literally need that defibrillator.

Lucky sits on top of the counter, drawing the ire of some of the Viejas, but at this point Lucky can set the house on fire and I'll be okay with it as long as James can pull this off.

He unwraps a tray at a time. First up are deep fried scallops with a sweet relish.

"Sky told me you have over two hundred people. My thinking is that we do lots of small plates centered around a really big protein."

Everyone is too busy nodding and making yummy noises to form any coherent sentences. "What protein?" Pepe asks.

"I was thinking of doing a pernil, Latin style. Everyone loves roasted pork. Forty-eight hour marinade. You already have the pit in the backyard. My buddy can get me two of those, and bam. We're set there."

Pepe blows on one of the scallops. "We can have the bartenders make Mai Tais! I'm digging the luau switch. Still beachy, but more tropical. What else do you have under there?"

James pulls back the foil on his famous lamb pops.

Those pretty much evaporate. The lamb pops are followed by the most succulent crab cakes I've ever had. The meat flakes right off with the right amount of crunch. But I have to say that the best is the tray of lobster taquitos.

"Sky said you wanted an Italian dish, so I have some veal meatballs that'll knock your socks off. If they don't, then let's just say that the recipe came from my sous chef, Nunzio."

The meatballs vanish in seconds.

"Are you guys happy?" I ask Pepe and Tony.

I take their smiling, stuffed faces as an answer. I think the answer to keeping my family happy is good food and good wine. Why has this taken me so long to figure out? They decimate the food like they haven't been fed in a week.

While James signs a couple of autographs, Lucky pulls me into the living room.

"So?" she asks.

"So?" I say.

She slaps my arm. "How are things with the sexy roofer?"

"He's not just a roofer," I say. "He's a carpenter, too."

"I do love a man who works with his hands. It just makes them know how to hold you a little bit better."

"Tell me about it."

"Bring him over tonight. James'll make dinner, obvs. Can you bring some of that Goose Walk wine? I had some the other day and let's just say there isn't any left."

"Anything," I tell her. "You saved my skin."

Her gray eyes are bright and happy. "What are friends for?"

* * *

Later that night when the family is gathered around for dinner, I go to my room to change into my bathing suit. As I tie my bikini strings, the door to my bedroom opens and Xandro stands at the door.

"Excuse you?" I hiss.

He stands up straight. "Hey, Sky. Sorry. I was looking for the bathroom."

I grab the dress on my bed and throw it on, knowing that it's useless. He's already seen me.

"Don't be shy, babe." He leans against my doorframe. "I've seen you in your bikini when you go for your little swims. It's like underwear that you're allowed to get wet in."

His words make my skin crawl. "Well, we're not in the pool. You're in my bedroom. Now get out."

"Where are you off to tonight? Dinner's almost ready. I missed the fancy schmancy chef lunch. I was out on my partner's boat."

"Out, Xandro."

"I heard your little roofer took everyone wine tasting."

I shove extra clothes into a backpack. Everything about this is wrong. Xandro standing in my bedroom is wrong. Xandro in this house is wrong. His eyes are drunk with lust and it makes me feel more than naked, it makes me feel exposed.

"It's nice that he's trying to get your mom to like him. But it's never going to work. That's not how our mothers are."

"You don't know anything about my family," I raise my voice. "You think that because you knew me when we were little kids you have a right to barge into my life? You're delusional."

"You're wrong Sky. I know a whole lot about your family. I know that when your mother couldn't afford to buy food she'd come down the hall and my mom would give her a plate for you. I know that your uncle used to sneak guys into the apartment when none of you were paying attention. Everyone talked about it."

"Are you trying to make a point?" I step closer to him with balled fists. "Or are you trying to really piss me off?"

"I'm trying to make you see that you and I have history. Aren't you tired of going through relationships that'll never go anywhere? Your mom told me how your last boyfriend cheated on you. Do you think that this guy is any different?"

LOVE ON THE LEDGE

I laugh in his face. My phone buzzes. Hayden is probably downstairs.

"Don't you have a model who needs a new boob job?"

"Sky, do you know why I'm even bothering with you?"

I roll my eyes. "Why?"

"Because you are already perfect. Everything about your face, your body, it doesn't need any work. With me you'd have everything. You wouldn't have to work. We could buy a house for your mom. Hey, our moms could even live together."

"Is this how you talk to women?" I ask. "Because it isn't getting you anywhere."

I step back. He follows. He grabs my arm, squeezing too hard. With my free hand I slap him and he lets go.

"Xandro, I'm not interested in you."

"That's unacceptable, Sky."

He reaches for me, but I swing my bag at him. "Don't touch me. Not ever."

Just then River walks past the hall on her way to the bathroom. She notices my door open and catches my eye. She does a 180 and comes right in. "Hey, Ricky Martin. What's up?"

I don't hear his reply because my heart feels like it's hammering in my ears. He blows a kiss at me and walks back downstairs.

"What was that?" she asks.

"That's a problem."

"We have to say something." She turns around but I stop her.

"Not right now."

"Sky, the creep was in your room. Unless you're going to tell me that you invited him in here, we have to tell someone and make him stop trying to court you or whatever he thinks he's doing."

"I'm going to talk to my mom, but not when he's in the house. She doesn't get what he's like. He's only like that when no one's around."

"Has he done this before?"

I shake my head. "Not like this. This is extreme. But he

says things to me, like he thinks we're written in the stars or something. It's seriously unhinged."

She studies my face. I fear she's not going to listen. I fear she's going to run downstairs and break something over his head. "Fine. But, if he pulls this again, I'll rip him to shreds."

And I know that she means it.

CHAPTER 30

"Are you okay?" Hayden asks when I'm in the car. "You seem off."

I smile and kiss his face in response. He doesn't believe me a hundred percent, but we drive to Lucky's anyway. Hayden and I strip down to our swimwear and join them in the hot tub.

"What smells amazing?" Hayden asks.

"Short ribs," James answers. He leans back with an arm around Lucky.

Hayden tries to pull me closer to him, but my body is rigid. Xandro really threw me off. That, and my forearm hurts where he grabbed me. I keep it submerged in the bubbles.

Lucky widens her eyes at me, which confirms my suspicions that I am, in fact, acting weird.

"I've heard a lot about your cooking," Hayden tells James. "My mom goes crazy over you when you're on TV."

James chuckles, but brushes it off. "They make everything look harder with really tight cuts. Like on the last episode when I was down to the wire, I still had two minutes on the clock, but they made it look like five seconds."

Lucky slaps him on the back of the head. "Stop ruining TV magic!"

"Shut your pretty face."

"You shut *your* pretty face."

They both shut each other up at the same time with a kiss.

"You wouldn't think so from looking at them now," I tell Hayden, "but these two didn't get off to such a great start."

"People surprise you," Hayden says, looking at me.

"Chef Big Head over here was the one who rejected me first."

James makes a face. "I seem to recall someone stealing my coffee."

"It wasn't even yours."

"See?" I tell Hayden.

They share a laugh when the timer buzzes. James steps out of the hot tub. "Hope you guys are hungry."

Lucky winks at me. "I'll go get us another round. There are towels over on the bench."

"They're really great," Hayden tells me.

"See? I know people, too," I tell him.

He nips at my ear. I take a deep breath and push Xandro's face out of my mind.

"It was weird not seeing you all day," he says. "I'm used to watching you drink your coffee at your balcony. You're like the princess and I'm the farm boy."

"Does this mean I can order you around?"

He nods, and this time I let him pull me onto his lap. He touches his nose to mine. "As you wish."

I wrap my arms around his neck and press my breasts against his chest. He brushes my hair back, droplets of water trailing down my face. "You're so beautiful."

"Thank you, farm boy."

He laughs and lets me go for a moment. "I got you something."

"Really?"

He leans over to where his jeans are folded on the chair beside us. "Really. I was going to give it to you later, but these two are so lovey dovey that I feel the need to step up my game."

I splash a little. "Goody. Give it."

"Don't get that excited. It's not much."

He pulls out a silver bracelet with turquoise beads.

"Oh, Hayden."

He takes my hand gently and secures it around my wrist. "You wear a lot of blue, so…"

I brush his hair back and look into his eyes. "It's my favorite color."

He takes my hand and kisses the inside of my wrist. One, two, three, he trails those kisses up my arm. I shut my eyes, enjoying the feel of his mouth on my skin, the water bubbling all around us, the fire crackling in the center of the yard. Then it stops and I'm forced to open my eyes.

"What's wrong?"

His thumb traces the green thumb mark on my forearm. "What happened here?"

He holds me like I'm made of glass. My mouth is suddenly dry.

"Sky…"

I pull my hand back towards my chest. Hayden takes me off his lap so that we're facing each other. Between the hot tub and his stare, I'm hotter than should be comfortable. I don't want to lie to him, but this is also my problem to take care of. So I tell him.

"I've already warned him that he needs to stop."

"You told me, Sky," Hayden says. "You told me that if this guy got aggressive you'd tell me."

He starts to stand. I grab his wrist. "Where are you going?"

"I'm going to give him a matching bruise."

"Hayden," I yell. "Please. Tonight is perfect. I'm going to talk to my mother tomorrow and tell her to uninvite him from the wedding. Please don't go."

He looks at my hand on his. He steps out of the hot tub and looks up at the night sky with his hands placed on his hips, like he's asking the heavens for patience.

Then he turns to me. "Is that what you want?"

I nod. "I want to enjoy you. Every minute of you."

He holds his hand for me to take and helps me out of the pool. He kisses each of my hands. "Then I'll stay. I'm yours, Sky."

It's the first time a guy has ever said this to me before. Usually it feels like a tug of war, like I'm trying to get a guy to look, kiss, speak to me the way Hayden does. In his kiss, it's like he's giving himself over to me without having to fight over it. When someone gives you their heart so willingly, well, it's a lot of pressure to take. Now that I'm on the other side of it, I know. But I also know that I'm giving myself right back.

In my kiss, I want him to know that I'm his, too.

CHAPTER 31

I wake up to a shriek.

Doors swing open on both floors. My cousins and aunts and uncles lean their heads out of their doors, rubbing crust out of their eyes and yawning their morning breath into the hall.

"What happened?" Leti asks.

Elena shrugs. "Sounded like it came from downstairs."

"The butler did it," Yunior jokes.

I lead the troops downstairs where Pepe is sitting in the living room with his hands over his eyes. There's an unwrapped package on the coffee table. Packaging kernels litter the glass and floor.

Uncle Tony runs to him, a long navy bathrobe training the ground. "Baby, what's wrong?"

We all gather around them. When they see that no one is dead, half of the family goes back to their rooms to sleep.

"This just got delivered."

"What?" I ask, with a jolt in my voice. I run around the couch and sit on the other side of him. There, in the center of the package, are two cake toppers. They're truly beautiful things. The groom has white hair with tiny glasses just like the ones Uncle Tony wears. It has a navy blue tux like the one they're going to wear. It's from a company that specializes in making toppers look as close to the couple as possible.

Pepe starts to sob.

The problem is that the second cake topper is a girl. She's dark-skinned like Pepe with glowing dark hair and a beautiful wedding gown.

"They did it on purpose," Pepe cries.

I hear Leti say she'll make him some tea, as if tea is supposed to calm him down.

"Oh, my love," Tony says, stroking Pepe's back. "That's crazy talk."

"Don't tell me that I'm being crazy. We ordered them together! You saw that I designed two men with two tuxes. Not this stupid bitch." He takes the bride from me and throws it into the fireplace.

Tony shakes his head. This is one of those situations where he doesn't know what to do, even though he always knows what to do.

I lean my head on Pepe's shoulder. He shakes from crying.

Cousin Steve sinks into the couch across from us and turns on the TV. "What's the big deal? Just get a new one."

I take the remote from his hand and slap it on the back of his head. "Go to your fucking room."

"What the fuck?"

"I'm not kidding. All of you. If you're not going to be helpful, then go somewhere else." One by one they return to their rooms, cursing me under their breaths. Leti returns with tea for Tony and Pepe, sugar cubes in each cup.

"I'll get new ones," I say. "Better ones. I promise."

Tony takes my hand and squeezes. "Thank you, baby."

"It's all going wrong," Pepe says. "Nothing's going as we planned."

"It's a learning process," Tony says, rubbing Pepe's shoulders. "It's going to be fine."

"No, it's not. It's like trying to fix a beautiful dress with scraps."

Tony shushes him softly. "Love, you don't mean that."

My heart hurts for them. This is my fault. If I didn't keep secrets from them, Pepe wouldn't feel like this.

"I'll fix this." I turn on the fireplace and throw in the other topper. Something about watching them both melt and burn in the fire makes Pepe calm down. "See? All gone."

After breakfast I get dressed, intent on going into town to find replacements. After that I'm going to talk to my mother about Xandro. After that, I'm going to make sure Leti has a DJ.

After that, I'll get my army of cousins started on the centerpieces. After that, my final dress fitting, the wedding rehearsal, and then boom. Wedding.

But when I get downstairs, Xandro is already talking to my mother.

"Sky, Xandro's heading to town. I told him you were going to run an errand."

My senses go into panic mode. "No, I'm fine."

She dismisses me with a wave of her hand. "Your cousins took all the cars to the outlets."

"River can take me."

"River's gone."

I curse her in my head. "I'll walk."

"Sky, you're being rude."

I'll tell her what's rude. Rude is storming my room without knocking. Rude is forcing a man I don't want into my life. Rude is dismissing the guy that I actually have feelings for.

But I know when I'm trapped. "Fine."

I storm out the house and get into Xandro's car.

• • •

"You don't have to look so pissed," Xandro says. "I'm sorry about yesterday. I was drinking."

"That's your answer?"

Xandro shakes his head as he parks in front of the bakery. "What do you want me to say?"

"I want you to stop whatever it is you're doing and admit that you and I are never going to happen."

When I slam the door to his car, he quickly follows me up the street. "Look, Sky. I said I was sorry. Let me make it right."

He puts his arm around me. Couples and teen girls walk around with great big smiles on their faces. The sun shines, and an ice cream truck announces that summer isn't over yet. All the while, Xandro forces me into walking with him. Why is it that I'd rather not make a scene than admit I feel threatened? What do I scream? Help! A handsome plastic surgeon is trying to take me out to lunch! Half the passersby would kill to swap places with me.

"Let's get something to eat." He pulls me into a small but swanky Italian place up the block. The waitress quickly gives us a seat in the back.

My heart thunders in my chest and I can't keep my feet from shaking. "Xandro, what can I do to make you go away?"

He takes the menu and examines it as if I haven't said anything. He asks the waitress for bottled sparkling water, a Caprese salad for me and the beef carpaccio for him, and two glasses of their best sauvignon blanc.

"I'm not drinking," I tell the waitress.

"Just bring it out," he tells her.

The waitress doesn't know what to do. She looks at me with fear in her eyes. Either way she's going to look bad in front of her boss. She's young, new, and used to being bossed around. I resign myself. I tell her to bring it, but there's no way I'm drinking it.

"Sky," Xandro says. "Do you know how embarrassing it is that you've chosen some day-worker over me?"

"He's not a day worker, and even if he was, it's none of your business."

"You're unbelievable, you know. I'm offering you the world, and here you are. This makes our arrangement a little difficult."

I lean forward. I decide I don't care if I make a scene. I don't care if the whole of the Hamptons can hear me. "We don't have an arrangement. You're nothing to me. Actually... you are something."

A smile breaks his face.

"You're a huge pain in my ass, and you're getting in the way of my errand."

"Don't be stupid, Sky. Your mother will never approve of your choice in men. What would you rather bring home, a surgeon or a meathead with a hammer?"

The runner and waitress bring out our food. She sets the glasses on the table so quickly that the wine slides over the sides. I stew in my rage. The worst thing is that I know Xandro doesn't want me, not truly. He wants the idea of me—a girl who came from the same place he did. Someone his mother will approve of, because I bet my soul his nice Catholic mother doesn't like any of the kind of girls he brings home. I'm his solution. But I'm also rejecting him. And his ego, his need to look good, is bigger than his need to please his mother.

"I'd rather bring home anyone but you," I say, smiling.

He scoffs in my face and takes a long sip from his wine. "No wonder your ex cheated on you. You don't know how to show a man what he's worth."

It's like my hand is in control of the rest of me, and I watch it throw my glass of wine in Xandro's face. I set down my empty glass on the table and grab the fork. I place it over his hand and press down, just enough that he squeals, but not enough to draw blood.

"I need you to listen to me, because so far, you haven't. You're going to stay away from me. You're going to drop the idea of dating me. You're going to tell my mother that you met someone else. Say whatever you want, I don't care. But if you ever try to touch me, ever again, just remember—you might know how to cut people up. But I know how to put you into a long, long sleep and make it look like an accident. Do we understand each other?"

He licks the wine droplets off his lips and finally nods. I lift the fork and set it back onto its place beside my plate. I take my napkin and drop it in his lap. Everyone in the restaurant is looking at us, but no one moves. No one asks if I'm okay. No one speaks to me on my way out. I take a bill from my purse and hand it to the hostess. "Sorry for the mess."

As I leave, I know I'm not sorry at all.

CHAPTER 32

I go into every craft store, bakery, and even the lone thrift store in walking distance, but I don't find a wedding topper. When I'm done, I call River to come pick me up. She doesn't say where she is, but she drops whatever it is. If I call Hayden I'll have to tell him what just happened, and I'm still too shook up.

River isn't any better. "Are you fucking kidding? I'm driving back. I'm going to bash his windows in."

I put my hand over hers on the steering wheel. "Stop. It's done. He's not going to be a problem."

She suddenly breaks into maniacal laugher. "Did you really threaten to kill him?"

"Technically, I said a long, long sleep. I wasn't lying. I know how."

She shakes her head. "You could never hurt anyone."

"You're right. But in that moment, I really felt like I could. It felt good, standing up for myself."

She puts a hand on my shoulder and her knee up to the wheel. "That's my girl."

"Now the real problem is that I don't know what to do about this cake topper thing."

"The real problem?" River asks. "Girl, if that's your worst worry right now, I'd say count your blessings."

* * *

But I've spoken too soon.

When we get back home, everyone is scattered around the house pretending not to eavesdrop on Pepe and Tony shouting at each other.

I walk towards their bedroom where the door is slightly ajar. My mom stands there with her arms crossed. She shakes her head when she sees me and walks away, suggesting I do the same.

But how can I stay away when I've never seen them fight like this? Tony and Pepe are my ideal couple. They're everything that I've ever wanted for myself. Love and understanding and happiness. Not what Uncle Felix and his trophy wife have. Not what Aunt Cecy has. Not what my mother and my father had.

"You're making too big a deal over nothing," Tony tells Pepe.

I can still hear Pepe crying. "You don't understand. How can you not understand?"

"I'm trying, but you're not making any sense."

River and I look at each other. We sit on the floor with our heads pressed against the wall. It brings back memories of locking myself in the bathroom, listening to my parents fight. Before he left for good, the other woman hovering in the doorway smacking her gum and checking her reflection in the mirror of the door, my mom and dad fought every day. She would tell him that he was a terrible husband, but he could still be a good father.

He didn't want to be a father, though. He wanted the kind of life he dreamed of back in Ecuador. He wanted to have women adore him. He wanted to earn a paycheck and then spend it on himself. He wanted to be free.

"*Dejame en paz,*" was the last thing he ever shouted at us. *Leave me in peace.*

So we left him in peace, and he left us in pieces.

River holds my hand as we listen to Pepe shout, "I am making sense! This was supposed to be us. And it's ruined. We won't be able to get another set on such short notice."

"Yes we can. We can try."

"If you don't see why this matters, then why are we even getting married at all?"

"You don't mean that."

Then there's silence, and I don't think I can listen to any more of it. I know that it's selfish, but if Pepe and Tony can't make it work, then I fear there isn't a lot of hope for the rest of us.

CHAPTER 33

Me: *Can you come over?*

Hayden: *Two minutes.*

Me: *Can you make it one?*

Hayden: *Firing up the jet.*

It's the middle of the night, and for the first time in days the house is quiet. It's not the kind of peace and quiet that I wanted. It's stagnant and sad and I wish they'd all go back to making a ruckus. I need a distraction. As I wait for Hayden, I think that he's more than a distraction. He's a need I didn't know I was missing.

Hayden climbs through my balcony and stops there. I'm lying down in a white lace teddy that contrasts against my tan skin. I curled my hair so the ends bounce when I prop myself on the bed.

There's a bunch of flowers in his hand. "Wow."

I smooth out the fabric, even though it's lace and there aren't any wrinkles to be found. I feel a little weird wearing it. I put it on because I wanted to feel sexy. Originally, I'd bought it when Bradley and I were still together. I only just pulled the tag off, too. It was too beautiful, too expensive to throw away. Besides, it would have a new memory, not the old one.

I hoped.

"You look incredible." Hayden walks to me slowly, like he's treading water. "Remind me again what I did to deserve you?"

He crouches on my bed and places a kiss on my lips. I pull him by his shirt. He loses his balance and falls on top of me, recovering just as quickly. I tug on it to pull it off his shoulders. I'm so tired of being sad. I want to feel something that makes me happy, and being with Hayden makes me happy.

He climbs on top of me and rests his elbows on either side of my head. Pins my waist with his. The light that comes in from the window makes his eyes brilliant. It's like looking at an angel, the one that fell right at my feet.

"Hayden," I whisper. I push up my hips so that he can feel how much I want him without me having to say it. "Hayden."

My eyes flutter as he kisses my cheeks. "Sweet Sky. What's all this?"

I smile against his kisses. "Don't you like it?"

He slides down to kiss the top of my breasts. His hands grab my waist and squeeze in that way that drives me crazy. I can feel his kisses right through the white lace. He parts my legs with his hands and kisses the inside of my thighs. He looms over me, and I love how big his frame is compared to mine. I press my hands on his hard abs. I undo the button of his jeans and tug on them. I catch the waistband of his boxers with my teeth and pull. He moans when I reach in and grab his dick, pull it out, and stroke it.

I want to remember what seeing Hayden naked for the first time is like. It's like every inch of his body was carefully crafted to perfection. Thin blond hairs trail from his belly button, an arrow that shows me where I need to go. When I press a kiss to the head of his penis, it lengthens. I have a desperate need to know what Hayden tastes like, and when he says my name, like he's begging, I can't take it anymore.

I take him into my mouth. I get on my knees on the bed to get at a better angle. I grab his shaft and suck on the tip. He moans, and I take my mouth off. I press a finger to my lips. His eyes are far off and dreamy. His hand threads through my hair and tugs, guiding me back to him.

I grab his hardness and massage it with both hands, letting the tip rest on my tongue.

"Shit," he whispers.

I love the way he reacts to me. Love that he tugs my hair some more. Love the wetness that follows his grunts. His precum tastes sweet. Leti says that's what happens when guys eat lots of fruit. I lick the wet trail and take his length as far as it can. I relax the back of my throat so I don't gag.

He pulls on my hair so hard that I moan. The moan vibrates against his tender skin and his dick throbs in my mouth. I wet my finger with my tongue and trace tiny circles around the sensitive skin of his head.

"Sky, you're driving me crazy."

"That's the point."

He bites his lip and grabs me, pushing me onto my back. He finds the snaps that keep my teddy together and pulls them open.

"Sky," he whispers in my ear. His warm breath makes me tingle. "I want to know what you feel like."

His finger traces a line through my wetness until he finds my clit. When I arch my back, he presses down in slow, delicious circles.

"Hayden," I tell him. "I need you now."

He nuzzles into my neck. "As you wish."

His thick, strong finger slides into my pussy. My walls squeeze around him. I ask for more and he inserts another finger. I bite back a moan. I grab the mattress with one hand and his dick with the other. I move my hand up and down. He presses harder against my body, sliding a third finger in.

He bites my ear and in response, I jerk him off faster. He hooks his fingers inside of me. I don't know if it's the combination of getting each other off, or if he found the mythical g-spot, but I start to come undone. My center pulses as I come, wet, all over his hand.

"Sky," he says. "Sky…"

"Come," I whisper. I close my eyes, lost in the feel of his fingers inside me, touching a part of me that's coming awake. He moans against my ear, and I grab onto him as he comes on my belly. I trace the slippery top of his head, and watch his eyes lust after me. I bring the finger to my lips and taste him.

"You are so fucking sexy." He collapses beside me.

I giggle, and stretch into the delicious feel of his body in my bed. "You."

He reaches over me for something on my bedside table. "I

brought these for you. You sounded upset."

I laugh quietly. "How can you tell? We were texting."

"I can tell."

I take the two roses and smell them. They're a deep red and fully bloomed. I trace their petals along his skin. I feel something that goes beyond the orgasm he just gave me. It's a spark that I'm afraid to light, but it's trying desperately to be seen.

"Hayden?"

He's started to drift off to sleep. "Hmm?"

"Will you be my date to the wedding?"

CHAPTER 34

In the morning I watch Hayden sleep.

If he's beautiful to look at when he's awake, then I don't know what to call this. His face is completely tranquil. His mouth is slightly open. That bottom lip is so kissable that I lean forward and do it. When I lean back, my Prince Charming answers me with a tiny snore. God, even that's cute. He spreads out his whole body. My thin white sheet does little to cover his morning wood.

There's a knock on my door. I jump up and reach for my bathrobe. I brush my hair a bit. I open it up a crack. It's only Leti.

"Hey, hooker. Everyone's going to the beach. We need to air out the bad juju from the house."

"Oh, I'm not feeling so hot. See you later." I start to close the door on her face, but she catches a peek of the sleeping god on my bed.

She shakes her fists and squees.

"Shh," I whisper.

"Okay, Sky," Leti says dramatically. "Feel better."

Subtle. I lock the door behind her and go back to bed. I can hardly sleep with him just laying down in my bed. It's like leaving out a piece of cake and expecting me not to eat it.

I trace a finger along his erect shaft. A smile spreads across his face. He grabs my hand and brings it up to his face to kiss. "Hey you."

I rest my head on his shoulder. "Excellent news. Everyone's going to the beach, so we have the house all to ourselves."

"That's an interesting development." He turns lazily towards me and pulls me into a strong hug. "How come?"

"I think after yesterday's fiasco, they need to all get out of the house."

He lifts his head to meet my eyes. "What happened?"

What didn't happen? "The cake topper came but it was a hetero couple. Pepe thought it was a personal attack. I think that when they were filling out the form online, they didn't change the second one's sex, but there's no way to really find out. I went out yesterday to try to get one, but nothing. Isn't this a big wedding town?"

"Earlier in the season maybe." He kisses my shoulder. The white lace teddy is on the floor, but I still wear the matching bra. His hands find my breasts and squeeze. "So I have you all to myself today?"

I press myself against him, sling a leg over his side to press him into me. "Yep. Do you have to do anything today?"

"Not that I can think of, but I'm not at full brain power right now." His hands trail down my spine and cup my ass. "Oh, wait."

"Nooo, no waiting."

He chuckles. "This is good, I promise."

"Okay."

"I have a surprise for you tonight. Gazebo at nine."

I nod, but I'm not thinking that far ahead right now. I'm more interested in the way he turns me on my back and holds my hands over my head. His weight makes my breath catch. I love how solid he feels. He presses into me. I part my legs to give him better access.

"God, you're fantastic." His dick presses against my wetness, teasing me.

"And you're not even in me yet," I laugh.

This feels nice, being able to make light of something that means a lot to me. I've never been able to just have sex with any guy that I find attractive. River tells me it's a waste of my youth, that one day I'll be married and stuck with the same chump. Leti wants to be able to say that she's fucked a guy in every country she travels to.

Me? I need to feel the *spark*. With Hayden, it's more than that though. It's full on fireworks. When he looks at me, I know he doesn't want to be anywhere else. When he looks at me, I feel like he's committing this moment to memory, because I'm doing the same thing.

Which is why, as much as I'd hate to ruin the moment, I have to pull back from his kiss.

"I'm on birth control," I say.

"So am I," he says.

"Hayden…"

He wraps his arms around me and flips us so he's on the bed and I'm on top. I sit up to straddle him. I lean forward so the ends of my hair tickle his chest. He reaches up to touch my breasts.

"Sky, you're the first girl in months. After I found out my ex was cheating on me, I got tested. I'm clean as a whistle. You?"

The minute I saw Bradley and Stella together, I went to my unit and had a test done. "Me, too. Nurse's orders."

I press my breasts against him and kiss him. Then, our stomachs grumble in synchrony.

"I'd be embarrassed," he says, "if your stomach growl wasn't louder than mine."

"Why don't you make yourself comfortable, and I'll make some breakfast."

He grabs my hand and pulls me hard against his lips. "Hurry, or I'll come and get you."

I untangle myself from the Adonis in my bed, throw my bathrobe back on, and head downstairs.

There is a most definitely bounce in my step. I'm going to have sex with Hayden Robertson. The thought makes me giddy and wet. Sure, I've been horny before. But that's nothing a bottle of wine and a battery-operated device can't take care of. Being with Hayden soothes parts of me I thought were permanently damaged.

As I crack eggs in a pan and throw in salt, pepper, and a little bit of Adobo, I realize that you can't let someone else damage you. Even when your heart breaks, it still belongs to you. You have to take it back and mend it yourself, because no one is going to do it for you. Letting myself get close to Hayden makes me feel awake, like the sun is just a little bit brighter.

I wait for the toast to toast, and the scrambled eggs to scramble. I grab the orange juice and put in a splash of prosecco because that's how I feel—like a bottle of bubbly ready to burst.

The doorbell rings. It's early for mail, but things have been arriving non-stop all summer. I tie my bathrobe so that I don't give the delivery person a peep show. I set the eggs off the fire, feeling as badass as James Hughes.

When I open the door, I feel like I'm still dreaming. No, this isn't a dream. This is a nightmare. The fright of him makes me jump. I drop my glass and it splatters on the ceramic tiled floor. I go to shut the door, to push him back and slam it in his face, but he doesn't go. He's stronger.

"Sky, listen to me," Bradley says. "Just give me a chance."

When I step back, pain shoots up and down my leg. I see blood, but I have to keep walking back.

"Get out."

He looks the same, but not. His hair is longer than usual. He's grown facial hair, which makes him look older. His clothes are rumpled, like he slept in them and then drove the five hours to get here.

"Sky, baby, I know you don't want to see me, but I promise. I promise that I'm not with anyone. Losing you was the worst mistake I've ever make. I love you, Sky. I love you."

I step back, dragging glass and blood in a zigzag trail. The pain in my foot gets so sharp that I let myself fall down. Everything I've been trying to hold onto, all the happiness I've found in the last months, comes undone at the seams.

Bradley reaches for me. I've forgotten what his touch feels like. It's something I've pushed so far away that he might as well be a stranger.

"Sky, you're hurt."

I slap his hands away. "You have no right to be here. Get out!"

"Sky?" Hayden shouts from upstairs. The steps creak with his weight. He's running. He stands at the top of the steps looking down at us. He sees the glass. The blood. He's wrapped a towel around his waist.

"Who the fuck is this?" Bradley asks.

"Get out, Bradley!" I'm stuck on repeat, but I'm too stunned to say anything else.

"Not until you tell me who this is!"

Hayden looks from me to Bradley. Hayden is mine. That's what I should say. He's mine. Instead, I force myself to stand, balancing on my good foot.

"You're a real piece of work, Sky," Bradley says. "You tell me that I lost faith in us, that I broke us, but look at you, moving on perfectly well."

I laugh in his face. "Did you think I'd sit around for the rest of my life waiting for you? You broke us, Bradley. I would never in a million years, if you were the last breathing man left on this planet, want anything to do with you."

He steps back, like my words slapped him. "You don't mean that."

"Why?" I ask, not to him but to the heavens. "Why can't you take no for an answer? It's you and it's Xandro. It's like you're not fucking happy unless you're the one ending things. Well you don't get that, okay? I get to end it. *I* get to end it."

"You're being hysterical," Bradley tells me.

Hayden looks at me like he doesn't recognize me. I know that if I ask him to, he'll physically remove Bradley. But Hayden isn't my lackey. He's my—love? How can I love anyone when my life is a mess?

"Get out." It's final, and he hears it. He turns around and slams the door behind him.

CHAPTER 35

Hayden catches me before I fall back down on the floor.

"My kit is in my room."

He carries me up the steps and gently sets me on the bed. Our romantic breakfast is cold, but I'm not hungry anymore. Hayden comes back with the kit and opens it up for me. I fold my foot so I can see the damage.

"I need a warm washcloth and the tweezers on the sink."

I whimper when I pull out the biggest piece of glass. I rip an antiseptic wipe, just like I did for Hayden the first time we met. I've done this to so many people while telling them it only hurts for a second. I feel like a bitch because it hurts for more than a second. It burns like hell.

Hayden comes back with the other things I need. I bring my foot closer to my face. Normally, I'd want him to be impressed that I'm so flexible, but by the seriousness of his face, I don't even begin to guess what he's thinking.

"Napkin please."

He goes and brings one to me. I pull out two smaller shards of bloody glass and set them on the napkin.

"Can I do anything else?"

I shake my head. "It's not too bad."

"Why do feet bleed so much?" Hayden asks.

"Blood vessels closer to the skin."

"Oh."

When I'm satisfied that there isn't any more glass in there, I wash it with the wet cloth and bandage my foot. I pack everything back up, and throw away anything with blood on it. I pull the sheets off the bed. There's probably no saving them, but I'll give it a try.

Hayden stands against the wall and I sit on the edge of the mattress.

"Are we going to talk about it?" he asks.

I feel tired. A dull ache starts to fill my head, my heart. I might have wrapped my foot too tightly because it feels like my heart is throbbing in my sole.

"Do you remember the ex I talked about? From Boston?"

"That was him?"

I nod. "He's been calling and texting, which is why I have my phone turned off most of the time."

"Sky, why didn't you say anything?"

"Because!" I shout defensively. "I didn't think he was going to show up here."

He's quiet for a little while. I want to be alone. No, I need to be alone.

"What did you mean...about Xandro?"

I sigh. "When I went to look for the cake toppers my mom forced me to go with him. He pulled me into a restaurant. I felt trapped. What was I supposed to do? Scream that he wanted to take me to lunch?"

"Yes," Hayden says. "You should have. No one should make you do anything that you don't want to do."

"Well, after hearing a lecture about how I have no right to reject him, I threw my wine in his face and put him in his place. He's not going to bother me anymore."

"You promised me, Sky. You promised that if he got out of hand you would tell me about it or get help. Now there are guys coming out of the woodwork."

I stand up to face him, but I hobble. He helps me stand, but I don't want to be touched. I don't want anything. "You make it sound like there's a fucking army knocking on my door. I didn't ask for Xandro, okay? I didn't ask Bradley to come here. I just want to be alone."

Hayden stands up straight. He doesn't know what to do with his hands so he keeps one holding up his towel and one over his chest where my bite marks have left an imprint. My heart is racing in my chest and my thoughts are zooming all over the place. I need time to think. This house is so big, and yet, it feels so small.

"This is my fault," I say. "I should've been concentrating on the wedding, not fooling around."

"Fooling around?" he asks. "Is that what I am to you? Just fooling around with the help?"

My heart breaks again. "I didn't mean it like that."

"Yes, you did."

"Don't tell me what I meant, Hayden. You just storm into my life saying all of these things that make me feel like there's nothing wrong with me. Then you get jealous—"

"I told you why."

"Yes, and I've been there. I know what it's like."

"I'm sorry, Sky. Should I not treat you the way I have? Have I been *too* good to you? That's what you're complaining about, right? That there must be something wrong with me because I'm not your cheating ex-boyfriend or some jerk who forces himself on you. Maybe if I were more like that you'd find it in your heart to love me."

"I…"

I do love you. It's on the tip of my tongue. Looking at Hayden, hurting him, it tears me up inside. I want to take all of my words back. I didn't mean anything. I want to tell him that I love him. That beyond time or reason, he's made a place for himself in my heart. Not because he forced his way there, but because he earned it.

"Hayden."

He picks up his clothes from the floor. He's going to go. He's going to go and I know that if I let him, he won't come back.

My words are lodged in my throat. I can't really breathe. Maybe it's best. Maybe I haven't given myself enough time to be alone. I might be over Bradley, but seeing him again made all of that hurt resurface. I never want to feel that way again.

Hayden stands at the door. He's giving me a chance to ask him to stay. When I don't, he shakes his head and turns around.

He says, "Goodbye, Sky."

CHAPTER 36

For the next two days, I don't hear from Hayden.

When Steven and Yunior think it'd be funny to skateboard off the roof and into the pool, only to dislodge a couple of shingles and sprain a pinky and ankle respectively, Robertson Roofers sends two guys we've never seen before.

I sit by the pool with my cellphone in hand and a stack of purchase orders. Leti keeps avoiding me about the DJ.

"He'll be there. I promise." She kisses me on the cheek.

"So it's booked?"

"Yep! Uncle Tony wrote a check already."

"Yeah, you have no faith in your family," Yunior tells me.

"I'm sorry if I don't take life advice from a guy who sprained his ankle skating off a roof. You're lucky you can still walk in the ceremony."

Yunior presses a finger on my shoulder and hisses. "Yeesh! Ice cold. Stay away from that one."

"Will you kids quiet down?" Pepe asks. "I can't hear myself think."

Pepe paces around the pool, biting his thumbnail. His silk robe is like a tail following him as he spins in circles.

"Relax, Pepe," I tell him.

Over on the lawn, Uncle Tony is directing the delivery guys where to put the rented tables and chairs.

"Elena, Juliet," I say. "Be useful and go help Uncle Tony unfold some chairs."

"But we just applied sunscreen," Juliet says.

"Oh, good, you won't get sunburned while you're helping." I shoo them away.

Maria makes it clear she's not lifting a finger. She unfolds her magazine and looks over the edge at me.

"What?" I snap.

She shrugs. "I just haven't seen your little roofer boy since he finished his work. He must've gotten what he needed."

At the mention of Hayden, I try to hide my sadness by giving her the finger. When my phone beeps, my entire being is on alert hoping for his name to pop up on my screen. It's Lucky.

"Hey," I say.

"Can I come over? James and Chris are in cooking mode and I pretty much don't exist."

"If you want to help arrange seashells, then be my guest."

* * *

"You are extra pensive, Sky," Lucky says. Her long black hair is up in a ponytail and she's wearing a David Bowie t-shirt. River and Leti are also on centerpiece duty, but mostly gluing their fingers to shells instead of the candles.

"Yeah, she's been extra secretive," River says. "Even for her."

Looking at their eyes, I can't hide it anymore.

"I have to tell you guys something." So I tell them about Bradley's surprise visit. How Hayden was there. How I cut my foot. How I told Hayden we were just fooling around.

"You're an idiot," River tells me. That hurts.

"You big liar who lies!" Leti shouts. "You said you stepped on a nail by the pool."

I shrug. "I'm sorry."

Lucky stands, holding a glue gun, looking very much like she's going to seal my lips shut so I stop making mistakes. "Why didn't you tell me? I could talk to him. I'm sure he's staying at his frat brother's place. It's not too far."

"No," I say. "We're not going after Bradley. I made it clear."

"Some guys don't know how to take no for an answer," River says, pressing a large conch shell around the base of the candle.

I hate the way she says that. Like she knows firsthand. I

stare at her, willing her to look me in the eye, but she keeps hot gluing shells.

"I'm going to tell you firsthand," Lucky says, pointing a finger at me. "Guys like Hayden, like James, they don't come around often. You have to dig through so many scumbags."

"Preach," Leti says.

"But I don't know where I'm going to be at the end of the summer. I don't know if I should stay in New York. I'm pretty certain I don't want to keep nursing. I just feel like there's something missing from my life, and it has nothing to do with a boyfriend. I want to do something that I love, and I love helping people. But I became a nurse because my mother told me to."

"You have to stop living life by your mom," Leti tells me. "I do it, and my mom doesn't like it, but she still wants me to be happy."

"Yeah, but you've always done whatever you wanted." I hold a blue seashell, the special one that Hayden picked out. I keep it in my palm. This one isn't going on a centerpiece. There's a natural hole at the top. I take off my bracelet and it slides right on. A perfect fit.

"I just met him," I say. "Maybe it's one of those things where you're still in the honeymoon phase. Maybe I can't see that it's just hormonal."

"You're being an idiot," River says. "Didn't I tell her she was being an idiot? Sky, I'm a world-class fuck-up. Right now, I can't even deal with my own shit, so I'm going to focus on yours. If you never want to see Hayden again, then don't. But believe me, I haven't seen you this happy or smile as hard as you have since he showed up. If that boy wasn't a miracle sent from the gods, then I don't know what he is."

Looking at the three of them, I know that I can't lie to myself. Everything I felt with Hayden was real. "I should have told him when I had the chance."

"Told him what?"

"That I love him."

Leti squeals. "Girl, I told you. Didn't I tell you?"

"He was so hurt," I shake my head.

"Then unhurt him," River says.

I think of Bradley begging me to take him back. Nothing he said would ever change my mind. What would make Hayden change his?

"Even if he says no," Lucky says, "at least you know you made an effort."

River takes out a cigarette and leans back. She lights it, blows a trail of smoke upward. "You already know what I'm going to say."

"That I'm an idiot?"

"No," she smiles dryly. "That I love you and I want you to be happy."

"Be happy." Lucky says it like happiness is a thing to be examined and dissected. "Once you take away the games and the drama, could it really be that simple?"

I don't know, but I'm going to have to give it a try.

CHAPTER 37

Me: *I miss you. Can we talk?*

That night, Hayden never answers, so I busy myself with things that have to get done. The wedding is in two days and the house is louder than ever. I manage to overnight a simple wedding topper that I think Pepe and Tony won't hate.

It's hard not to think about Hayden when the bridesmaids' "suite" is the same room where he fell through. Our dresses are hung and tagged in the closet. I make sure the steamer works. Check the bathroom for toiletries and makeup bags. I stack the boxes of centerpieces on top of each other.

I make a mental checklist:

String lights and lanterns all around the yard.

Finish centerpieces.

Finalize arrival time with DJ and photographer.

New topper.

James and his staff will arrive as early as humanly possible, as promised by Lucky.

The tuxes are all in the opposite end of the house.

The pool and pool house are clean and ready.

Table and chairs are laid out and decorated with garland.

The gazebo…

The ceremony is going to take place in the gazebo that Hayden built. I have to go to the store in the morning and pick up an extra string of lights to decorate it.

I check my phone for the zillionth time and still nothing. I wanted to be left alone and I got my wish. Leti did warn me about what I put out to the Universe.

I unzip the dress with my name on it and try it on one more time. Sure, it's not my wedding, but it's definitely a white dress.

I let my hair down from the tangled bun at the top of my head. I've been planning my wedding since I was five and I decided to marry John Smith from Disney's Pocahontas. She's the Disney princess who looks the most like me, after all. Back then I didn't know that the real Pocahontas was a teenager and John Smith wasn't a blond. And also was a horrible human. But for a little while, that was my fantasy.

Little girls spend so much time fantasizing that no one remembers to tell us that there will come a day when you can't separate the princes from the frogs. That even when you do everything right and follow the right steps, you can end up starting over. They tell us so often that we shouldn't make mistakes. Mistakes ruin your life, from accidental pregnancy to kissing too many boys to getting the wrong grade to wearing the wrong clothes.

More than anything, I want to tell these girls that it's okay to fuck up. It's okay to start over. And I have a better understanding of what I want to do with my life.

"You look beautiful."

I jump when I hear my mother, and turn to see her standing at the door. She's in her pajamas, her hair in rollers.

"Your dress is here, too."

"Pshh. He's made me try that thing on a hundred times."

"He's just nervous. He wants everything to be perfect."

"We all do. As perfect as we can get, with this family…you never know, *nena.*"

"I'm just going to change and go to bed."

"Sky, wait." She stands in front of me. My mom is so small. So was my dad. I don't know where I got my height from. She holds my face in her hands. "I'm sorry, *mija.*"

"Why?"

"I wasn't happy when you told me you quit your job."

I roll my eyes.

"Listen to me, Sky. I wasn't happy. But it has nothing to do with me. I was afraid for you. I don't want you to have the kind of life I had. I don't want you to come home every night with your hands cracked and bleeding because the factory is so dry. I don't want you staying up late, wondering where your husband is. I thought Xandro was a good boy, a family boy."

"What made you change your mind?"

"He told me you spilled a drink in his face."

I nod. "He's not wrong."

"I don't always agree with you," she says. "But I know I raised you right. You would never have done that in public unless he was being fresh. *Descarado.*"

"It's okay, Ma."

She makes a face, like she's still not pleased. "Does this mean you're going back to work soon?"

"Actually," I say. "I was going to join the circus. I'm halfway there being around you people."

"Be careful now," she says, pursing her lips. "Go to the pool. Something just arrived for you."

"Me? This late?"

She sucks her teeth, even though every time I did it, I got smacked in the head. "Ay, go. *Ándale.* You think too much, my Sky."

• • •

I change out of my dress and run out to the back. My pulse quickens with my steps as I pull open the back doors.

"Hey," I say, breathless.

Hayden stands at the edge of the pool wearing a white t-shirt and blue jeans. In his hands is a small wooden box. The night breeze urges me closer to him. My insides feel like a pinball machine, with my heart as the metal ball getting knocked around from corner to corner. Right now, it's in the back of my ribcage.

"I have a wedding present for your uncles. I just didn't know if it was appropriate for me to give it to them."

"Oh," I say. I can be cool and casual. I can ignore that my heart has now been ricocheted to my stomach and all the lights in my pinball-machine-self are going haywire from his nearness. "Thank you. I can give it to them."

I hold my hand out but he won't give it.

ZORAIDA CÓRDOVA

"Sky," he says, deflating a little. "This is stupid. I miss you. I should have texted you back but I wanted to surprise you. Then on the way over here I realized that my non-response would have come off as not wanting to talk to you."

I breathe deeply, taking control back over my body and heart. I close the distance between us and wrap my arms around him. I bury my face in his chest. I press my hand on his back. I'm relieved when he holds me back.

"Those were pretty terrible days being without you."

I nod into his chest. God, I missed his smell. I missed the smell of wood and soap and everything earthy. I missed the way he anchors me.

"Come," he says, holding my hand and leading me towards the gazebo. "Surprise isn't done yet."

We walk across the damp grass where crickets chirp their mating calls. He leads me through the dark, up the steps of the gazebo. It smells like fresh varnish. I run my hand along the smooth wood, the intricate designs that make it so one-of-a kind.

"It's beautiful," I tell him.

When I turn he isn't there. I'm at the center of the gazebo in the middle of the night. Most of the lights in the house are off. There's just the moon and the blue glow of the pool.

"Hayden?"

"Hang on," his voice calls out from somewhere in the dark. I can hear him fumble with something. He yelps, like he cut himself. Then a final, "Here goes."

The lights come on. Dozens of tiny lights are strung around the top of the gazebo. It makes the backyard look like it's ready for a fairytale wedding.

Hayden returns to me. "Do you like it?"

"It's amazing. I mean, I'm not getting married here, but I would. I mean. You know what I mean."

"I do." He grabs me by the waist and hoists me up to him, pressing his lips to my lips. Damn, I've missed them. Every inch of them.

"Hayden, I'm sorry about what I said. I didn't mean it."

"I'm sorry I walked away from you." He cups my face. I

love the way he looks at me. I can feel his adoration. I don't have to guess. "I made it about me when you're the one getting hit on by every guy on Long Island."

"Not every guy," I say.

"Either way. Can you forgive me for leaving?"

"Can you forgive me for not telling you right then and there how I feel about you?"

"Depends. How do you feel?" He tilts me back to expose the tender skin of my neck.

My body responds to him right away, all tingly and wet. "That you're mine and I'm yours. That you brighten my day with the way you smile at me. That I want you to kiss me every day for as long as humanly possible."

And he does. He kisses me from my neck, to my jaw, to my mouth. He smells sweet, like he was eating candy before he got here. "That's it?"

I smack his chest. "What do you mean? Now it's your turn."

I realize that, this whole time, we've been swaying. The music is a simple thing—the breeze against trees, crickets, the ripple of the pool, the quick beats of our hearts.

"I feel really happy that I didn't quit my dad's company like I said I would. I wasn't supposed to be on the job that day. If I hadn't been, I never would have met you. I'm not big on meant-to-be. But if this is it, then I'm a believer. I believe that you are strong and independent. I believe that I've never known anyone quite like you. I believe that I love you, and that alone makes me want to be a better man "

Hayden loves me.

I love Hayden.

It's easier than science.

I wrap my arms around his neck. "Good. Because I love you, too."

CHAPTER 38

I lead Hayden up the stairs and into my bedroom, rushing him through the door when I hear footsteps creak down the hall.

"You haven't even seen the present for your uncles," he tells me.

"I'm busy." That's right. I am busy. I'm busy pulling his shirt over his head. Touching each distinct muscle that flexes under my skin.

He catches my bottom lip and tugs on it. "Sky."

I pull back just enough to feel the cool air between us. "Yes?"

"It's important to you too." He holds the wooden box between us. I'd much rather have his wood between us. "After that, you can have your way with me."

"Promise?"

He bites my shoulder as a response.

Now that he's here and has forgiven me, I can't think of anything else. He has to lift me off his lap and set me on the bed. I jokingly protest, but now I'm interested in what's inside the box. I recognize Hayden's beautiful carving. There's a P and T in an elegant script. I love the idea of Hayden sitting there, working with his hands to make this. Lucky's right, men who work with their hands sure know how to use them.

I open it to find two wooden figurines nestled on a blue velvet cloth. At first, I don't know what I'm supposed to be looking at. The first one is about four inches tall and made of a light brown wood. The face isn't really distinct but it's a beautiful carving nonetheless. The second one is a little bit shorter and made from mahogany. Each one has the initials carved into their hearts—a T and a P.

"This is them," I say. I turn to kiss him, but he's already

halfway there. "Thank you."

"I wanted your approval. Should we give it to them at the wedding rehearsal or save it as a surprise?"

I smile against his lips so our teeth smack together. I fall back in a fit of giggles. "Wedding day. They'll love it so much."

"Shhh. You're going to get us caught."

I roll my eyes. "Half the house is out partying."

"I only just got your mom to like me."

I look at him suspiciously. "Yeah, how'd you do that?"

He leans back on my bed, spreading out that glorious body for me. "I can be charming when I want to be."

"Hayden."

"I told her that I loved you. That I just want you to be happy, even if it's not with me."

I set the cake toppers on my dresser and lock the door. In the dark of my room with the soft blue pool light coming in through the balcony, I know there is one thing that I want. I pull the straps of my dress off my shoulder. I really love in movies when they do that, and cut to the dress falling to the floor. Hayden follows the fabric. It slides past my breasts, down my waist, hips, and lands on the floor in a pool of chiffon.

Hayden unbuckles his belt.

I grab my breasts to make my nipples hard, then explore my own body with my hands. I wrap my hands across my waist, trail them down my hips. I hook my thumbs on the edge of my thong.

Hayden undoes the button and fly of his jeans.

I pull my panties down, wiggle my hips. I take two steps forward, leaving my clothes behind. He reaches for me, but I wave my finger at him. I take courage from the lust in his eyes. I watch him watch me massage my clit.

"Come here," he tells me.

"Make me."

He's up in a shot. It makes my breath catch. He hoists me up in the air. I wrap my legs around his waist. His dick curls upward. He slides it up and down between my wetness. The tip presses into me and I gasp. I dig my nails into his back to hold on. He pulls back.

"God, you're so tight."

I yelp when he lifts me higher on the wall. He drives me crazy with the way he bites my neck and moans in my ear.

"Hayden, I need you."

"I need you."

"Get inside me."

He thrusts his pelvis up. He catches my scream with his lips. It's kind of nice trying to be quiet when all I want to do is shout. I feel his head inside of me. He slides in slowly, achingly, making room for the rest of him. It hurts a little, in the most delicious kind of way.

"Baby," he whispers. "Baby, you feel so good."

He pulls me away from the wall and throws me onto the bed, never pulling out. His hands pin mine over my head. I open up wider and he picks up his speed. He's so slick that he slides out once. For a moment, Hayden disappears. He pulls out, leaving me sprawled on the bed.

"Hayden?"

His hands grab my thighs, and then that mouth, that beautiful mouth of his covers my pussy. It's just a tease, because he returns, climbing on top of me.

"I couldn't help myself. I needed to taste you again."

He kisses me, lifting a leg over his shoulder. His dick slides back in, and this time he drives it in as far as possible. He kisses away the pain with his lips, and in this moment, I've never wanted someone more in my whole life. It swirls inside me and tightens in the pit of my stomach.

"Look at me, baby." His eyes are so blue. "I love you, Sky."

I answer him with a kiss. In that kiss I want to convey all the love I have for him. It comes in a rush, like the last few weeks. I hold onto it. "I'm coming."

My insides pulse around his length. He chuckles against my ear. "I know, baby. Come for me."

He thrusts into me until the ripple of my orgasm makes me crash. I press him deeper into me by pressing my feet on his ass.

When Hayden comes, he shuts his eyes. Even without looking, he finds my lips. We're sweaty and wet and exhausted. But for the first time in a long time, it feels so, so good.

CHAPTER 39

Hayden leaves in the middle of the night.

I wake up to a note that says. "See you at rehearsal, Love."

My mom might be warming up to him, but seeing Hayden walk out of my bedroom in the morning with a post-coital smile plastered all over his face won't do us any favors.

While I brush my teeth, River comes in and sits on the toilet.

"I happened to wake up this morning," she says, "and saw an extremely shirtless Hayden sneaking out the house. He's not much for covert missions. Does he ever wear a shirt?"

I rinse and spit. "He does! But it doesn't stay on for very long."

"I take it you've made up."

"We made up and a half."

"Good for you, babe. Get yours."

I set my brush back in the cup holder and sit on the bathtub ledge. "What's up?"

She holds onto the sides of the toilet, looks down at her lap. "I need your help."

I brace for the Thing that River's been holding back since she got here.

She licks her lips. In the white bathroom light she looks like a broken doll. Her curls hang tangled and her lips are dry.

"I fucked up," she says. Her foot starts to tremble. I place my hand on her knee to make it stop. "It's Will."

"River," I say. "Did you pay him?"

"I tried. I went to Smitty's. They wouldn't cash my chips."

"Why not?"

"I kind of told the dealer to go fuck his mother the last time I was there. Anyway, Mad let me play again, and I won back the three hundred, but Will wouldn't take it. He said 'this one's on the house.' Sky, what if he kills me?"

"He's not going to hurt you, River."

"I have to go. I don't know where, but I have to go."

Outside the bathroom Elena and Maria are fighting over a hairdryer. Pepe is knocking on doors to make sure everyone remembers to dress properly tonight because there will be pictures. No one knows what's going on in here, what's going on with River. It's like day and night.

"Does he know where you're staying?"

"I don't think so. But it's a small town. Not hard to figure out."

I'm concerned that River will never be able to stop gambling. More than that, that she'll meet someone worse than Will. I've been scared for River since the day she put a cherry bomb in Frankie Morales's mailbox because he touched my boobs in gym.

"No one's going to come for you."

"I found this thing." She tucks her hair back. "It's a rehab center in West Bumblefuck, Montana. I still haven't touched the money from my dad's life insurance…"

I choke laugh. When did I stop noticing that River was so lost? "I'm sorry, Riv. I've been so wrapped up in my shit that I haven't been taking care of you."

River takes my hands in her. "That was never your job."

"I know. But you're my sister."

"Besides, everyone knows I'm the fist, Leti's the fury, and you're the heart."

I pull her into a hug. I can feel her tremble, like a deep cold has reached down to her bones.

"I'm going to talk to Hayden. He seems to know everyone around here. Maybe he can help get Will off your back."

"I tell you all the time not to be an idiot," she says. "I just haven't figured how to follow my own advice."

I grab her face and kiss her forehead. "Everything is going to be fine."

She tries to smile. "I've missed your optimism."

I leave her to shower. I tell myself that everything is going to be okay. River has always taken care of herself. She lets us in when she's afraid, but doesn't always accept help. It's the first time she's sought out help like this. I can't shake the feeling that she isn't asking for help, she's preparing to run.

CHAPTER 40

For the rehearsal dinner, I light long white taper candles all over the dining room. We add two more tables to accommodate the whole family. Pepe keeps fiddling with his three-piece suit while Tony tries to speak Spanish to our great-aunt Victoria. Tony's family is smaller than ours. He's got a couple of cousins who'll show up tomorrow, but that's about it.

"Check this mix," Yunior says. "I've been working on some stuff with my friends."

It's a mix of some old school songs and techno. "Is this what they teach you at business school?"

He puts his finger to his lips. "Don't let my mom hear you. She'd go crazy if she knew I was doing something other than homework."

"Some things never change," I say, promising to keep his secret.

Yunior proclaims himself the DJ for tonight and hooks up his iPod to the stereo. I remind him that Pitbull isn't exactly dinner music, but he acts like he can't hear me.

James and Lucky arrive at the same time as Hayden. James and Hayden both wear their "I'm not trying but I still look good" button downs and jeans. Lucky opts for dress shorts and a navy blue tunic.

"I'll wear a dress tomorrow, I swear," she says.

"You guys look great." I'm already looking past them and at Hayden. I think about being with him last night and get excited. He holds my arms out and looks me up and down, leaning in close so that only I can hear him.

"I miss the white lace."

I can feel myself blush. "Can I trust you to behave yourself?"

"Don't worry about me. I make friends quickly."

I leave him to shoot the shit with my cousins and James. River and Lucky are naturally drawn to each other. Lucky's done her fair share of traveling, so River picks her brain. An alarm goes off in my head, but then Daisy and two of the other kids run into the table with all the glassware. When a dozen glasses come crashing to the ground, my mom shoos the kids away to their designated table and helps me get a box of new ones.

"You've got enough here to start your own restaurant," James tells Pepe.

Pepe smiles widely. "I just wanted to be prepared."

"Steven," I yell. "Where's the box of champagne?"

He pulls one headphone out of his ear.

"I know you heard me," I tell him.

He rolls his eyes and goes to do as I ask.

Leti rounds the kitchen corner with a bottle of wine in her hand.

"What are you doing?" I ask.

She shrugs. "This one's mine."

I pull the bottle from her and pour myself a glass. "So far only a few glasses are shattered."

"Stop expecting the worst."

"Have you met us?"

She smiles, and the light catches the star on her canine. "Have you talked to River?"

I nod and drink my champagne. "She'll be fine."

"I looked up the place in Montana. They have horses. It's a sixty day program."

"When is she going?"

"She didn't say. I feel like I should go with her. Like drive her there."

Leti shakes her head. "I wish I could. I'm going to be in Puerto Rico next week."

"What the hell are you going over there for?"

She winks. "Gary invited me."

I clink my glass to hers. From here, we watch our family sit down and drink. Las Viejas made trays of empanadas and fried shrimp for appetizers. Tony chats with one of his cousins, his hand wrapped around Pepe. Pepe takes long sips from his drink. Maria is staring at her nails, still bitter she wasn't asked to be a bridesmaid. My mom stacks five empanadas on Hayden's plate. River throws her head back and laughs at something Lucky says.

"You did it, kid," Leti tells me.

"The wedding's tomorrow," I remind her.

"Give yourself a break." She pushes me out of the kitchen and into the dining room. "Sky's going to make a speech!"

There's no sense being angry with her, even for a minute. Sure, I don't like speaking in public, but I love Pepe and Tony, and if I've learned anything these last few weeks is that when you love someone you have to tell them. Even if you think they already know. "I love you" are the most beautiful words you can say to someone when you truly mean them.

"I had my doubts at the beginning of the summer," I said. "Not about the wedding, but that you could fit the entire family in a house and everyone would survive."

Aunt Cecy raises her glass. "*Todavia es temprano, eh!*" *The night's still young.*

"As the maid of honor, I really wanted to do a great job. When I was a little girl, Pepe was the one who helped me do my homework. He helped me fix my hair when *someone* decided to give me bangs."

"Me too!" Leti shouts.

"That's because you were the one doing the cutting, Leti." Everyone laughs, which gives me a little confidence. "You know, my Ma was a hard worker. She had two jobs and never complained that she didn't have any sleep. She's the strongest woman I know, but even a superwoman needs a little help. That's always where Pepe came in."

I turn to him and lift my glass. "Pepe, you've been more than an uncle to me. You're my father, my brother, and my best friend. Watching you and Uncle Tony finally be able to get married is a dream. Tony, you've changed our lives by making Pepe so happy. From you, we can learn that love is truly unexpected. You guys are my best example of a happily-ever-after. To Pepe and Tony."

"To Pepe and Tony," every cheers.

Pepe takes his napkin and dabs at the corners of his eyes.

Tony stands. "Thank you all for coming and being part of our, well, wedding month, really. Sky, you've been fantastic at everything you've done. Thank you for brining James and Lucky and Hayden into our lives."

Hayden squeezes my hand under the table.

"It's a fantastic feeling," Tony says, "to find the person you belong with out of all the people on this planet. It only took me fifty years and a lot of missed lunches, but Pepe, my love, I can't to wait to share my life with you forever."

We cheers again, and clink our forks against glasses until they kiss.

• • •

For hours we eat and drink and drink and eat.

Then, we just drink. The party spills out to the backyard, even though Pepe threatens murder on anyone who messes up the wedding setup.

The grooms are sleeping in separate rooms. Pepe in the pool house and Tony in the regular house. You know, because they want to be traditional or something.

River strips down to her bikini and grabs one of the pool beds for herself. It comes with a cup holder for her champagne. Daisy and the younger kids cannonball on the other end. It's like everyone has taken to the romance of the night. The gazebo is lit, and the lights around the pool are set to change colors. I watch the blue fade to purple to pink to red and then start over.

Pepe rushes past us in a hurry.

"Hey!" I call after him. He turns around in a flurry.

"Hey, *bebé*." He twists his fingers the way he does moments before his runway shows. "I'm turning in. I have a champagne headache."

"Yeah, tomorrow's not a good day to be hungover," I say. "Not that anyone's going to listen to me."

He looks from me to Hayden, then back to me. Pepe pulls

me into a bone-crushing hug. I can feel his heart race.

"Are you okay?"

He nods. "You know that I love you, right?"

"Yeah, I know."

"You know that no matter what happens I'll always be here for you. And Leti and River. All of you. You're my babies."

I smooth his cheek with my hand. "I know. Go get some sleep. I'll wake you up for breakfast."

He kisses my cheek and goes off into the pool house. The lights are off in minutes.

"So," Hayden says, cozying up to my pool chair. "How hard would it be to get you all to myself?"

I tap my finger on my chin. "Hmmm. Very hard."

He leans into my ear, his breath tickling my skin. "I want to taste you right now."

His hand slides up my dress and squeezes my thigh. Yunior walks by just then and says, "I see that."

Hayden waves at him. "Hey, how's it going?"

I sigh. "I think we're going to have to wait till all the kids are asleep."

Hayden turns my face to his with his finger. "I'll wait as long as I have to."

CHAPTER 41

When most of the family has gone to sleep, with the exception of a handful who think they're in the swimming portion of the Olympics, I nudge Hayden to meet me in my room.

Leti purrs in my direction. She splashes some water at me.

"There had better not be any puke in the pool when I wake up," I warn her.

"I promise, Mommy Dearest."

"I love you!" River shouts from her pool bed.

In my room, Hayden is sprawled on my bed totally naked and erect. He smiles with his arms behind his head. I slink to the bed and crawl onto the mattress. I rake my nails up his thick, muscular legs. In this position, in this light, he looks like a bronze sculpture. He's a god holding the weight of the world. I never want to see him dressed again.

"You're all ready for me," I say, positioning myself between his legs. I let my hands wander up and down his abdomen without touching his dick once.

I lick it once from the shaft to the tip, loving the way it jerks in my direction.

"Aw, baby, you're killing me."

"You said you'd wait as long as you have to."

He whimpers. I know I'm being a little mean, but I want to savor this moment. I've imagined this while I watched him working shirtless. Me getting on my knees and pulling down his pants. But this is different. Hayden is on my bed like my own personal buffet.

I grab the base of his shaft and cover the head with my mouth. I lick it in slow circles, over and over until a bead of pre cum bubbles to the surface. He arches his back, shoving his dick further into my mouth. I pull back and gasp, moving my hand up and down.

He reaches for my face, traces a thumb across my wet lips. "You're so fucking beautiful."

I give him a squeeze, then take him into my mouth again. Going down on Hayden is an entirely new sensation to me. I love the way his skin feels on my tongue. The way it gets thicker and harder every time I lick him. The way his legs tremble as I pick up my speed and add quick flicks of my tongue on the underside of his pink head. It's like the start of an earthquake the way he shakes, pushes up his pelvis, grabs onto my hair and pulls.

I'll never get tired of hearing Hayden say my name.

"I'm going to come," he warns me. Gives me a chance to move out of the way.

I shake my head. I let my moan vibrate against his head as his warmth fills my mouth.

"I love you," he says between shallow breaths. "I love you, Sky."

I swallow and place a wet kiss on his exhausted dick. "Look, it's going back to sleep."

Hayden chuckles. "Not while you're around."

"It's hot as hell in here." I get up to open the balcony doors. No one can see into the room, thankfully. Everyone's deserted the pool except River, who smokes on one of the beach chairs, Leti, who's asleep with a champagne glass in hand, and an unidentified cousin passed out in a bed of tulips.

Before I return back to my delicious man, I notice something weird. The light of the pool house is on. Pepe should be sleeping.

"I think I should go to talk to my uncle," I tell Hayden. "What kind of maid of honor would I be if I let him stew in his nerves?"

Hayden stands and wraps his arms around me. His sweet sweat is intoxicating. I lick the skin on his chest and promise to return.

Before I run downstairs, I run into the bathroom to rinse with mouthwash and spray some perfume. Pepe might be cool like my brother, but I can't just show up reeking of oral sex.

"Hey," River says. "Done moaning and groaning?"

"Shut up. I'm going to check on Pepe."

"I'm sure he's fine. He's probably steaming his suit for the ten thousandth time."

Still, something isn't sitting right with me, and not just because I swallowed…well…

I go to knock on the pool house door but it's slightly ajar. I turn to go back. Maybe he and Tony are in there getting it on before the wedding. But when all I hear is crickets, I decide to go in. Everything is spotless. The bed is made. The tux is hung. There's a full glass of water on Pepe's work desk along with a piece of paper and an uncapped marker.

I'M SORRY.

There's the beginning of another word. I—something. But the marker bleeds, like he kept it pressed to the paper and then never finished. My heart thunders in my chest. I ball the paper up and run outside.

"River," I whisper shout. She's so startled she slips off her inflatable bed and splashes into the pool. Leti starts awake.

"What?"

River spits water as she swims to the edge of the pool. "What the actual fuck?"

I bend down and try to whisper with as much panic as possible. "Pepe's gone."

"No!" Leti shouts and River slaps a hand over her mouth.

"No one can know." I show them the piece of paper.

"I can't believe it." River rips it up into little pieces and lights it in the ashtray. I watch it go up in flame, then ash, then tendrils of smoke twisting in the air.

"Come on," I say. "We have to go find him."

CHAPTER 42

"Are you sure he's gone?" Hayden gets dressed as soon as he sees my face when I return.

"I just peeked into Tony's room. He's knocked out."

"Where do you think he went?"

"I don't know, but not far. All the cars are still out front."

"We'll take mine."

"No. I don't want anyone to wake up if they hear an engine. River and Leti are already downstairs."

I don't wait for him to follow me, I just know that I have to get Pepe back here before sunrise. As quietly as we can, we're out the door.

"Split up," I say. "You two go right and we'll go left."

We take off like racehorses. The roads are pitch-black, and nearly every house we pass is quiet. There aren't many streetlights, so I shine the flashlight in my phone. It isn't much, but at least we won't get run over.

"Oh God," I say, panicked. "What if he gets run over? What if I don't find him?"

"We'll find him," Hayden says. "Here, make this right. This is the way to the beach."

"I can't believe he did this." Suddenly, I start to cry. I don't like when people see me cry, so I'm glad for the cover of night. "I wanted them to be the couple that made it, you know? I guess that's pretty selfish."

"That's not selfish at all." He grabs me and pulls me into a hug. Something digs into my back. He holds up the box with the wooden cake toppers. "Oh, sorry. I just thought this might help."

After a few minutes of empty road, I shine a light on a blazer. I want to scream at the thought that he might be run over. Hayden picks it up and I break into a jog. My chest hurts and my feet are throbbing. There's his tie. I run fast. Up where the road becomes a hill is Pepe.

He's trying to unbutton his shirt. I can hear him crying as I approach. He jumps when I touch him.

"It's me," I say. "It's Sky."

He bats his hands in front of his face and shakes his head. Crystal tears run down his face. He can't breathe.

"Look at me," I tell him, forcing him to focus his eyes on me. "Pepe, look at me please."

He gulps the air around him and nods.

"I need you to breathe." I stand beside him and rub circles on his back. "A little at a time, okay? I'm right here."

Slowly, he inhales.

"You're doing great. Take your time."

I put my hand out, silently asking Hayden to hang back. The last thing he needs is another surprise.

"Come, sit."

On the sidewalk filled with gravel and sand, Pepe sits in his favorite suit. His breaths are long and steady now.

"I'm sorry."

I rub his back. "What happened?"

"I just—" He starts to cry again. "I just was lying there thinking about everything that was said. I love Tony, so, so much that it physically hurts me to think about something going wrong. My dad walked out on us when we were kids. Your dad. Maria's dad. We're a family that gets left, Sky. What if Tony leaves me?"

"He's won't." It's something I don't have the authority to promise, but I have to believe in this.

"Maybe not like that, but what if he dies? What if something happens to him and I can't help him? What if I do something wrong? What if it doesn't end like I thought it would? What if loving someone isn't enough to make it work?"

A car drives by on the opposite side of the road. I wonder where River and Leti are right about now. I wonder if anyone in the house has noticed that we're gone.

"You never left," I tell him.

He looks up at me with swollen dark eyes.

"You never left me. I didn't leave you. The people that left us, they weren't family. I know that you're scared of being hurt, but isn't that the whole point of getting married? You're literally trusting another person not to break your heart, like, forever."

His laugh is snotty and wet, but at least he laughs. "I'm afraid, *nena.*"

"You told me that I had to do what makes me happy. Does Tony make you happy?"

"Yes," he says without hesitation.

"Then forget about the things that you can't control. All you have to worry about is walking down that aisle and looking at the man you love and starting your life together. The only thing that should stop you from getting married tomorrow is if you don't want to."

"I do want to," he cries.

"Then, as River likes to tell me, stop being an idiot."

"Oh, *nena.*" He hugs me. "I'm so thankful you found me when you did. I just lost it."

Hayden clears his throat. Pepe jumps and scrambles to his feet.

"It's just Hayden," I say.

Pepe rubs his face with his hands. "Oh, God. No. I'm so embarrassed."

"I guess it's not a good time to tell you that Leti and River are out looking for you, too? That's it though, I promise."

"We were going to wait till tomorrow," Hayden tells him. "But I figured you might want to see this now to clear your head."

Pepe takes the wooden box and opens it slowly. I shine the phone light so he can get a good look at it. He covers his mouth and starts to cry again.

Hayden looks panicked. "I'm sorry if you don't like it. You don't have to use them."

"No, no!" He shuts the box and presses it against his chest. "They're beautiful. They're *us.*"

CHAPTER 43

The wedding orchestra lulls the wedding guests to sit. The orchestra was Tony's surprise gift to Pepe.

A tall, slender pianist, a blonde with a harp, and a short violinist who reminds me of Captain Jack Sparrow start to play a Beatles medley.

Two hundred plus guests are lined up in neat rows, waiting for the wedding party to walk past the pool, down the cobblestone path, and to the lit gazebo. If I crane my head, I can see the back of Hayden's head sitting beside Lucky and James. I clutch my bouquet and breathe in the sweet smell of roses.

"Don't you feel a little funny wearing white?" Steve asks.

I turn and quiet him with a snarl.

Behind me, Leti fidgets with the buttons on the back of her dress. "Something's itching me."

"Maybe you got crabs," Yunior says.

The terrible thing about having your cousins as wedding partners is hearing their endless commentary. The best thing about it is having your cousins there.

"That's not where you get crabs, you idiot," she says, slapping him in the gut.

Behind them there's even more snickering. I turn around. "Will you all shut up for once?"

I take Steve's arm when the band slows down their instruments and start the beginning of Led Zepplin's "All of My Love."

"I picked this," River whispers from the back.

"Thank you dear," I hear Tony say.

As I walk down the aisle, bracing my smile for pictures, I let myself sigh with relief. I even smile at Xandro, who's brought a date who could be on the cover of Maxim. Good for you, bro.

I take the first few steps to the open gazebo. I have to admire the way Hayden designed it with the wedding party in mind. I smile at the minister, take my place on the tier, and watch the rest of the party file in. Leti is Leti, and waves like she's in the middle of a ticker-tape parade. Junior throws up a peace sign, which the photographer takes twenty photos of. River gives me her naturally mischievous smile and lets go of her partner's arm as soon as possible. She got stuck with Uncle Tony's cousin who smells like garlic. Then there's Elena and Juliet, who take selfies as they go down the aisle.

"Jesus," I sigh, drawing the officiate's ire.

The harpist sets her instrument to the side and pulls out a ukulele. Someone in the crowd giggles. She starts off Israel Kamakawiwo'ole's "Over the Rainbow" with a quick strum. Then Captain Jack joins in on the violin, swaying to the beat. Tony starts his procession on the arm of his cousin Isabella. He holds his head up high as the music swells. His smile is so wide that I know if I did one thing well this summer, it was helping save my Uncle Pepe from making the biggest mistake of his life.

Tony kisses my cheek and takes his place at the altar.

Pepe starts to walk down the aisle with my mother giving him away. When I look at them, I realize that I might not have grown up with a traditional mother and father, but they were still pretty perfect. My mom's dress is a beautiful salmon color that compliments her dark skin. They both have the same dark eyes and full lips. The same wide smiles. My mom kisses Tony on both cheeks and takes a seat in the front row.

As he gets up on the altar, Pepe grabs my hand, and I give it a squeeze of encouragement.

Then they face each other, and say their "I Do's."

• • •

After the ceremony comes the dancing. The bottles of champagne that overflow like fountains. My cousins fawn over the fashion models who have come for Pepe. Las Viejas *tut tut* at the tiny summer dresses that they don't approve of for a wedding. Because *now's* the time to be conservative.

"Ladies and gentlemen," a familiar voice says over the mic. Yunior is standing at the DJ tent. He's got giant headphones with customized, bedazzled Y's on each ear. I look over at Leti. I guess she knew Yunior's secret way before I did. "Can I have your attention please? We are going to welcome the *illest* couple this side of New York for their first dance as husband and wife."

The record skips, and Yunior hits the mic. "My bad."

Pepe and Tony shake their heads in his direction. Nothing like family.

"I'm going to kill him," I say, starting to march off to the DJ tent, but Hayden pulls me back.

"Easy, tiger," River says. She takes a comfortable seat where she can smoke without people complaining.

Tony and Pepe start to dance to "You Are So Beautiful." One by one, everyone starts dancing. Hayden pulls me into his big, strong arms, and we sway to ballads, salsas, merengues, and hip hop songs. I don't notice the sunset until the backyard comes alive with lights.

"Sky," Hayden says, pulling back to inspect me. I've gone rigid. "What's wrong?"

Slowly, all the guests turn to the gazebo, where a fire has started. Everyone starts to scream.

"Fire!" they shout.

Hayden's already on his phone calling 911. Tony runs inside the house for a fire extinguisher. Leti dives for the garden hose, but gets tangled up and falls in the pool. Some of my cousins are behind the gazebo, too scared to walk around the fire.

"Sky, come back!"

I run to the gazebo where the kids are and usher them to safety.

"Everyone get back!" I shout. Then I go back to make sure I didn't miss anyone.

The hair on my back prickles like someone's standing behind me. I whip around, but there's no one there. I turn to run back to the front of the house, but I trip on something. A bottle of lighter fluid.

I was right. There's someone behind me. I see him running into the woods, but I don't see anything but a bald head and a beard.

Hands grab me from the back and I scream.

"It's me!" Hayden says. "Baby, it's me."

He pulls me back as half a dozen firemen spray the gazebo. By the time it's done it's nothing but splinters and a pile of ash. Luckily, nothing else was damaged.

I look at the shocked faces of the weddings guests, but I don't see her. Hayden tries to hold me back, but I pull away. There's no time to explain. I run to the front of the house. There's an empty spot in the driveway. River's car is gone.

River is gone.

CHAPTER 44

I tell the police what I saw—a bald man running through the woods. They take the bottle of lighter fluid, but don't promise much. I don't tell them that River was here. I don't tell them that he was looking for her. I don't even know when she left, but I hope that she's long gone right now.

Because nothing else was ruined, Tony and Pepe keep the party going. The only way to face something terrible is with a celebration. Pepe did say he wanted to give everyone a wedding to talk about, and even a little fire hasn't dampened the drunken happiness in the air.

I wrap my arms around Hayden's waist. "I'm sorry your masterpiece went up in flames."

He shakes his head. "This? My masterpiece has yet to come, baby."

He rubs my hands, pulling me into a deep kiss. I take a minute to go into my room to change. My phone is in my charger. I have three messages from Bradley. With all the things that have happened, he's the last thing I need. I hit delete.

There's one from River. It's time-stamped way before the fire. It says, *Going rogue.*

I want to tell her about what happened, but she needs a clean slate. So all I say is, *I love you.* When I go back downstairs, I hug my mother. I hug Tony and Pepe. I even hug Maria.

I take Hayden to the middle of the buzzing dance floor. The smell of backyard torches mingles with the charred smell of the wood, but no one seems to mind.

"This one goes out to my favorite cousin, Sky," Yunior says and starts playing the Talking Heads's "Burning Down the House."

I give him a thumbs up. My grandma twirls with Pepe's assistant, Vera, and Lucky pulls James away from the buffet to the dance floor. Leti screams when she realizes the star on her tooth fell out during the commotion, though I suspect Gary might've swallowed it.

"I love you," I tell him. The words feel true, and I want to say them over and over again.

"Does that mean you're staying?" Hayden picks me up and spins me in the air. My belly fills with that fluttering of new love.

I haven't made a decision. Not quite yet. I know that I want to go back to school, and I've blown my chances at the fall semester. But there's going to be the spring. I know I want to help girls like me, like River, like my cousins. I want to let them know that they're going to be okay.

Being a nurse has changed my life, even if it wasn't what I wanted to do with my life. I know how to dress cuts, and I've delivered babies into this world as many times as I've patched up bullet wounds. I've become more interested in the wounds that people can't see.

"Yes and no," I tell him. "I was thinking of taking a trip. Maybe Greece, and then who knows? My passport is sadly stamp-less."

He crosses his fingers with mine. "Oh."

"Come with me?"

He kisses me. "Good thing you asked. I was already trying to come up with ways to fit myself in your suitcase. I love you, Sky."

I hold him tightly. I'm not sure where we'll end up, but a kiss is a good place to start.

WANT TO SEE MORE HAYDEN AND SKY?

Leave a review to receive a bonus short story
featuring their globetrotting adventure!

Email a link to the review to **zoraidawrites@gmail.com** and
Zoraida Córdova will personally send you the short story!

ACKNOWLEDGMENTS

This book is very close to my heart. I wanted to write about a girl who had a very crazy, but very loving family just like me. Thank you to my family who supports me in this crazy journey to follow my dream. Mom, Joe, Mami Aleja, Danny, and the usual suspects.

Thank you to the Robeos for inspiring Tony and Pepe's wedding. I took a few liberties with the characters, but their essence is all you. You are the one couple that makes me believe in True Love.

Adrienne Rosado, the Little Mongoose that Could. Laura Duane, Sarah Masterson Hally, Brielle Benton, Hannah Black, and the wonderful team at Diversion Books. Thank you for letting my girls on the verge have a home. Najla Qamber for finding the perfect couple and creating a stunning cover. To my writing friends at Write-o-Rama, NA Hideaway, and NAAU.

Robert Lettrick for your unflinching belief not just in my words, but also in me.

To my family at Flashdancers and New York Dolls—Bobby, Grace, Lauren, Kat, Sandy, Penny, Mona, Sasa, Mike, The Three B's, Ethan, Julissa, Tommy, Anita, Kim, Patricia, and many more. Thank you, from the bottom of my heart, for all of your support over the years.

As always, to all the readers, bloggers, and book lovers that make it possible for girls like me to tell stories.

And finally, for everyone out there searching for love. I hope you find your Happily Ever After.

ON THE VERGE: Book One

LUCK
on the
LINE

ZORAIDA CÓRDOVA

"With a perfect blend of humor, drama and heat, *Luck on the Line* is a welcome and much needed addition to the new adult genre."
—*RT Book Reviews*

Despite her name, Lucky Pierce has always felt a little cursed. Refusing to settle for less or settle down, she changes jobs as often as she changes boyfriends. When her celebrity chef mother challenges her to finish something, Lucky agrees to help her launch Boston's next hot restaurant, The Star. Even if it means working with the infuriating, egotistical, and undeniably sexy head chef.

James loves being known as Boston's hottest bad boy in the kitchen, but if he wants to build a reputation as a serious chef, he has to make this restaurant work and keep his scandalous past out of the headlines. Getting involved with his boss's spoiled, sharp-tongued daughter is definitely not on the menu.

As the launch of The Star looms and the tension and chemistry heat up in the kitchen, they're going to need more than a little luck to keep everything from boiling over.

CPSIA information can be obtained at www.ICGtesting.com
Printed in the USA
BVOW07s0836240415

397604BV00004B/73/P